# Lessons from a Tour Guide

## KRISTEN JENNINGS

Edited by Cara Lockwood (Edit-my-novel.com)
Cover Design and Illustration by Kylie Sek
Interior Formatting by Sarah Symonds (dragonflyformats.com)

Trade Paperback ISBN:979-8-9929437-0-2
Ebook ISBN: 979-8-9929437-1-9

First Edition June 2025

*To anyone who ever felt like their job was not enough. Real enough, serious enough, meaningful enough. You are enough, and the impact you make in this world does not go unnoticed.*

*And for anyone who has worn the Royal Stewart tartan, thank you. Your passion and gift for storytelling shaped me into the writer I am today. May the clack of your heels be a signal that someone amazing approaches.*

# Author's Note

Hanna's name is of Hebrew origin and is pronounced with a hard H at the beginning. While the majority of characters in the book refer to her as Hanna, she is called Ana by Spanish-speaking characters, and Anna by French-speakers as is appropriate for their languages. These are intentional spellings and I worked with native-speakers of all three languages to ensure proper use of the name variations. Any errors are my own and do not reflect on them.

# 1
## Early is On Time

HANNA'S first mistake that morning was taking the train.

"*Shitshitshitshit*," Hanna muttered under her breath while checking her watch for the millionth time. Was it too much to ask that the laws of nature bend just a little bit for her? Slowing down the rotation of the earth around the sun, making the minute hand creep forward instead of maintaining its steady tick did not seem too large a request.

As a rule, Hanna only wore an analog watch, wound daily as part of her nightly ritual. Who needed a fancy digital watch–with their step counters and constant harassment to "*take a moment to breathe*"–anyway? Stick to the basics, the tried and true, as her father liked to remind her. A gift for her sixteenth birthday, the thin leather band was worn with age, the brown color faded and stretched along the holes and edges. Bluebirds ticked their way along the watch face from the ends of the hands, circling the birdhouse at the center. It was inexpensive and did not match the polished nude heels or conservative navy sheath dress that Hanna wore, but it was priceless. Her one small concession to the appearance she strove to maintain.

Currently, the watch mocked her, beating in time with the click of her heels across the cobblestone pavement. Perpetually on time, which actually meant ten minutes early, Hanna cursed the train for taking longer than usual to get her from Long Beach to San Diego. Honestly, after years of traveling for work, she should have anticipated this. The greater Los Angeles area was notorious for bad traffic, apparently even when one bypassed the freeway.

When she booked this meeting, taking the train seemed like a great idea. As a vacation concierge, affectionately known as a tour guide, Hanna never needed to own a car. Public transportation worked smoothly in most of the countries she visited, even in parts of the United States, but Los Angeles had to make a statement. Making her only two minutes early to one of the most important meetings of her career.

For over ten years, Hanna worked for Trips Ahoy, a trip planning company catering to groups who wanted to visit the top tourist destinations in the world without the stress of planning it themselves. But now, with the retirement of her boss and mentor Stephanie Ricci, Hanna was ready to start her own business. She just had to nail the first client meeting.

Slowing her stride a block before the cafe where she was meeting the client, Hanna stepped to the side and pulled out her compact mirror. *Never look rushed, even if you are.* Stephanie's smoky voice was clear in her mind, even though she was miles away on a vacation in the tropics. The round pocket mirror with a ring of vines etched around the edge was a gift for Hanna's first tour. A reminder to always look her best and to never, ever, forget to check her teeth after eating.

Holding the mirror at arm's length, Hanna used her free hand to smooth back a few strands of hair that pulled away from her thick curls and checked that her makeup was in place. Nodding to herself after confirming everything looked as it should, she smoothed down her dress and resumed her walk at a natural pace. If anyone thought it strange that she stopped on the side of the road to check her hair and makeup, Hanna did not care. Impressing Hazel Eversham was too important.

A short, firecracker of a woman, Hazel embodied everything

Hanna wanted to be when she grew up. Well...grew up more than a functioning twenty-eight year old who was rarely in one place long enough to have a long-term lease, thrifted designer clothing, and had a Google spreadsheet organizing her favorite take-out places. Hazel was wealthy, adventurous, and didn't take shit from anyone.

She first met the silver haired force of nature septuagenarian on a tour through Rome and Venice designed for older adults.

At the end of the first day, Hazel pulled Hanna aside and told Hanna that if she wanted to watch winded old people shuffle from place to place, she would have moved to a retirement community.

"I want to drink wine poured by an attractive Italian man. Can you set that up?" Hazel asked with a straight face. Hanna instantly liked her. Whenever the group had a free afternoon or evening, Hanna provided Hazel with activity suggestions to match her lively spirit.

Which was exactly the type of service Luxe Travel specialized in. Although she offered samples of potential tours on her website, whether Hanna was leading the tour herself, or booking it on behalf of a family and providing them the itinerary to follow themselves, each tour from Luxe Travel was customized to every group. She conducted preliminary questionnaires with each group, generated an itinerary for the clients to review, then booked the travel arrangements. Before Hazel contacted her, Hanna had planned several trips for a few clients that followed her on social media, and beyond a few follow-up questions and phone calls for emergencies, they trusted her to book them fantastic vacations.

But itinerary-only tours were not enough. Hanna needed to start booking trips for private tour groups to get her business off the ground.

Which was why she was meeting Hazel at an adorable tea shop in San Diego. She was referred to the owners by friends, curating relationships with quality, locally-run businesses (a cornerstone of her business plan), and knew it would impress her long-time client with its combination of comfortable tables, tasteful decorations, and

3

impeccable food and beverages. Pushing open the frosted glass doors with brushed-gold handles, Hanna made her way to the host stand and introduced herself.

Glancing up from the tablet concealed behind the polished countertop, the host smiled warmly at Hanna. "Right this way. The other members of your party are already seated."

Quickly masking her surprise at the plural *guests*, Hanna pasted on her warmest smile and followed the host to a table seated near the front windows, affording the best view without residing near the bustle of the kitchen and entrance. She could hear Hazel before she saw her, a twinkling laugh hitting Hanna's ears as she rounded the corner and spotted Hazel's white and grey braid swaying as she laughed.

Seated across from Hazel was a man in a light-blue shirt that stretched across his shoulders as he gestured toward his table partner. Thick brown hair, cut shorter on the sides and carefully styled on top, swayed slightly as he shook his head. Although he was facing away from her and Hanna could not see his expression, it looked like he did not agree with whatever Hazel was laughing at. Based on the hand he placed on Hazel's arm, Hanna could tell that they were familiar, and she wondered why the mysterious man was at her meeting.

Considering that Hazel wanted her assistance planning a trip to Paris with her friends from a women's entrepreneurial club, the man's presence at the table did not bode well. Pulling back her shoulders, Hanna took a calming breath. She had not made it this far in her career without the ability to pivot as unexpected challenges arose, but her heart still beat faster in her chest with anxious energy. As the host led her into the table's line of sight, Hanna saw the moment Hazel's blue eyes found her, lighting up with recognition and joy.

"Hanna!" The older woman stood in a graceful motion and stepped around the table to pull her into a hug. Scents of rum and ginger floated on a cloud of Hazel's perfume as Hanna breathed around her vise-like grip. For someone who barely reached Hanna's chin, Hazel could hug like a bear.

"How is it possible that you get prettier every time I see you?" Pulling back so that she could take a good look at Hanna, Hazel chuckled good-naturedly. "The perks of being young."

"Please, you are hardly old," Hanna teased. "Do not forget that you were staying out later than I was in Italy."

As always, Hazel's makeup was applied subtly to enhance her features rather than outshine them. The wrinkles around her eyes were testaments to the years of love and laughter she celebrated with her late-husband and family.

"You flatter me," Hazel replied with a wave of her hand. "Please, continue."

They shared a laugh that resonated across the room. It was one of the reasons Hanna enjoyed working with Hazel. She loved her unexpected humor and familiarity. But, she could not let herself get too close. That was a lesson Hanna learned years ago.

The sound of chair legs sliding against the floor interrupted Hanna's next comment and reminded her that there was an unknown variable in her plan to secure Hazel's business. No, they were very much not alone as the man with thick, dark hair rose from the table.

"Oh! How forgetful of me." Hazel never forgot anything in the entire time Hanna had known her. "I brought someone for you to meet." Turning towards her guest, Hazel's eyes and smile brightened as she gestured between the man and Hanna. "This is Noah. My grandson."

Muscle memory was Hanna's best friend as she faced Noah, her hand moving on autopilot to shake his hand as her brain turned off. Clean, callused fingers engulfed hers, wrapping tightly in a firm grip that sent a shiver up her spine. Forearms dusted with dark hair were exposed by the rolled sleeves of his button-up. A shirt that amplified the defined muscles of his arms. The motion of his bicep flexing as their hands connected shook Hanna out of her haze.

*Pull it together*, she chastised herself. This was no way to act around a client's family member. Certainly not the way to act before

5

her business was even off the ground. Mistakes were a luxury she could not afford.

Putting on a professional smile, Hanna made her second mistake of the day. Looking at Noah Eversham's face was more distracting than his arms. Eyes the color of a cloudless sky peered down at her beneath dark lashes, flashing with a spark of something she could not put her finger on. His hair somehow looked thicker from the front, sloping gracefully away from his forehead, matching the dusting of scruff along his sculpted jaw.

Countless cities and faces across the world left Hanna desensitized to handsome men, or so she thought before laying eyes on Noah. Looking at him was like staring at artwork, beautiful and untouchable. He would have been the most handsome man Hanna had ever laid eyes on, if not for the scowl on his face.

Widening her own smile to overcompensate for his lack of one, Hanna broke the silence.

"Hanna Poole. It's a pleasure to meet you." She made sure to emphasize the hard H in her name, knowing that most people mispronounced it as Hannah instead of the correct Hebrew pronunciation.

"Noah. My grandmother speaks highly of you, the infamous trip planner."

She bristled at the description. Granted, a large portion of her job was to plan trips for people, but coming from his mouth the title sounded like an insult. There was a reason her business cards said *Vacation Concierge*. Rude as the comment was, Hanna would not respond in kind.

"I am honored that Hazel speaks so highly of me. Shall we sit? This tea shop has been run by the same family for over seventy-five years and I was told their scones rival any you can find in England."

As she sat, Hanna watched as Noah held out the chair for his grandmother, trapping Hanna between them at the table. Placing her purse behind her on the chair, Hanna folded her hands in her lap, allowing the host to set the menu in the center of the table before explaining the options for shareable versus individual high tea. Having reviewed the menu online in advance, Hanna gestured for Hazel to look at the menu first.

"Do you always take your clients to establishments you've never visited?" Noah's smooth voice was a contradiction to his harsh words. The subtle bite to his tone had Hanna's eyes flashing to his. Where did he get off being rude to her not five minutes after being introduced? Couldn't a girl order some tea before getting subjected to the inquisition?

Hanna kept her tone syrupy sweet as she replied. "Pardon me?" Beneath the table, her hands wound around the napkin to resist the urge to pick at her fingernails.

Watching her with the unflinching gaze of someone assessing an opponent for a weakness, Noah smirked. "You said that you've 'been told' about their scones. Shouldn't someone whose job it is to guide people around places they have never been rely on more than just hearsay? We could get that information from Google."

Remaining calm and composed in any situation was part of Hanna's job. Several members of a group partied too hard the night before a river cruise? Hana passed around pedialyte, advil, and motion sickness medication. People yelling in her face about their inability to get closer to the Mona Lisa? Nothing attentive listening and a few well placed elbows to the people around them could not solve.

But Hanna's blood pounded at the nerve this man had to doubt her skill. Something about the insults coming from that perfectly sensuous mouth ignited her temper and Hanna ground her teeth to hold back a fiery retort.

Smacking her menu against her grandson's arm, Hazel leveled a glare at Noah. "Don't be rude. I let you join us so that Hanna could alleviate the concerns you have with my trip, not insult her. If you cannot be polite then leave. I raised you better than that."

That was interesting news. Hanna wanted to ponder this revelation, but her brain was stuck on the word "concerns" repeating in her mind like a glitch. Concerns were normal, particularly when it came to traveling. But Hazel made it sound like Noah's concerns might prevent the trip from happening. Which was not good. Hazel had many connections, including wealthy and influential friends, that could help Hanna launch her company.

Knowing that Stephanie wanted to retire soon, and dreaming of becoming her own boss, Hanna spent the last couple of years growing her social media presence, curating content designed to showcase the places she visited and tips for traveling. While there was some money in promoting products or places, it was not all Hanna wanted to do. If she had, Hanna would have remained with Trips Ahoy after a large company bought it from Stephanie. When Hazel reached out after seeing the announcement for Luxe Travel, Hanna knew that securing her business would establish credibility and bring in more clients.

She was so busy thinking through various scenarios and justification for her services that Hanna almost missed Noah speaking.

"I'm sorry, mémé, you know that I worry about you." Noah's voice softened as he spoke to his grandmother, then firmed again as he faced Hanna. "Ms. Poole, I apologize for suggesting that you do not know how to do your job without giving you a chance to prove you can."

All the words were correct, but they still sounded like he was not willing to give her that chance. This was not the first time a member of a group expressed doubt over her ability as a guide and it would not be the last. Repeated instances meant that Hanna's rebuttal was practically scripted.

"Thank you, and please call me Hanna. I understand that my job does not make sense to a lot of people, but I can address any questions you might have. Rest assured that Hazel's trip will be everything she and her friends are hoping for."

"Which we are looking forward to!" Hazel clasped her hands together with youthful enthusiasm. She was finally fulfilling her dream to travel the world, and Hanna felt her own enthusiasm for travel flourish under the sunlight of Hazel's joy. There were only so many times she could see the same tourist destinations, the novelty having worn off long ago, but getting to show those places to people for the first time, seeing the light in their eyes, made it all worth it.

At that moment, their waitress came and introduced herself, explaining the menu options and asking if they had any questions before ordering.

Hazel glanced at the menu before smiling at Noah and Hanna, her gold watch glinting in the light as she tucked a strand of hair behind her ear. "Sharing would be fun, and the jasmine tea sounds lovely. Does that work for you two?"

"Anything you want," Noah agreed. He looked at Hazel with such obvious affection that Hanna suspected he always found a way to make sure Hazel got whatever she wanted.

They both turned to face Hanna with an unspoken question in their eyes.

Outwardly, Hanna agreed with their selection. Inwardly, she worried that she would be stuck drinking tea that she did not enjoy. At least their sandwiches and scones were served individually.

When the waitress left to put in their order, Hazel started the conversation back up. "So, Hanna, what have you been up to since I saw you in Greece?"

"A little bit of everything. More trips around Europe, then a few in Japan before the end of my last season with Trips Ahoy. After that, I focused on opening Luxe Travel, so it's been nonstop paperwork."

Hazel reached over to clasp her hand. "Congratulations, again. Selfishly, I am glad that you are opening your own company, because it means I get to keep experiencing your wonderful trips. When Stephanie announced that she was retiring and selling her company, I was worried that I would lose you and have to travel to new places with someone else."

The compliment filled Hanna with pride, warming her against the chill of air conditioning. "I am happy to hear it. Stephanie was my mentor for so long that I knew I did not want to work for anyone else. Plus, with the blog gaining traction, it was the right time to break out on my own. Thank you again for booking your next trip with me. I will make sure it is unforgettable."

Mostly forgotten, Noah reminded Hanna of his presence with a quiet scoff, low enough that Hazel could not hear it from her side of the table. It helped that Hazel was gushing about Hanna's blog, her words drowning out the sound as she told Hanna how she shared each post on Facebook. Seemed like posting on that aging platform still had its benefits.

When Hazel excused herself to freshen up before the food arrived, Hanna decided to address the elephant in the room and face Noah and his surly attitude head on.

"Is something wrong?" Hanna turned to him.

The last pretense of polite blandness wiped off his face the moment Hazel was out of view, a glare turning his eyes into sharp blades. "You mean, beyond your plan to scam my grandmother and her friends out of thousands of dollars with this sham of a tour company?"

He sounded disgusted, and hot anger burned in Hanna's chest. Biting her tongue when their waitress arrived to deliver their food and tea, Hanna stewed in her anger. The gall this man had. It was only years of customer service experience that allowed her to keep her expression neutral as Hanna pitched her voice low, struggling to maintain an even tone.

"Scam? Luxe Travel is a legitimate company and I would be more than happy to supply a copy of our business license for you to validate. All of the locations that I take tours on are personally vetted and I always provide options for travel insurance. Reservations are logged into the client's portal so they have access to the information at any time. I have a program for recording all monetary transactions and pay for top of the line security software to protect my clients–"

"But you don't have many clients yet, do you?" His lips twitched with a smug smile. "And all those promises of travel insurance and a valid business license mean nothing if you declare bankruptcy.

Who's to say you do not take their money, your business folds, and then you pocket their money without any refunds?"

An angry flush bloomed on her neck and chest. Noah was lucky the only knife on the table was too dull to stab him with. He possessed the uncanny ability to get under her skin in a way no guest had before.

"I would never do that. Hazel has gone on trips with me before and I have never done anything untrustworthy."

Leaning forward in his chair, Noah's face was now close enough that Hanna could see a light dusting of freckles across the bridge of his nose. She blamed her outrage on the warmth that pumped through her veins. It was not because Hanna found Noah attractive. Not this rude, judgemental jerk.

His tone matched his icy stare. "That was when you worked for an established company. Credible. I find it suspicious that instead of sticking with them, under new management, you decided to start over with no backing, no reputation besides your own. My grandmother might trust you, but I don't, and I will not let you take advantage of her."

"I have reviews posted on my website from previous clients, as well as a recommendation from Stephanie Ricci. I have been in this business for over ten years and I know what I am doing. If you do not trust your grandmother's judgment, then the only other option for you is to go on a tour and see for yourself that the experience I provide is worth it."

Hanna's breath was uneven, her chest rising rapidly as she defended herself. Inviting him on a tour came out of her mouth without permission. She could imagine nothing worse than being forced to endure his presence for a prolonged period of time. Hanna was confident he felt the same way about her. Knowing that she said everything she could, Hanna sat back in her chair, smoothing the napkin over her skirt as if nothing Noah said could ruffle her feathers. The proverbial ball was in his court now.

The click of Hazel's short heels against the floor warned Hanna of her approach and provided relief from whatever Noah was preparing to say.

"How lovely," Hazel remarked over the food, sitting down as Noah poured her a cup of tea. "I hope you two got to know each other better while I was gone." Her arched brow indicated that she noticed the tension from the other occupants of the table and the sparkle in her eye set off warning bells in Hanna's mind.

Noah grinned like he was about to reveal a secret, and it set every nerve in Hanna's body on high alert. "Of course. We were just discussing your trip to France." He paused. "And how great it would be if I joined you."

# 2

# *A Smile is Your Best Accessory*

"A CABARET?" Noah said the word like a question and accusation rolled into one, jumping right into the conversation without so much as a hello.

Twirling a pen in her fingers, Hanna forced herself to smile. After all, you can apparently hear a smile through the phone. "Good afternoon, Mr. Eversham." It put a small smile on her face to hear Noah's muted sigh at her splenda-sweet response. "What can I help you with?"

Perhaps give him directions to the nearest cliff to walk off?

"You could start by explaining what a cabaret is doing on the itinerary."

"Yes, it was on your grandmother's list of 'must do's' in Paris."

Since their meeting a week ago, Noah called every day. Sometimes multiple times a day, all so that he could "check in" on the planning process. He wanted to be involved in every step, no matter how many times she informed him that people hired her specifically so that they did not have to deal with the small details. Despite that, Noah wanted confirmation of every booking and each day's itinerary for the fourteen day trip, which she uploaded to the online client portal. Giving Noah access to this portal, in addition to Hazel, was clearly a mistake.

There was a sound of shuffling papers in the background. "And you thought that was an appropriate activity for women their age? One of them might have a heart attack."

"Last I checked, they were grown adults who could make their own decisions. If a cabaret is what Hazel wants, it is my job to book her the best possible, not critique her choices."

Silence filled her ear for a blessed moment.

"Where is it?"

"Paris."

An exasperated sigh came through the line.

"Where specifically?"

This time her smile was genuine. She should not take so much joy from pushing Noah's buttons, but he made it so easy.

"Montmartre."

She heard him typing.

"The name?"

Hanna told him.

More typing.

Registering what all the typing was for, Hanna gasped. "Are you looking it up? It is a real place, I assure you."

If you could hear a smile through the phone, then Hanna knew she could hear Noah smirking.

"Just making sure it is the best, since that's what my grandmother is paying you for. Although I do not see why she needs you when you can book directly on their website."

The nerve of this man. Contrary to what one overinvolved, over-protective, and arrogant grandson thought, this was not Hanna's first time planning a vacation. Trips Ahoy catered to groups looking for a cookie cutter experience, which meant that Hanna was giving the same set of tours each season. Japan and Korea in the spring, Europe in the summer, and South America in the winter, the history and stories of each landmark memorized to the point where she could recite them in her sleep. When guiding groups became a routine as stale as an open bag of crackers, Hanna looked for ways to keep them fresh and exciting.

That was when she asked Stephanie if she could design a new tour. Her first attempt never made it past the planning stages, receiving critique that it included too many activities in too short of a timeframe. Guests did not want to get carted from place to place like mail delivery, viewing sights like they were on a conveyor belt. After a period of self-doubt, where Hanna spiraled into thinking that she would never accomplish anything, Stephanie sat her down so they could work on revising the tour together. It took several drafts, but eventually she had a tour worth booking. Most of the tours Hanna created while at Trips Ahoy were wildly popular.

So, there was no reason for Noah to hover like a parent waiting for their teen to come home after their first date. Case in point, Dolly Parton's "9 to 5" usually brought her nothing but joy, but when the cheery ringtone rang minutes ago, all it did was grate on her last nerve. Now, her heart rate increased each time she saw his name on the screen of her phone and she took every opportunity to kill him with kindness in hopes that he gave up whatever quest he was on. And the flush of her face was caused by the fury that grew each time he doubted her, not the way his voice reminded her of sitting on the beach on a warm summer day.

It was the fifth time Noah called.

Today.

Hanna responded as if he never made the pointed jab at the necessity of her services. "Was there anything else you wanted to discuss, Mr. Eversham? Or can I get back to the job your grandmother hired me to do?"

A throat-clearing reminded Hanna that she should tone down the sass and pay attention to the guest on the other end of the phone. "I wanted to discuss the recent additions you added to our itinerary, unless you had something better to do?"

"I have as much time as you need," she said, standing and starting to pace across her room. All ten feet of it. She was spending too much time surrounded by four walls and needed to get outside. Launching a luxury travel company involved more time indoors than she was accustomed to. "I was just about to head out for coffee, would you like to meet up and we can go over your questions in person?"

Noah agreed to meet her at a location of her choosing, and it gave Hanna an idea. She needed to gain his trust so that he would stop interrupting her work and actually let her plan this trip. Four months before the trip would feel like an eternity if she had to defend every choice she was making. Meeting in person would provide a chance to show him the type of experiences Luxe Travel provided. It only took a few calls to set something up, and there was a smile on her face as Hanna texted the location information to Noah.

When they met at the coffee shop an hour later, Noah was wearing another crisp button down, this one a deep maroon that brought out his tan, the shine of his shoe and glare of his dark sunglasses practically blinding Hanna in the bright light. Apparently, when she asked him to dress casually, that meant slacks. Hanna could not wait to see him messy.

"Thank you for meeting me," Noah said while pushing his sunglasses on top of his swept back hair. Her memory did not do justice to his beautiful blue eyes, and just one look into them sent a jolt of energy through her body that caffeine could not accomplish. The decadent scent of roasting coffee beans poured out from the entrance as a couple excited the shop, the whir and hiss of coffee machines filling the air around them.

Hanna felt Noah's solid presence behind her as he reached for the door and held it open for her. "Anything for my most involved client."

Hanna was disappointed when her joke was met with silence. This man was harder to crack than a closed pistachio. Trips were more difficult with people who did not know how to have a good time. If she could not get Noah to relax, he would bring the vibe of the entire group down.

"Aren't I your only client?" Was that an attempt at humor? Hanna smothered a laugh.

"Technically, your grandmother is the client. You are just a bonus." Hanna looked over her shoulder with a cheeky grin and nearly tripped over the threshold at the sight of the right side of his mouth curving up. There was hope for him yet. Hanna's new mission in life was to get a full smile out of this man.

Clearing his throat, Noah settled a frown back on his face. "Speaking of my grandmother, I had a few questions about the activities–"

"*Ana!*" A short woman with black hair curling wildly around her round face called out in Spanish. Pilar Espinosa bustled around the counter to approach them with open arms, her simple black apron dusted with coffee grounds. An immigrant from Peru, Pilar's accented English never failed to remind Hanna of her own mother, and she felt a pang of homesickness when she realized it had been weeks since she last spoke to her parents.

Pilar fired off rapid questions in the spaces between kissing Hanna's cheeks. "*How are you? Are you eating enough? You look too skinny. It's been too long since you visited. How is your business? And who is this handsome man? A boyfriend?*"

"*No, Pilar,*" Hanna answered in Spanish, switching back to English at the look of confusion on Noah's face. "Do you remember the tour I was planning, with Hazel and her friends? This is Hazel's grandson, Noah. He is coming on the tour with us."

"A pleasure to meet you, Ms...?" Noah charmed Pilar instantly with his half-smile and sparkling eyes, a blush dusting her face as she swatted his arm. As cute as it was to watch Pilar flirt with Noah, Hanna felt something close to jealousy swirling in her chest despite the reality that Pilar was old enough to be Noah's mother.

"Everyone calls me Pilar. I haven't been a Ms. in a long time. You are in good hands with my Ana, she is the best there is. Single, too. Sit, sit. Let me get you some coffee and alfajores."

Now it was Hanna's turn to blush. The last thing she needed was

Pilar trying to set her up with a client's grandson. She had enough difficulty avoiding the topic of her dating life with her own parents. Watching the smaller woman herd Noah towards a table was amusing, and Hanna laughed at the desperate look he sent her way.

"Pilar," she chided. "Noah and I are here to meet with Daniel. I called him an hour ago to let him know we were coming."

"*Mijo*," Pilar yelled. "Your guests are here."

The door to the kitchen swung open as Daniel came into view, wiping his forearm against his brow and spreading a streak of flour across his brown skin. "Is it Ana?"

When he saw her, Daniel's face split into a wide grin. "It's been too long."

Opening her arms for a hug, Hanna kissed Daniel on the cheeks before wiping away the flour on his forehead with a napkin from her purse. He smelled like delicious coffee and baked goods. "Your mother said the same thing. Now that I am back in town, I promise to stop in regularly." Over Daniel's shoulders, Hanna saw Noah's jaw clench and eyes narrow as he watched them. Strange that he did not bat an eye when Pilar kissed her. As she pulled away from her friend, Hanna turned him toward Noah. "This is the client I told you about, Noah. Noah, this is Daniel Espinosa, the owner of Terrenos Frescos."

Hanna watched as Noah unclenched his jaw and extended his hand toward Daniel. Nearly a foot shorter, Daniel still managed to pull Noah into a hug, greeting him as if they were old friends. "*Bienvenidos*. Welcome. Any friend of Ana's is a friend of mine. I don't open my kitchen for just anyone, you know."

Only a few years younger than Hanna, Daniel prided himself on maintaining a spotless shop. Terrenos Frescos was decorated in playful colors. Vibrant artwork from artisans hung on the clay colored walls. Dark wood booths with mismatched throw pillows woven in geometric patterns lined the walls, and square tables with cushioned seats filled the open space. A long counter ran almost the entire length of the back wall, the coffee machines, racks of mugs, and a pastry cabinet giving patrons a tantalizing glimpse of what the shop offered.

Warm and inviting, the authenticity that Daniel and Pilar created was what initially drew Hanna to the shop. She continued coming because they provided something no coffee chain could, they made her feel like family.

More customers made their way into the shop, and Pilar went over to greet them, welcoming them in like old friends. Realizing that they were starting to get in the way, Hanna stepped to the side, angling her body in a way that encouraged Noah to do the same.

"Thank you again for letting us come on such short notice," she said to Daniel.

He waved off the thanks, ushering them towards the kitchen. "For you? Anything."

At Noah's quirked brow, Hanna felt the need to explain, "I have frequented this shop for years and always make a point to mention it on social media." She did not add that after the pandemic, there was a downturn in business that almost had Daniel closing the shop, and Hanna used the power of her follower count to promote the shop and host a GoFundMe. "Local, family-owned businesses are rich in history and good for the community. These are the places that people should be visiting, and I do what I can to increase their visibility."

"And that's what you do on your trips?"

She looked over her shoulder at him with a satisfied smile. Asking questions like that meant he cared, and caring brought him one step closer to not treating her like a scam artist. "Exactly. Which brings me to the purpose of our visit today."

Noah looked around the room, sharp eyes taking in the spotless countertops and appliances. "I thought we were meeting to discuss my concerns for the trip. And get coffee."

"Yes, but why just get coffee when you can learn how to make it."

His eyes widened in surprise before he turned back to survey the room in light of the new information. As if he could sense the tension between the two, Daniel was uncharacteristically quiet, moving about the space to grab what they needed for the lesson. Usually, her friend would keep up a continuous string of conversation, asking about her recent tours and regaling her with stories about his spouse, Marco, and their toddler, Maya.

The kitchen was small, with counters lining every available wall and wooden shelves with spices, earthen dishware, and utensils mounted above them. Where the main room was a vibrant riot of colors, the kitchen was stark, clean white lines and stainless steel appliances. A refrigerator held what ingredients they would need for the small selection of pastries and sandwiches they offered, and planters with fresh herbs were set in each of the three windows.

Pulling on the apron that Daniel handed her, Hanna explained, "I wanted to give you a taste of what kinds of excursions I can book for tour groups. Daniel graciously offered to teach us about the different types of coffee beans grown in Peru, and then we get to make our own coffee to enjoy with alfajores. Daniel?"

One of the key characteristics of a successful vacation concierge is knowing when to yield the floor to someone with more expertise than you. She was a spotlight, not the main attraction.

Affable as his mother, Daniel launched into the history of his favorite subject, coffee. He often joked that coffee ran through his veins, but considering that his extended family owned a coffee farm in Cusco, and how much of the beverage he consumed each day, Hanna suspected that it might be true. When he was a child, Daniel and Pilar visited Peru every summer, where he got into mischief with cousins and learned the family trade. He shared stories about days spent harvesting the pods, cradling them in his hands.

Glancing at Noah from the corner of her eye, Hanna was pleasantly surprised to see his eyes fixed on Daniel, giving him his full attention and listening earnestly. When Daniel began explaining how each variety of bean had different flavor notes, and that variation in fermentation changed the complexity of the flavor, Noah leaned forward, asking specific questions that had Daniel beaming with pride. Practically bursting with glee at having someone to share this passion with, Daniel had Noah sniff each jar of coffee beans, encouraging him to guess what flavors he could smell. It was like watching a teacher finally get an enthusiastic student, their energy building off one another.

The best part was that Hanna could tell Noah's curiosity was genuine. As much of a grump as he was towards her, Noah showed nothing but sincere kindness to Daniel and Pilar. He followed Daniel's instructions precisely, carefully pouring out water over pre-ground beans into a coffee press, waiting to pour it into sampling cups. The smell of freshly roasted coffee barely roused Hanna from the fixation she had on watching Noah's long, slender fingers wrap around the carafe or handle the delicate cups. They looked so small in his large hands, and she wondered what else would look–

Nope. Absolutely not.

Hanna could not lust after a client. Particularly not one who treated her job like an unwanted charge on a bill.

Stuffing away the wayward thoughts into an imaginary box in her brain, stored in a corner where it should collect enough dust to impress a crumbling European castle, Hanna refocused on the lesson in coffee making. Daniel gave her the abbreviated version years ago, but he was obviously enjoying the opportunity to take them through what was his version of the extended edition of Lord of the Rings.

When it finally came time to try the coffee, Hanna watched Noah intently, curious to see what his coffee preference was. At the tea shop, he added a splash of milk and a generous scoop of sugar to his cup, so Hanna had an inkling how he would react to the bold taste of the coffee.

Daniel placed a jar of beans below Noah's nose. "Here, smell the beans before you take a sip and try to guess which roast you are drinking."

Before taking a sip, Noah lifted first the various beans, then the brew to his nose, inhaling deeply in an attempt to smell the scents that Daniel explained earlier. When the first burst of flavor hit his tongue, Noah winced slightly before masking the reaction. Running a hand over his stubbled jaw and clearing his throat, Noah returned the cup to its place in the lineup.

"It's rather bold, but I think I tasted vanilla and...citrus?" His eyes ran along the row of jars before pointing to one. "This one?"

Having noticed Noah's initial wince, Daniel's enthusiasm had deflated, but he perked back up again at the correct guess.

"Yes! That is our house roast, more acidic than most people are used to, but we balance it with the vanilla and citrus. Here, try this one next." Daniel nudged another cup forward.

After his experience with the last cup, Noah glanced at Hanna without reaching for the cup. "Why don't you try this one?"

Based on his hesitation, Hanna guessed that he was concerned the next cup would be too bitter for his liking, and was trying to get her to fall on the proverbial sword for him. Travel was all about trying new things, and Hanna knew from experience that the next roast was softer.

Shaking her head with an encouraging smile, Hanna replied, "Me? No, this experience is for you. Besides, I have my own cup."

Noah frowned down at the row of cups, looking at them like they insulted him. He swallowed before lifting up the next cup, and Hanna had to stifle a laugh. The man truly did not like bitter drinks. Beside her, Daniel turned away with a cough that sounded suspiciously like a laugh.

Despite his initial reluctance, Noah's eyes widened in surprise when he tasted the coffee.

"It's...sweeter than I expected. And, almost floral?"

This time, Daniel let out a deep laugh. "Better than you were expecting, no?"

A flush spread over Noah's cheekbones. "Yes," he said sheepishly. "It might be one of the best cups of coffee I have ever tasted. But I wouldn't say no to a little creamer."

"You two go sit down and I'll bring you a fresh cup along with our homemade creamer." Daniel clapped Noah on the shoulder before waving them out of the kitchen.

Placing her apron on the peg near the swinging door, Hanna looked over her shoulder at Noah. "So, what did you think?"

"I was surprised. When you offered to meet for coffee, I was expecting a quick meeting, not a lesson on coffee beans. But I enjoy learning from people who are passionate about their craft. It gave me an appreciation for Daniel's heritage and the struggles small farmers are experiencing."

He pulled out her chair before sitting across from her.

Hanna mentally high-fived herself. Bringing him to Terrenos Frescos was part of her plan to convince him that her company was legitimate and added value to people's vacations. Admitting that he enjoyed the experience was a step in the right direction, and Hanna felt tension release from her shoulders at the thought of him not fighting her over every decision.

"But–" Noah's blue gaze focused on her. "–that doesn't mean I trust you yet."

Annnndd, there went all the progress Hanna thought she was making.

She wanted to bang her head against the wall, which would probably yield more than the stubborn man across from her. But strong outbursts of emotions never got women anywhere in the world.

Instead, Hanna folded her hands neatly on the table, assuming a posture of confidence before responding calmly. "Trust takes time. I understand your hesitancy when it comes to this trip." A lie. "I can also understand why you might be considering other travel agencies for your grandmother to use." Another lie. "But, part of what Luxe Travels offers, what *I* offer, are unique experiences that you cannot get elsewhere. Visiting a country is one thing, but immersing yourself in the culture and lifestyle gives you rich and rewarding experiences. Experiences like this."

She gestured to the cafe around them, Pilar chatting with customers at another table while Daniel brought out their fresh drinks. "You can get coffee anywhere, but getting to meet the owners, families who have worked the land for generations, and use your own hands to make something is priceless."

A crease formed between his eyebrows and Noah regarded her skeptically. "Sure, but my grandmother doesn't need you for that. Why not just cut out the middle-woman, you, and arrange everything on her own?"

Wow. It was like Noah did not even care that he was insulting her career choice to her face. Sure, her family constantly treated her job like it was a side project on her way to a "real" career, but having a relative stranger say she was expendable hurt more than Hanna wanted to admit. Moving one hand under the table, Hanna began spinning the plain gold band on her middle finger with her thumb, letting the smooth touch of the warm metal steady her heartbeat.

She understood his concern, paying someone for a task she could do herself was a luxury Hanna could not afford, but Noah and his grandmother could. "Because I save people the hassle and headache of having to arrange it on their own. Plus, do you see anyone else going into the kitchen?" She gave a pointed look around them. Silence sat between them for a beat.

"No." The answer was pulled out of him like a stubborn dog refusing to let go of a tennis ball even though it wanted to continue playing fetch.

"Exactly, because it isn't offered to just anyone. When people take a tour with me, they don't just get my planning and translation skills, they also get my connections. You work in business, right?"

He nodded, shoulders tightening as he realized she was going to put him in his place. Clients usually held the upper hand, controlling her means of receiving steady income, but she relished the instances where she got to lay out a tactful "I told you so." And something about this particular man, the way they rubbed each other wrong, made this moment even more enjoyable. She felt a little shiver of delight through her body.

"Then you understand how valuable relationships and networking are. Have you been to Paris before? Do you have hours to book reservations to the Louvre, Eiffel Tour, and countless other places Hazel and her friends want to go? Would you like to research dozens of private car services to find one that is reliable and can accommodate a wheelchair? I have been at this job for a long time, and work hard to seek out places and people that offer something outside the typical tourist trap box. Businesses trust me to bring groups who genuinely care about exploring and trying new things, and groups trust me to take them to hidden gems in some of the most well-known places of the world. What I provide is more than just 'trip planning.' I create unforgettable memories for people, crafting experiences catering to their unique interests."

Hanna could feel the heat rising in her face from the impassioned speech, her heart pounding somewhere in her throat. At certain points, Hanna had allowed her frustration to slip into her tone, some-thing that she worked diligently to keep at bay around guests. As Stephanie had to often remind her when she was a fresh-faced teenager co-guiding groups, "People don't pay us to lecture them like naughty school children. They want a guide who is polite, polished, and pretty."

But, when she lifted her eyes to look at Noah again, having briefly lowered them to her cup when taking a calming breath, Hanna saw a muscle in his jaw twitch. Definitely not a good sign. Saying goodbye to any dreams of launching her business with a splash, Hanna prepared for him to call Hazel and fire her on the spot.

His blue eyes blazed like the hottest fire and Hanna felt warmth pool in her core as he continued to stare at her. Noah's jaw flexed like he was puzzling out what words to skewer her with. But when his lips parted, it was not with the verbal set down Hanna expected.

"You are right, I do not have time for that. Nor do I think my grandmother would want to go on a trip that I planned for her." The mention of his grandmother softened the hard set of his face. "If she heard how I was talking to you." He shuddered. "Well, let's just leave it that I'm grateful she isn't here."

Hanna knew she should laugh politely when he gave a self-deprecating laugh, but she merely regarded him warily. None of what he was saying sounded like he was firing her, but neither was he apologizing for his behavior.

"Look," he continued, "I am well aware that you don't like me, and I do not trust that you aren't looking to use my grandmother for her money. But, that is no excuse for me to talk to you the way I did. I am sorry."

Noah ran a hand through his thick hair, the once styled look now artfully waved.

"Thank you." Hanna watched his shoulders relax. "Whether you like it or not, Hazel hired me, not you, and I am going to continue planning an amazing vacation for her and her friends."

Before he could interject, Hanna plowed on. "But, that does not mean that I want you to fight me every step of the way. Each delay costs time and effort, which could limit the options I am able to book. Hazel already provided her credit card information and paid the deposit, and I know you've double checked that there were no recent fraudulent charges."

Honestly, it spoke highly of him that he was protective of his grandmother. There were too many convincing scammers and hackers out there. So, although a large part of her was frustrated that Noah's protectiveness was impacting her job, Hanna was also envious that Hazel had someone in her life that cared enough to intervene. In a family dedicated to non-profit work, with both parents medical professionals, Hanna grew up on a steady diet of self-sufficiency and over-achieving. Her parents and siblings gave so much to the world around them, that Hanna often felt left behind.

Running out of both time and options, Hanna asked, "What else can I do to convince you that I'm not out to steal your grandmother's money?"

Noah regarded her for a moment.

"How about we make a deal? I'll stop questioning every decision you make, if–" He paused to look at her, the effect of his full attention like a cyclone pulling Hanna into his blue eyes. "You stop acting like Tour Guide Barbie."

She stumbled over her words as her brain fought to catch up with what he said. "Excuse me? Tour Guide Barbie? You think I'm acting fake?"

If only she did live in Barbie World where everything was fantastic and went her way. Then she could escape this carousel of a conversation.

Nodding, Noah took a sip of his coffee, wrapping his hands around the cup when he was done. "That's part of the reason I am having trouble trusting you." His eyes scrutinized her, as if looking close enough would reveal cracks in her armor.

Could he see how she used flawless makeup–not too heavy–a chic wardrobe, thrifted, and practiced politeness to shore up any crumbling facades?

"How can I trust you when I do not know how much of this is your real personality, or just a persona for clients. There are glimpses of the real you, flashes that make me feel like I can trust you, but then you close up and I am left wondering what to believe. To me, honesty is more important than being likable."

Noah wanted the real version of her? Impossible. No one wanted that. Hanna was not even sure *she* knew who that person fully was. So much of her job was dedicated to being whoever the group wanted her to be. Everyone wanted the fun, upbeat, always happy and positive woman who had enough energy to power a small town. Not the version that called people out for their bad behavior.

"So you like it when I call you out for being an asshole?"

Noah's mouth lifted in that half-smile Hanna was beginning to crave. Almost as if it was a reward for the thoughts that popped out of her mouth, unfiltered.

"Oddly enough, I do. I can admit when I'm being an asshole, and should be called out for it." He placed his hands palm down in the middle of the table. "At least your reactions are honest when you are calling me out, and I promise that this will not negatively impact your job."

"Really?" She regarded him skeptically. "Even if I tell you that you need to let me do my job and stop acting like an overbearing parent, you will not ask Hazel to fire me?"

"No, because at least I know you are being honest. Do we have a deal, no more fake personality around me?"

"In return, do you think you can withhold pestering me long enough for me to get my job done?"

"I'll try," he replied with a smirk. "Think you can convince me this is all worth the price?"

The spark of competition made Hanna's heart skip a beat.

"Definitely." Their hands met briefly in the space between them, what should have been a professional gesture instead sent a zap of pleasure up her arm before spreading through the network of nerves, lighting up every receptor in her body. Maybe the challenge would not be convincing him that her tour was worth it, but convincing herself that the chemistry between them was not worth exploring.

While they finished their coffee, Hanna and Noah chatted about random topics. Straying from her process when vetting activities to what movies they watched recently. As they stood to leave, Hanna watched Noah subtly slide several bills underneath the empty cups. Even though she told him that the experience was her treat, Noah insisted that quality service should be rewarded, and it was sweet that he did not appear to want recognition for his generosity.

At the door, they parted with a wave.

"Talk to you soon," Noah called out.

"Not too soon," Hanna replied.

His laughter echoed in Hanna's head the entire ride back to her apartment.

# 3
## *Make Time for Friends*

WHEN SHE GOT HOME, Hanna's landlord was in the kitchen chopping vegetables. Hair in a pile of ebony curls atop her head, Sarah called out a greeting as Hanna hung her purse and keys on their designated hooks. After inheriting the three-bedroom craftsman home from her aunt while she was still in medical school, Sarah started renting out the two extra bedrooms to cover the cost of property taxes and utilities. Hanna found out about the room through another guide, Will, who took seasonal jobs with companies that specialized in outdoor adventure treks.

When someone traveled as much as Hanna did, it seemed pointless to pay rent for a place that she was not at the majority of her time. Which is what made renting from Sarah so unique. Hanna and Will filled out a calendar with the dates they would need the rooms, and Sarah rented them to traveling nurses the rest of the time. The room was impersonal and all of Hanna's possessions could fit into two suitcases and a backpack, but it worked for her. She did not need any frills, just someplace that was safe, did not cost her entire paycheck, and a reasonable distance to the airport.

The scent of chana masala simmering in a pot hit Hanna's nose, her stomach grumbling as she stepped into her house shoes and wandered into the kitchen, flipping through her small pile of mail as she went.

Bill, bill, spam about her nonexistent car's extended warranty, and an envelope addressed from Trips Ahoy. This was not the first time she received communication from the new company that bought out her former employer, opting to keep the name in the buyout. During the initial phases of the process, Hanna was contacted with an optional contract of employment to stay with the company, but she declined in favor of starting her own business. They reached out again after the buyout was complete, with a minimal increase in benefits package, but Hanna declined again. Hanna thought they must be desperate if they were reaching out to her again, but she had no interest in returning to work for them. Tossing the mail onto Sarah's shredding pile, Hanna joined her in the kitchen.

"How was work?" Pulling dishes from the cupboard, Hanna began setting the table for three, having seen Will's keys and shoes by the door.

"Crazy." Sarah passed her a bowl of steaming basmati rice. "There is a stomach bug going around again so it was back to back puking kids. What about you, any new clients?"

Adjusting the napkins on the table, Hanna told her about the trip to Terrenos Frescos with Noah. Sarah knew about her previous interactions with Noah, having heard the story over another shared dinner. They both grew up in households where shared meals were sacred, and anytime they were both home Sarah and Hanna made a point to eat together.

"He did say that he would try to bother me less though, which is a good thing. It would be nice to finally get through a day without his 'Good morning, Ms. Poole. Think of any new ways to steal from my grandmother, Ms. Poole?'" Hanna tried, and failed, to emulate his deep voice. "Gah, that man is so infuriating."

Sarah smiled knowingly. "He certainly knows how to get under your skin."

Rolling her eyes at the understatement, Hanna adjusted the

silverware until it sat perfectly on the folded napkins. Will lovingly teased her about making such a fuss over a dinner with roommates, but Hanna felt that dressing up an ordinary occasion elevated it into something special. And everyone could use more of something special.

"That's not even the worst part." Hanna filled water glasses while Sarah spooned the food into bowls. "He said that I was untrustworthy because I acted like, and I quote, 'Tour Guide Barbie.'"

"Hah! He's got you pegged there." Will's bright hair and even brighter smile were the first things anyone noticed when he walked into a room. Perpetually tanned from spending the majority of his time outdoors, his long blonde hair, straight white teeth, and blue-green eyes stood out in vivid contrast.

Hanna shot him a glare as he sauntered into the kitchen, grabbing the bowl from Sarah and placing it on the table before sinking into a chair, legs stretched out in front of him while his arms draped over the back of the chair. Courtesy of his Nordic ancestors, Will had a figure that took up space, well over six feet tall and the muscle definition to support it. Hours spent rock climbing, horseback riding, zip lining, any sport or physical activity really, meant that Will stayed fit, something that the groups he led on expeditions appreciated.

"No, he doesn't. I am a living, breathing person, not a plastic doll." She even had the jiggle in her hips and butt to prove it.

"Sure, but you always act so controlled and perfect. Happy and peppy with your matching accessories." They had known each other long enough that Hanna knew Will did not mean it in a hurtful way.

Hanna's mouth was open to snap back with a clever and mature response of "do not," but Will shifted in his seat, mimicking her straight posture, one ankle crossed over the other. Feeling her cheeks heat with a blush, Hanna conceded that he might have a point. But looking a certain way was part of her job and was not easy to turn off.

"Keep arguing and I won't share the naan with you." Ever the peacemaker in the group, Sarah interrupted any further back and forth and tore apart a piece of naan and dipped it in her bowl. "Did Noah say why it mattered so much to him how you acted?"

Midway through a bite, Hanna thought back on the conversation while she chewed. "He said that he could trust me more if he knew my reactions and personality were real, not just telling him what I thought he wanted to hear."

Which was not unreasonable. Getting called the name of a fictional toy that historically looked nothing like Hanna was not a compliment, but perhaps she was reacting so strongly because she knew there was truth to it, not because Noah meant it maliciously. No one questioned her demeanor before and it puzzled her that Noah did. They never worried that Hanna was stealing from them, in fact, one guest handed Hanna her black Amex card and told her to use it to purchase gifts for her family back home, completely trusting that Hanna would not misuse it.

Sarah waved a hand through the air. "And that's a bad thing?"

"No, but it's not like he has any room to judge! He showed up in slacks and a collared shirt when I specifically told him to dress casual. As if he looked any less polished with his perfect hair and perfectly trimmed beard, manicured hands and fancy watch." Hanna picked up her water glass and took a large gulp to cool the flush that was working its way up her body at the thought of how Noah looked at the coffee shop.

"Oh, that's the real reason he frustrates you. He's been getting under your skin when what you really want is for him to get into your pants." Will wagged his eyebrows suggestively.

Thanks to her combined Peruvian and Scottish heritage, Hanna's caramel colored skin could still turn as red as her sister's hair when embarrassed. "That would be completely inappropriate. He's a client."

"So?" Will did not bother with rules, preferring to live his life exactly as he wanted, breaking the hearts of many of his guests along the way.

Hanna tossed her balled up napkin at Will, which he caught

midair. He was just as annoying as her twin brothers. "Some of us would like to keep their jobs."

"Hasn't happened to me yet."

Yet another way the patriarchy won. Will could sleep with clients and get away with it, but Hanna knew that one rumor would be enough to destroy her reputation and derail her business. She made that mistake once, when she was a teenager and thought she was in love, and that one mistake almost cost her everything.

"The key word being 'yet,'" Sarah admonished Will. Though she was only a decade older than Hanna, and slightly more for Will, Sarah was the mom of the group, keeping them in line and doling out wisdom when they needed it. "One of these days your choices are going to catch up with you and you will realize that building something meaningful with a person is more rewarding than dozens of flings."

Hanna gave Will a smug smile, watching his eyes widen as if Sarah had wished great evil on him. She quickly swallowed her smile as Sarah turned towards her.

"And Hanna..." Sarah's dry hand found hers on the table. "Do not be afraid to open yourself to new experiences. Noah may not have phrased it well, but I agree with his sentiment. You hide yourself from others, only letting them see glimpses of the amazing person you are. The world will not end if you tell a guest that they are out of line or let yourself get closer to them. You work for yourself now, that means you do not have to tolerate people who are rude to you."

If only it were that easy. Life taught her that people only wanted her when she acted the way they desired, and at the first sign of something undesirable, they would leave.

# 4
## Guests are Paying Customers, Not Friends

HANNA HAD SPENT enough time in airports to know they were not the magical hub of transportation that cinema tries to convince everyone they are. Yes, they had the ability to take a person to far off places, removing them from the mundane of everyday life and whisking them to a dazzling new place for a brief stint in time, but they also made a person feel like cattle, prodded and shuffled from one location to the next.

Between standing in seemingly endless lines—surely the line for TSA was a portal into purgatory where frazzled passengers ran over your ankles with their luggage and coughs and sneezes came from every direction—and the bombardment of last minute shopping for the unprepared or bored, it was enough to stress anyone out. Frequent travelers knew the secrets of getting through with less headache, thank you advance check-in and TSA Precheck, but more often than not, Hanna did not give tours to frequent travelers.

Hence, the reason for her presence at the San Diego International Airport waiting for the tour group to arrive. Although Hazel and Noah traveled enough to navigate the chaos of international airports, Hazel's friends Lillian, Mai, and Daphne, did not. Hazel insisted that Hanna travel with them, instead of meeting them in Paris, to make sure that Mai, who used a wheelchair, did not

35

feel like a burden for the group. Checking her phone to verify that the private car she ordered for the group was arriving soon, Hanna pulled her carryon and matching backpack to the curb.

Moments later, a white SUV pulled up to the curb and Noah stepped out of the front passenger seat just as Hanna was reaching for the rear door handle.

"I've got it," he said, opening the door for the older women.

Casual dress must not be a term that Noah was familiar with, because he was once again dressed in slacks, button down shirt, and a long coat despite the fact they would be sitting on a plane for hours. Hanna hid a laugh in her shoulder as Noah leaned in to help his grandmother out of the vehicle just for the older woman to smack his arm at his fussing.

"I can get out on my own, no need to treat me like I've got one foot in the grave." In jeans and a soft sweater, Hazel was dressed more in line with what Hanna suggested in the packing list she sent to the group. "Hanna, so good to see you again."

Spiced perfume tickled her nose as Hanna bent slightly to accept Hazel's hug. "The pleasure is all mine. Are you excited for another trip?" She watched as Noah helped the other women get out of the vehicle, keeping an eye on the growing pile of luggage the driver was putting on the curb.

Hazel's eyes were lit from within, her excitement for the trip palpable. "After that amazing itinerary you put together? I have a feeling this trip is going to be the best yet. Between the art, food and wine, and shows, I hardly think we will get any sleep."

"Now, Hazel, not all of us can keep up with you." The smoky voice belonged to the elegant asian woman wheeling over to join them. Her dark hair was cut short and heavily dusted with gray, rich brown eyes twinkling with mischief as she regarded her friend. "You must be Hanna. Hazel has been talking about you non-stop since she first took a tour with you, hopefully you can help us keep her from going too crazy. I am Mai Kato, but you can call me Mai."

Hanna laughed at Hazel's pretend offense at her friend's

comment. "Lovely to meet you, Mai. My job is to make sure you all have fun, and I don't think there is anyone who could stop Hazel when she puts her mind to something." Hanna was pleased that Mai laughed at her joke.

"I like you already," Mai said with a pat on Hanna's hand.

"I liked her the moment she booked us a cabaret," said the tall woman stepping up to Hanna. Calloused hands clasped Hanna's as she found herself being drawn into another hug. Daphne Dupre smelled like sunshine and coconuts, her braided hair shining in the morning light. "I hope you brought your dancing shoes, missy, because these new knees are ready to boogie." She gave a little shimmy to illustrate her point, bracelets jingling on her wrists.

Here was a group of women who embraced life and were ready for a good time. It was groups like these why Hanna never got tired of traveling, they were infectious with their enthusiasm and she was caught in their orbit. Hanna wanted to be this full of life and joy when she was their age, living in the present and not taking a moment for granted.

"Be careful with my bags!" A sharp voice drew Hanna's attention away from the trio to the back of the vehicle where the driver was unloading the last suitcase from the trunk. Beside him was a thin woman dressed head to toe in cream, her platinum hair and gold jewelry looked like it belonged in a stock photo instead of the dirty curb of an airport.

With her face pinched with worry as the driver set a Louis Vuitton duffle bag on top of the matching suitcase, Hanna would have thought the item was the woman's first-born child, not a piece of luggage.

Not wanting to start the trip off on a sour note, Hanna strode forward to thank the driver and take over managing the suitcases.

"Lillian, right?" Hanna steered Lillian away from the driver with an arm around her shoulders. "Nice to meet you. My name is Hanna and if there is anything you need, please let me know. Hazel let me know that you were looking forward to touring the Louvre and Monet's gardens."

"Well, yes, I love art." The blonde turned over her shoulder to look back at her luggage. "Are you just going to leave our bags on the curb? Mine are very expensive."

Hanna suppressed an eye roll at the implication that she was abandoning the bags when they were two steps away. Based on Hazel's warnings, Hanna knew that Lillian's husband recently left her for a younger woman and was lashing out. It did not excuse the rudeness, but at least Hanna was prepared for it and would not take it personally.

"Your bags are in good hands. If you would like to join the others, I will get the bags so that you can all get checked in."

Having prepared two luggage carts in advance, Hanna was glad that she packed light. Based on the number of suitcases the four women brought, it would take some coordination to push both carts and her own bag. At least it was not that far to the luggage drop off.

A shadow covered the handles of the carts just before a pair of hands settled around hers on one cart. "That was neatly handled."

Noah did not look at her as he said it, instead focusing on the path in front of them as they navigated through the groups of people making their way into the check-in lobby, Hazel and her friends following behind them.

True to his word, after their meeting at the coffee shop, Noah kept their communication to a minimum, checking in only once or twice a week. Each time, he asked genuine questions, like how transportation for Mai would work, and their conversations ended with a clipped, "Thank you." More often than not, his texts about the trip would turn into calls where he would ask why Hanna selected particular establishments, and where her favorite places were to visit in the city. He seemed to enjoy hearing her talk and share stories about her travels, despite his one-word responses.

And true to her word, Hanna was working on being her real self with him. "Well, it is my job. Just wait until she sees what her bags look like after they've been in the belly of a plane." She could just imagine the meltdown now, the pristine luggage stood no chance against the grime of thousands of bags on conveyor belts.

Beside her, Noah covered a laugh with a cough, the edge of his mouth twitching. They approached the self-check bag kiosks and Hanna quickly tagged each of the women's bags, taking photos of the corresponding tags just in case.

"Where are yours?" Noah held his tagged luggage in one hand, a messenger bag slung over his shoulder. As Hanna worked her way through the group's bags, his large hand was always there to grab it and place it back on the luggage cart. Despite her initial reaction to tell him that she could manage it on her own, Hanna was not too proud to admit that it made the process smoother, and she thanked him as he lifted each bag. His eyebrow lifted in response, as if to tell her that the thanks was unnecessary.

Lifting her shoulder to gesture to her backpack and carry-on, Hanna replied, "This is all I brought."

"Just two bags?" Lillian looked at her in exaggerated horror. "How could you possibly have enough changes of clothes, let alone makeup and hair products?"

Taking a moment to start handing bags off to the counter attendant with a shared smile of customer service commiseration, Hanna turned back to the group. Even sweet Hazel was staring at her in confusion, the ability to travel minimally not in any of the women's vocabulary.

"I have everything I need. Since I travel often, I am used to packing just a few pieces that I can rotate and wash when needed. Packing light makes it easier for me to help all of you and I do not need to worry about saving room for souvenirs."

Not that there was anyone for her to buy souvenirs for even if she wanted to. Her family was spread out across the globe, her eldest sister the only one with a permanent address, and carrying around knick knacks for months before having an opportunity to mail them was not on the top of Hanna's to-do list. They would not want anything either, claiming that Hanna's safety was the most important gift. Her small group of friends was just as traveled as Hanna was, so they never wanted gifts, and Sarah only asked for chocolate, which was easily retrieved on the way to the airport before the return trip.

"Well," Daphne murmured, "I wish I had your self-control. I thought I would need to sit on my suitcase just to get it closed!"

Yeah, Hanna could tell based on the weight as she hefted it off the cart and onto the scale. Clearly, weight limits were not a concern to the group.

Mai laughed before waving a hand at the remaining luggage, of which only one suitcase was hers. "Were Noah and I the only ones who read Hanna's trip suggestions? Packing light was one of them."

"You always were good at memorizing rules, mostly so that you could figure out how to get around them," Hazel teased her friend affectionately, the quartet descending into giggles as they reminisced about past misadventures while Hanna finished unloading the luggage. This group was going to be a handful in the best way possible.

Warm breath tickled her ear–the only reason a shiver went down her spine, surely–as Noah leaned in to whisper, "Sure you can handle their brand of trouble?"

When she tipped her head back to look up at him, Hanna found Noah's face much closer than expected. Since he had to lean down to speak in her ear, Noah was eye level with her upturned face, their mouths inches apart. A flush burned its way across Hanna's chest, infusing her limbs with heat until she felt like she was melting from the inside out while her mouth went dry. This close, Hanna could see flecks of gold in Noah's eyes, tiny chips of warmth in otherwise cool eyes, and spotted a thin white scar along his hairline. Her fingers itched to trace it and Hanna clenched her fist to resist.

Close as they were, Hanna caught the flash in Noah's eyes, his pupils dilating as his mouth parted slightly. Was it possible that her proximity was doing similar things to his body? Did he feel this spark between them, too? Improbable as it was, Hanna knew nothing good would come from that line of thinking. Noah was her client.

*Technically, his grandmother is the client*, the devil on her shoulder whispered. Blinking away the errant thought, Hanna cleared her throat and stepped back.

"Handle it? Please. I encourage it." Leaving Noah to ponder that with a toss of her hair, Hanna corralled the group to take them through security.

Thanks to priority screening, the group was through TSA with minimal trouble and Hanna let out a sigh of relief that while the group did not heed her directions to pack light, they had at least listened to what could and could not go in a carry on. Pushing Mai's wheelchair through the automatic doors into the first class lounge, Hanna was glad they were through one of the trickiest hurdles for traveling. How a group got through the check in and security processes was telling for how they would manage waiting for more popular experiences, like the line for the Eiffel Tower elevator.

"Welcome, ladies and gentleman." The counter representative smiled politely and extended a hand across the counter, eyes sweeping over the group with a flash of approval. "May I see your tickets?"

"Of course." Hanna handed them over before reaching for her phone. While the rest of the group could access the lounge due to their first class seats, Hanna had purchased a lounge pass for herself. Saving money by flying economy was the responsible decision and it was not like Hazel or her friends would need Hanna on the flight. That was what the first class flight attendants were for.

That did not mean she wanted to draw attention to the fact that she was flying economy, so Hanna tried to discreetly slide her phone to the bespectacled man across the counter from her.

But, as her father would say, God had a different plan for her today.

"I am sorry, miss, but your ticket does not give you access to the lounge." The representative gave her a pitying smile, completely ignoring her phone, while sliding her ticket back. "There are still seats in first class available if you would like to upgrade your ticket? Your companions are welcome to wait in the lounge for you."

All conversation stopped, the silence in the small lobby deafening as embarrassment flooded Hanna's face and caused a small sheen of sweat to form on her skin. This reminded her of one of her first solo tours, where Hanna mixed up the date/month order on a reservation and was told by the hotel staff–in front of the entire party–that she made a mistake and there were no rooms available at that hotel. A small miracle that their group was the only one in the room, but Hanna could feel the weight of seven pairs of eyes staring at her.

"Hanna, darling." Hazel stepped up beside her, setting a comforting hand on her arm. "Is everything alright?"

Now would be a great time for Hanna to discover she secretly had invisibility powers. Or the capability to time travel.

Refusing to let Hazel see how much this humiliated her, Hanna stuffed down her feelings. "Just a small misunderstanding. Why don't you and the others continue into the lounge? I have you all checked in and will join you in a moment."

"Are you sure? We do not mind waiting for you." Mixed looks of sympathy and impatience–thank you, Lillian–lined the other women's faces.

"I am sure." Hanna nudged them toward the elevators. "Go enjoy a mimosa!"

Hanna waited for the elevator doors to close before she turned back to the counter...and ran smack into Noah's chest.

"Noah!" His name came out as a surprised squeak. "What are you still doing here? Go with Hazel, I will be there in a few minutes." What had she done in life to deserve his presence for this embarrassing moment? The last thing she needed was for him to see this and add it to his list of reasons why they should not have hired her.

He wrapped his hands around her shoulders and gently moved Hanna to the side. "What is the problem?" His question was addressed to the representative still holding Hanna's ticket.

"Your companion has a ticket for economy class and cannot join you in the lounge. As I was just explaining to her, there are still seats available for your flight if she would like to upgrade."

"Economy?" Noah's eyes flashed to hers, something unreadable in their depths. He was probably angry that her peasant status was showing. "Why aren't you with us?"

"Because I am trying to start a business and it would be irresponsible to pay for first class," she hissed at him, pitching her voice low in the hope that the representatives could not hear her. Noah's frown deepened and Hanna fought back a glare of her own. Just when she thought he was beginning to like her.

The representative watched them with the hidden glee of someone who was enjoying the drama unfolding in front of their eyes. "Would you like me to show you which options are available for upgrade?"

"That will not be necessary." Hanna slid in front of Noah. "As I was trying to show you on my phone, I purchased a lounge pass."

This time it was the representative's turn to flush with embarrassment. Reviewing the information on the screen, he scanned the pass and slid the phone back towards Hanna. "My apologies, miss. Please enjoy your stay in the lounge."

"Thank you, I will."

Wheeling her bag behind her, Hanna tried to make as graceful an exit as possible, only turning back to hold the elevator for Noah. Who was still standing at the counter.

At her raised eyebrow, he said, "Go ahead, I just had a question. It will only take a minute."

Grateful for the reprieve being alone in the elevator would give her, Hanna left Noah in the lobby, slumping against the cool wall once the doors closed. It was fine. *Everything is fine. People make mistakes,* Hanna reminded herself with several slow breaths. The hot flush slowly receded as Hanna's heart rate slowed. She hated making mistakes, particularly in front of others. Logically, she knew there was no shame in flying economy, but after years of traveling with people whose daily budget was more than her rent, Hanna could not shake the feeling of being on the outside looking in. Dressing the part went a long way to integrating with groups, but nothing would change the fact that she was not one of them. Never had been, never would be.

Every cell of her body wanted to hide away for a few hours while Hazel and the others forgot the interaction, but running away from discomfort was never the answer. She was an adult, dammit, and the next two weeks would be more awkward if she did not get it out of the way.

When the elevator doors opened, Hanna surveyed the polished space, the gleaming tiled floor curving like a river around a series of seating areas partially hidden by half-walls. Her shoes tapped against the floor as Hanna passed the buffet stations and square bar. Floor to ceiling windows overlooking the tarmac made the space look larger than it was, and Hanna soon found the group. Daphne and Hazel were seated in plush maroon chairs across from Mai, around a low table that reflected the room's light from its opal top. At the bar, Lillian was accepting four glasses of mimosas.

"Hanna, darling," Hazel called out as she joined them at the table, "is everything alright with your ticket?"

Tucking her skirt beneath her, Hanna settled into a chair before answering. "Yes, just a small misunderstanding. Nothing to worry about. I see you helped yourselves to the buffet, was there anything else I can get you?"

"No, but you should get something for yourself." Mai gestured with her fork to the omelet in front of her. "This is delicious."

Before Hanna could reply, Lillian came around the table, sliding a glass to each of her friends. "Well, that certainly does smell good. Hanna?" Her southern accent thickened the name as if she was mispronouncing it on purpose. "Would you get me one?"

"Let the girl sit a minute, Lillian," Daphne chided. "Go get one yourself."

"It's alright." Hanna was already rising from the chair. "What would you like on it?"

Lillian smiled smugly at the group before rattling off a list of ingredients. "See, she doesn't mind. It is her job after all."

*She* had a name and could answer for herself, but Hanna kept that thought to herself and went over to the food stations. While she waited for Lillian's omelet, Hanna filled a bowl with yogurt, granola, and fruit, food that was easy to eat while being continuously interrupted by questions.

A crisp ticket flapped in her peripheral vision. "Here."

Hanna groaned inwardly. Was it not enough that he stayed to witness her exchange with the desk agent, but now Noah had to interrupt her moment of peace waiting for food?

"I already have a ticket," she said, ignoring the proffered paper.

Noah leaned his hip against the counter, creating a perpendicular stand-off as his body faced her and she resolutely faced the omelet station.

"This one is better."

"Why? Because it was printed on first-class lounge paper? Thanks, but I'll stick with the one I have."

Flicking the ticket so that it danced in front of Hanna's face Noah replied, "No, because it is first-class."

"What?" Hanna pinched the paper between two fingers like it would burn her, studying the ink like the Rosetta Stone, rereading the words to make sure she was seeing them correctly. The words did not change. There was her name, their flight number, and a number for a seat in first class.

Out of the corner of her eye, Noah remained where he was, face unreadable as he watched for her reaction.

"Are you mocking me?" The only times Hanna flew better than economy was when she received an upgrade due to her frequent flier status. While she accounted for transportation expenses in her rates, Hanna knew that she could save money by taking a lower-status seat, and while she rarely traveled with guests on planes, none ever offered to upgrade her. To receive this from the man who accused her of trying to take his grandmother's money, or scam them into a free vacation was incomprehensible.

Noah's eyebrows lowered in confusion. "What? No. I would never do something like that."

"Then why give me this ticket? If I accept it, does that prove to you that I am using you for your money? Newsflash, I do not need your money to get on that plane. I had my own seat, using my own money, that I was perfectly happy with. Had I wanted to fly first class, I could have, and I do not need your pity to get there."

How dare he? Just because she was flying in economy did not make her less than him. Angry tears pricked the backs of her eyes and Hanna blinked rapidly to keep them from falling. It galled her how quickly he was able to poke at her insecurities, making her feel like a twelve-year-old again trying to fit in at a new school, getting laughed at for her twice-over hand-me-down clothing.

"Hanna, no. Look at me, please." The gentle pleading in his voice, something she never thought to hear in his tone, had Hanna's head turning against her will. "This is not pity, or me thinking less of you for flying economy. I did this because I did not think it was right for you to be in economy while we are in first class. You did all the planning for this trip and deserve a comfortable seat for a long flight. Heaven knows you will need all the rest you can get once we land and my grandmother's crew has you traipsing across Paris."

His eyes softened at the joke, small lines crinkling at the edges. Like a popped balloon, Hanna's anger deflated.

"How do you know this is not just some scheme to con you into getting me a better seat?"

"Because if you were that good of an actress, you would be winning Oscars, not taking an overeager group of seniors on a tour through Paris."

Hanna laughed, smile widening as a ghost of a smile flickered over Noah's face. "Don't be so sure, there is a lot you do not know about me. Layers of mystery."

Honestly, she did not mean for it to sound so suggestive, but even her own ears picked up on the husky tone of her voice. Energy snapped between them and Hanna's tongue darted out to lick her suddenly dry lips. Noah's eyes darkened as they watched the movement, Adam's apple moving over the open collar of his shirt. He took a step forward, his chest brushing against Hanna's arm on an inhale.

Taking shallow breaths to prevent touching him completely, Hanna was captive to his gaze. Now she understood why people fell under hypnotism. Caught in Noah's piercing stare, everything around her became muted, voices falling away into a dull murmur as her senses focused on the man in front of her. What would he feel like if she leaned into him? The hint of corded muscles underneath the layer of fabric was like a ghost, shifting in and out of focus in her memory. All she had to do to confirm their presence was move just a little closer.

"Miss...miss, your omelet is ready."

Oh gosh, had she really been so lost in thought that she did not notice the chef holding out the plate for her? At least she did not appear to be the only one affected by their proximity. While Hanna thanked the chef and grabbed the plate, Noah ran a hand through his hair and straightened his shirt, smoothing out invisible wrinkles.

Right over the place where Hanna's arm had touched.

When their eyes met, there were twin spots of pink above Noah's scruff and he quickly muttered something about meeting her at the table before turning to grab a plate of his own.

As long as neither of them mentioned the spark of chemistry between them, they could just ignore it. Right?

# 5

## There are No Excuses for Skipping your Skincare Routine

WRONG. Hanna was very wrong in thinking that she could avoid the inconvenient attraction she felt towards Noah. Especially not with them sitting side-by-side in an enclosed space for over ten hours. First class might have more space than economy, but not enough to separate her from the subtle hints of fresh soap that drifted from Noah's side of the divider.

Distracted while getting everyone else settled into their seats, and assuring Lillian several times that no one was going to steal her bag from the overhead bin, Hanna missed Noah stowing her bag and sliding into his seat. The seat that, with a quick glance at her ticket, happened to be directly next to hers.

Great.

Now she would have to keep her guard up for the duration of the flight. It was one of the reasons she preferred traveling separate from her groups whenever possible. Sitting two rows behind them meant that it was more likely they would come get her–potentially catching her sleeping with her mouth open–if they needed something. Hanna wondered if Noah planned it that way, hoping to catch her diabolical plotting.

"Champagne?" A smiling flight attendant offered from behind, jolting Hanna back into the moment, where she realized with a pang of embarrassment that she was still standing in the aisle.

Being in the way, particularly of someone trying to do their job, was something Hanna strove to avoid at all costs. She hated being an inconvenience. *See,* her brain tried to warn her, *being around Noah is already causing problems.* Quickly placing her backpack down so that she could step into the seating area, Hanna's gaze caught on the subject of her wayward thoughts.

Over the small side table and half-wall that separated them, Noah was frowning, eyebrows pulled tight as fathomless blue eyes clocked the tray of champagne flutes before landing on Hanna. The stick in the mud probably frowned at the idea of drinking so early in the day. Not that she overly indulged around guests anyways, but they were flying to Paris, where day drinking was practically a hobby. Besides, it was not like Hazel never saw her drink. The woman was often the instigator for ordering multiple bottles of wine with a group, affectionately teasing Hanna for only having one glass.

Struck with the impulsive desire to ruffle Noah's feathers, Hanna turned to the flight attendant with a warm smile and accepted a proffered glass. Before setting it down on her table, Hanna raised it slightly towards Noah and took a small sip. His mouth tightened in a thin line before he adjusted in his seat, bending to retrieve something from his bag.

A petty victory, but it had Hanna smiling nonetheless.

Once they were safely at ten-thousand feet, her laptop came out and Hanna spent the first hours of the flight managing client inquiries and trips through her website. Flying was like existing in a time warp, where minutes seemed both condensed and stretched into forever. Solidifying reservations and inputting the details into the itineraries for several groups, Hanna blinked in surprise when she checked the flight map and saw that it was time for lunch.

Used to the physical demands of tours, Hanna forgot how much her body protested sitting for long hours. Her legs were stiff and her ass felt flat as a compacted box, tingling with needle-like pricks as she shifted in the seat. She really needed to set a timer or something to remember to move when work absorbed her focus. Stretching her neck and shoulders to get the blood flowing back to her stiff muscles, Hanna let out a soft groan when she got to a particularly sore area.

Damn.

Maybe not so soft when a chuckle came from her left.

"Okay over there?" Noah had a book open in his lap, a finger holding his place on the page. Hanna found herself curious to know what type of reading material he enjoyed. Probably something infinitely dull and serious, like finance.

Twisting in her seat to stretch her back and face him, Hanna replied, "Just not a fan of sitting for hours on end. Nothing some movement and stretching cannot solve."

Noah watched her carefully, giving away nothing of the thoughts behind his eyes. "That makes sense for your job. You seemed pretty absorbed in what you were doing."

The statement sounded more like a question, as if Noah wanted to know what she was working on but did not want to outright ask.

"Work has a way of doing that," Hanna answered with a small laugh.

Thick eyebrows curved down. "I thought everything was booked for our tour?"

"It is. This was for other groups."

Noah's frown deepened. "Other groups? You're planning other trips while on ours?"

So much for his apparent shift in attitude towards her. It sounded like he was accusing her of not giving her full attention to them. That bothered Hanna. When she was with a group, all her focus was on them. Getting them what they needed and what they never realized they wanted. They were paying for her time and expertise, and Hanna always delivered. What she did in the few hours that were hers alone was no one's business but her own.

Rushing to defend herself, Hanna kept her voice low due to the close proximity of other passengers. "No, I am planning other trips while confined to a plane. Unless you want me to get up and give your grandmother and her friends a tour of the first-class cabin, I thought I would use my free time however I saw fit. Rest assured, once we land my time and energy are dedicated to your group, and my other clients know that."

"Hanna, I didn't–"

Whatever he was going to say was interrupted by the arrival of their food and drinks. Oblivious to the tension between them, or ignoring it, the flight attendants asked them if there was anything else they could bring. Taking the opportunity to slip away while Noah asked a question, Hanna escaped to the lavatory to wash her hands and gather her thoughts.

She thought they declared a truce, and though Noah largely stayed out of the planning process after their meeting, it seemed like his attitude towards her ability to do her job had not wavered. Hanna thought they were making progress, their phone conversations about hobbies and interests bringing them closer to understanding each other as people, not just as client and guide.

Dabbing some water on her heated neck, Hanna knew that she could not let him get a rise out of her. The last thing she wanted was Hazel or her friends to catch her arguing with Noah. The review practically wrote itself, *Unprofessional and ill-tempered. Difficult to work with.*

Resolved to keep to her side of their partition and raise the divider, Hanna returned to her seat.

Only to find Noah waiting for her.

"I'm sorry." He offered her a small plate of chocolates.

With a resigned sigh, Hanna took the plate and sat down. "Noah, you don't have to–"

"Please." Picking up the chocolate dusted with gold shavings, Hanna nodded for him to continue. Something about his earnest expression had her anger melting. "If I learned anything from talking with you the last few weeks, it's that you care deeply for all your groups. My question came from a place of curiosity over how your business is run, not a commentary on your work ethic or integrity. I know we are still learning to trust each other and I apologize that it came out harsher than intended."

Reflecting on what he said, Hanna recognized that she misinterpreted what Noah meant before. She was used to defending her job and abilities as a businesswoman, and reacted strongly to the perceived slight.

Offering Noah one of the chocolates, Hanna said, "Thank you. I'm sorry for jumping to conclusions without asking you what you meant. Something to work on."

Her heart fluttered when he gave her one of his lopsided smiles, their hands brushing as Noah took the chocolate. When Noah placed the chocolate in his mouth, licking the melted chocolate off his fingers, Hanna's lungs stopped working. And the man was not even aware of the effect he had on her, eyes closed as he savored the treat.

Was the air in the cabin getting thinner or was it just Hanna?

Head buzzing, Hanna almost missed his next question, her hyperfixation on his lips signaling her to pay attention as she saw them forming words.

"So, what made you want to become a tour guide?" Apparently finished with dessert, Noah started on his lunch.

Not quite ready to get into the full backstory of her career choice, Hanna decided to give him the abridged version that all her guests received. "A passion born from necessity, I suppose. I happened to be in the right place at the right time and helped out a tour guide from Trips Ahoy, who was impressed enough that they told me to apply for the job. One trip in and I fell in love. What about you?"

"I'm surprised my grandmother did not already tell you, I run the family company."

That made sense. Despite not knowing him long, Hanna could tell that Noah had a deep sense of commitment to his family as well as a sharp mind capable of handling the responsibilities of running a company.

"So we both run companies. Who would have guessed that we have something in common?"

Noah looked at her for a moment, staring deep into her eyes. "I guess we do."

Neither of them looked away, and Hanna could swear she saw a pleased glint in his eyes, the idea of them finding common ground breaking down a barrier of distrust so that she could see his deeper thoughts. With their tables on opposite sides of the same wall, they were forced close together and Hanna could see Noah's pupils dilate, blue disappearing beneath black. It was the only outward sign that their proximity affected him and Hanna felt her pulse race in response.

"Are you finished with your meal?"

Interrupted again by the overly helpful flight attendants.

Noah cleared his throat roughly before shifting back in his seat while Hanna launched herself away from Noah so quickly that she nearly collided with the flight attendant removing her dishes. Apologizing profusely, Hanna sought a topic of conversation to steer them back onto neutral ground.

"What exactly does your company do?"

Noah regaled her with the ins and outs of owning a natural toiletry and cleaning brand, one he was working to get into international hotel spaces, until the lights began to dim, signaling that it was time to sleep.

Once she could hear Noah's gentle snores, Hanna let out a sigh of relief. Finally. The recycled plane air was drying out her skin and the desire to clean off her face was reaching unbearable heights. Scheduled to arrive in Paris in the afternoon, they would spend a few hours sightseeing before making their way to the hotel to retire before dinner, and Hanna needed to look just as refreshed getting off the plane as she did getting on. Anyone who wore makeup knew there was nothing less appealing than clogging your pores with day-old makeup. But, she had to wait until there was no chance of her guests seeing her before cleaning her face.

Retrieving her small bag of toiletries, Hanna made her way to the lavatory to brush her teeth and complete as thorough of a skin care routine as one could while in a confined space–where one did not want any of their personal items touching the shared countertop. Her hydrating face and eye masks could wait until she was back in her seat. Unwilling to turn on the light in case it woke Noah, Hanna opened a fresh pair of under-eye masks, the slippery material sliding against her fingers...

And landing on the floor.

Tipping her head back with a silent groan, Hanna leaned forward to retrieve the trash–and shed a silent tear for the wasted product–before slamming her head into the tray table.

"Shit!"

Well, she definitely could have been quieter, but damn that hurt.

Hanna glanced around to see if the noise disturbed anyone. Apart from the stern look an older businessman was giving her across the aisle–as if he had any room to judge considering his light was shining in people's faces–it seemed like Hanna was in the clear. Thank goodness. She worried for a moment that the sound and concurrent vibration of the table would disturb her seatmate, but it appeared not.

"You okay?"

The light next to her switched on as Noah's grumbling voice reached her ears. Wow, she really did not need to know how he sounded when he first woke up. Rough and sleepy. It filled her brain with images of him stretching in soft sheets, turning towards her with a smile as morning light highlighted the carved muscle of his-

Nope. *Stop that train of thought immediately*, Hanna warned herself.

She kept her head tilted away from the overhead light as she whispered, "Yep! Just a minor impact with the table. Nothing to worry about."

"Really? It sounded like you hit your head pretty hard. Here, let me check to make sure you aren't bleeding."

A shadow of an arm moved in her peripheral vision and Hanna panicked, worried what his touch would do to her. Forgetting about her makeup-free face, Hanna turned to face him.

"No need! See? Perfectly fine." She moved her head side to side as if that would illustrate her point. "Just go back to sleep. I am sorry that I woke you."

Compared to the rest of the dimly lit cabin, their seats were cocooned in a halo of light. Above the divider, Noah stared at her, his face partially shadowed. Hanna watched as his eyes tracked across her face, checking her over for injury. As he looked, a small wrinkle formed between his brows, a feature Hanna was beginning to notice appeared often. Blue eyes followed the waves of her hair, sliding down before journeying up, pausing on her lips, then cheeks, and finally her eyes.

In sync, a blush made its way up Hanna's throat and face, as if her blood was called to the surface of her skin by his lingering attention. She hoped that enough of her was shadowed to hide the red stain on her skin. The longer he stared without speaking, the more Hanna wanted to fidget. Was she bleeding? Was there something gross on the underside of the table that was now wedged in her hair?

Averting her gaze to discreetly run a hand through her hair, Hanna's eyes caught on the open package that lay on the floor after being dropped again when she hit her head.

Oh, no. Anything but this. Pulse hammering as awareness rushed through her body, Hanna squeezed her eyes shut to avoid reality for a moment. But when she opened them and saw her reflection on the television screen, her makeup-free face was staring back at her.

No wonder he was looking at her strangely. "Please pretend like this never happened."

Noah tilted his head in confusion. "Why not?"

Grimacing from the continued embarrassment, Hanna explained, "This isn't exactly the way I want my guests to see me. Not really the perfect, Tour Guide Barbie people want." Her laugh sounded brittle to her ears. Much like her clothing, Hanna wore makeup like armor, feeling unkept and almost naked when someone saw her without it on. Sans makeup, Hanna was told that she looked like a child. Not the professional image she wanted to project.

Noah's face softened in understanding, his chest rising and falling in a heavy breath before he straightened and looked at her with dark eyes.

"I see you, and I don't want a perfect, cookie-cutter tour guide. Remember, I asked you to be yourself, whoever that is. If you really want, I will not bring it up again. But, Hanna?"

The light shut off.

"It's my turn to be honest. The reason I was staring was not because I thought there was something wrong with you. I was admiring how utterly breathtaking you are. With or without makeup, you are perfect exactly as you are."

True to his promise to not bring it up again, Noah turned over in his bed, pulling the blanket up to his chin and falling asleep moments later.

Hanna frowned at the darkened seat next to hers, wondering if Noah was trying to catch her off-guard by saying something sweet. There had to be an ulterior motive to his compliment. He did not trust her. Right? Unless their weekly phone calls leading up to the trip softened Noah's gruff exterior. Turning over in her own chair, Hanna resolutely decided not to dwell on it. That line of thinking only led to confusion.

Long after Hanna finished her mid-flight facial and reclined her seat for sleep, Noah's words continued to dance through her brain, repeating over and over like the newest Sabrina Carpenter song. Until finally, the whispered remnants of *breathtaking* and *as you are* pulled her into a dreamless sleep.

# 6

# Stretching is the Difference Between an Expert and an Amateur

NO MATTER how much money or status you have, everyone gets a small thrill at seeing their name printed on a sign held by someone at the airport. At the sight of her name written in elegant cursive on a crisp, white board, held by Madeline the driver Hanna booked for the trip, Hazel squeezed Hanna's arm in thanks and turned to her friends in excitement.

"See, at least someone recognizes who the leader of this group is."

Daphne scoffed and looped her arm through Hazel's. "Leader? Hah! They only wrote that so you wouldn't forget what your name is."

"I've never forgotten anything in my life," Hazel shot back before Lillian and Mai joined in the good-natured teasing.

Red hair cut in a stylish bob, Madeline smiled as the group approached.

"*Bonjour*, you must be Madam Eversham and her lovely friends." Four heads nodded in agreement, their eyes wide in appreciation over her lyrical accent. "It is so nice to meet you all. My name is Madeline and I will be your chauffeur during your stay in France."

"Madeline, what a beautiful name," said Daphne.

"Were your parents fans of the children's books?" Mai asked.

While Madeline answered the group's questions—no, her father had a fondness for the sponge cake of the same name; yes, she was born and raised in Paris; her favorite thing to do was explore new restaurants, and yes, she had dined in the Eiffel Tower–Hanna led them towards their baggage carousel. Hanna met Madeline several years before at a housewarming party for a mutual friend. While sharing a story of a group who refused to walk anywhere, Hanna was interrupted by Madeline, who offered the services of her family's private car company. Efficient, accommodating, and always in touch with the best places to eat, Madeline quickly became one of Hanna's favorite contacts in the city.

"Anna." She also dropped the h in Hanna's name, as was practice for Latin-based languages. "It has been too long. Last time you were here I barely got to see you. This time, you will make time to go dancing, yes?"

Notes of citrus and bergamot settled around them as they exchanged air kisses. With a fond smile, Hanna pulled back from her friend's embrace.

"Perhaps. I am staying in the city for a few extra days." Hanna was in the process of booking a trip with a small family, the Delgados, who were vacationing in Europe and heard about her services from a friend. Taking a few days off between trips, it made sense to stay in Paris while the Delgados finalized which city, or cities, they wanted to hire Hanna for.

"Dancing?" Daphne bumped her hip playfully into Hanna's. "You've been holding out on us. Now we all have to go out and party."

Hazel gave her a puzzled look, brows furrowed in a way that her grandson must have inherited. "You told me you did not dance."

*Not with guests*, Hanna thought to herself. But, as she opened her mouth to respond, Madeline cut in.

"Not dance? Anna? She was born for the dance floor. Why, you should have seen her when–"

"*Madeline*," Hanna rushed to interrupt her in French, "*not in front of them, please.*" There were several possible endings to that sentence, and Hanna did not want any of them spoken out loud. Some stories were best kept between friends.

Madeline shrugged off the comment, as she was used to Hanna's detachment from her guests. *"Fine, but these seem like the type of women who would appreciate you having a bit of fun. Maybe you can start with Mr. Tall, Dark, and Handsome."*

Desperate for a distraction, Hanna glanced around. "Oh, look, our bags are here."

Clearing her throat around the awkward transition, Hanna stepped towards the moving carousel as the first of their bags came into view. Further discussion of dancing or other activities halted as bags were retrieved and the group loaded into Madeline's car. Then, the sights and sounds of Paris surrounded them as they began the slow crawl through traffic to their hotel.

As Madeline expertly navigated the streets, Hanna pointed out landmark destinations to the group, turning sideways in her seat to watch their faces light up brighter than the City of Lights with each view.

Well, all their faces except one.

Noah watched her with a slight frown on his face, not once turning to look out the window when Hanna gestured to each famous location.

"You shouldn't sit like that," he gestured to her unbuckled seat belt. Seated directly behind her, Noah leaned forward so that he spoke in her ear.

Turning even more so that she could look him directly in the eye, Hanna swallowed around the rapid pulse in her throat at their proximity. This close, she could practically count each of the dark lashes framing his gorgeous eyes, the blue popping against their dark frame. Not that she wanted to count them...that would be absurd, frivolous, and, oh, so tempting.

"I can sit however I want." Hanna redirected her frustrating attraction into this new battle with Noah. "Besides, I hardly see how it concerns you as long as I can do my job."

Without missing a beat, Hanna gestured to a famous cafe and explained its importance to the group. When Mai gushed over the flowers spilling across the awning and began telling her friends a story she heard about the cafe, Hanna was glad that the group had reservations there for later in the week.

"It's not safe," Noah said firmly. "You should also wear your seat belt." It took Hanna a moment to remind herself what they were talking about and she was about to retort that it was not his job to keep her safe when their eyes met. Above the firm set of his jaw and downturned lips, Noah's eyes were filled with worry. His dark brows drew lower as he glanced between Hanna's less than secure position on the chair, the lack of seat belt, and the road in front of them.

Each aggressive maneuver that Madeline made to navigate the streets of Paris sent pulses of fear through Noah's gaze. Was he worried about what would happen to their group if Hanna was injured, or could Noah's concern be for her?

Either way, Hanna's heart wanted to reach out and soothe the fear that was practically radiating off him.

"Okay," she said while maintaining eye contact as long as she could while turning to face the front. She reached up and pulled the seat belt down and fastened it with a click.

As she settled into the seat back, Hanna felt the brush of air against her ear as a whispered, "thank you" moved through her hair. Looking up, Hanna met Noah's gaze in the rear-view mirror and gave him a warm smile.

There was no helping the blush that stained her cheeks when he returned her smile with one of his own, lifting the dark clouds from his eyes. Hanna straightened in her seat before continuing her abbreviated tour of the city.

"–AND then, we realized that the microphones were still on! The interns caught the entire conversation, and bam, we were famous on the TikTok." Mai finished telling the story with a flourish of her wine glass, the liquid sloshing precariously near the edge as she descended into giggles.

Dabbing at tears of laughter from the corner of her own eyes, Hanna took a sip of water and made a mental note to look up the viral video of Mai and another museum board member asking if "slaps" meant that their intern wanted her to hit someone in their "Gen Z Writes the Script" video. With her soft voice and polished appearance, Mai's evident confusion over the slang was trending for its wholesomeness. If only they could see her now, pink cheeked and drinking the rest of the party under the table.

Well, the rest of the party with the exception of Hanna and Madeline, who both stopped after two glasses, waving off additional glasses with the excuse of work. Squeezed into a velvet-backed booth around a low table, the group was finishing an early dinner near their hotel. Before checking into their hotel and taking a short break to freshen up, Hanna took the group to the Arc de Triomphe and the Eiffel Tower, iconic locations that they would drive past multiple times over the next few days. Hanna felt it was best to get those locations out of the way as soon as possible so that the group was not distracted on their other excursions.

It also helped ease the group into the jet-lag, keeping them up until a reasonable hour without exhausting them.

"So, you're telling me..." Daphne's bracelets jangled as she waved her wrist. "That you had no idea what the words meant, yet you still agreed to be filmed? Sometimes when I talk to my grandniece and nephews, I swear it sounds like they are speaking a different language."

Tipping her head in Daphne's direction in agreement, Lillian said, "Agreed. It would be a cold day in hell before you caught me in one of those videos."

"That is because you don't know how to laugh at yourself," Hazel chided playfully. "Besides, if it gets kids interested in the museum, that seems worth it."

"Exactly," Mai agreed. "Several schools reached out after the video came out to inquire about field trips."

"That is wonderful!" Hanna grinned widely. "One of my favorite memories from school was visiting a museum."

School itself was not one of Hanna's favorite activities, nontraditional as her education was, but she remembered the day their homeschool group went to a museum. It was Hanna's first dip into the sea of exploration, all contained in one, magical building. At the museum, Hanna could pretend that she was in far off places, discovering a thirst for venturing into the unknown and learning about different cultures and cities. Limited by where her parent's jobs took the family, museums represented infinite possibilities, all in visually stunning format.

"Do you have a favorite?" Noah leaned around Hazel to ask.

Throughout the evening, Hanna exchanged limited words with Noah. As with any group on its first day, most of the evening was spent with the four friends catching up and a lot of questions directed at Hanna regarding her life outside of tours (practically nonexistent) and her most memorable tours—a woman, nameless, of course, who was indignant that they could not tour Buckingham Palace because the Queen was in residence and insisted that she was a friend of a friend of the Queen and that it wouldn't be a problem. Noah remained quiet, his observant eyes tracking the conversation in the soft light offered by the cylindrical lamps hanging from the low ceiling.

"A favorite...?" Hanna's hair slipped over her shoulder as she leaned forward, and Noah followed the movement of her fingers as she tucked it behind her ear.

Having the full force of his attention was unnerving, the lighting softening his gaze in a romantic way.

Resting his forearm on the table, exposed by rolled sleeves,

Noah's rich voice carried to Hanna. "Museum. I'm sure you have visited quite a few."

"I have, which makes it difficult to pick a favorite." Giving herself a moment to think, Hanna took another sip of water and Noah followed suit. Turning over the dozens of museums she had visited in her lifetime in her mind, Hanna struggled to select a favorite. Art, music, history, or science, they all had subcategories and niche subjects.

Turning back towards Noah, Hanna opened her mouth to answer, but the words caught in her throat. Lowering his glass to the table, Noah licked a drop of water from his lips, his tongue following the curve of his lower lip, leaving Hanna speechless. They were not even seated next to each other and yet it set Hanna's body aflame. Her bottom lip tingled with awareness as if he had caressed her lip, not his own. All too happy to encourage that line of thought, Hanna's imagination supplied an image of Noah leaning into her, no one between them, his large hand cupping her cheek, thumb pressing into her bottom lip to part her lips before swiping his tongue across it.

"...Hanna?"

She jolted out of her fantasy at the sound of Noah's voice, flushing deeper in embarrassment at having been caught thinking salacious thoughts about a guest. Not that he knew what she was thinking about, but just being distracted by the thought was enough. Refocusing, Hanna smoothed down her skirt reassuringly before replying.

"It is going to sound like a cliché, but the Louvre is my favorite museum. With the sheer number of exhibits and pieces on display, and in archives, I feel like I could visit over and over again and still have something new to see. The curators keep it fresh and interesting, even with statement pieces like Mona Lisa on display at all times."

"Then we are lucky to have you with us when we visit tomorrow."

With that reminder, Hanna discretely signaled the waiter for their check. Despite the boisterous attitude of the women, Hanna caught them stifling yawns throughout the meal and knew that they should get back to the hotel soon if they were going to start early the next day. Art lover or not, the Louvre was an all-day excursion.

"Your confidence in me is flattering, but fortunately for you there will be an actual art historian with us tomorrow. My love of the museum notwithstanding, there are limits to even my knowledge."

"And you have me." Lillian's voice broke through their bubble. "I studied art history in college, and my family donated many paintings to museums. You might have heard of the exhibit the Met put on last year with our collection."

Hanna was genuinely trying to like Lillian, but after listening to her brag about the wealth and prestige she married into the entire evening, the designer-obsessed older woman was quickly becoming her least favorite of the group. Entitlement was nothing new for Hanna, and she was used to letting it roll over her like fog, but compared to Hazel's normalcy, it was a jarring contrast. *People are who they are, mija,* Hanna's mother would say. *The only thing you can control is how you respond to them.*

With that in mind, Hanna gave Lillian a tight smile over her shoulder as they filed out of the booth. "How generous. I am sure it was a lovely exhibit and I look forward to hearing your insight tomorrow. It is always nice to have another expert in the group."

Puffed up with pride over the compliment, Lillian launched into a story about a mishap that occurred during the art donation as her friends trailed behind with indulgent smiles on their faces. The following day would be a blast, listening to Lillian act like she knew more than their guide and waltzing around like she owned the place as they saw some of the world's best artwork. Already, Hanna was mentally practicing deep breathing exercises to prevent stabbing Lillian with one of her pointy stilettos.

AFTER A DAY WALKING through the Louvre, Hanna removed her pair of sensible, low-heeled walking shoes, and sat on the chair in her hotel room, allowing herself a moment of stillness after the long day. Only a moment. Between the long flight with little movement and then a full day on her feet, Hanna knew that she needed to get back up and stretch before tightness settled into her muscles. Consistent stretching was the best way to prevent injury and chronic fatigue as a tour guide. It did not matter how great of shape you were in, stretching could make or break you.

With a small groan as she got back up, Hanna pulled out her gym clothes from the dresser and laced up her sneakers, slipping her phone and hotel key into the pocket of her leggings and scooping her hair into a ponytail. She would stretch in her room in a pinch, but if the hotel had a gym, like this one did, Hanna preferred to get out of her room. Not only did it mean more space, but it also helped provide delineations for her mental health. Bedrooms were for sleeping and getting ready, not work.

The gym was located on the top floor of the hotel, several sets of weights and a row of machines shining in the bright light of the room. When Hanna stepped into the room, she could see the pool glistening in the moonlight from outside the glass wall that separated the gym from the heated pool and spa. Other than the whir of air conditioning, it was quiet. Hanna had the room to herself.

Moving to the far wall, away from the equipment and with enough space to stretch freely, she set down her water bottle, phone, and room key and stood with her arms to the ceiling. Flowing from one position to the next, Hanna settled into the gentle rhythm that relaxed her body and mind, focusing on her breathing and the pull of her muscles. Later, Hanna would double check the bookings and schedule for the next day, as well as respond to messages from potential clients, but now, this time was just for her.

A sharp beep signaled the unlocking of the door a moment before it opened. Folded forward with her hands tucked under her feet, Hanna tipped her head sideways to greet the new arrival.

Noah stood just inside the doorway, hand paused halfway to his ear, one headphone dangling as he stared at Hanna. Dressed in a fitted T-shirt and loose gym shorts, Noah still managed to look polished, his hair styled just as perfectly as it was when she first saw him that morning. At least Hanna's workout just started and she was not a sweaty mess. Thoughts of different places, where being sweaty *with* Noah would be encouraged, flittered through her brain. Suddenly, the room felt hotter, the gently whirring air conditioning no match for the heat that sizzled between the room's two occupants.

"Sorry," Noah said, "I didn't think anyone would still be up. Do you mind if I join you?" He motioned towards one of the racks of weights and then towards the room at large, headphones swaying in the air.

Remaining upside down while talking to him felt like giving Noah the upperhand, so Hanna rose. "Not unless you plan on grunting like one of those obnoxious gym-bros. Otherwise, there is plenty of space for us both."

Cracking a smile, Noah stepped towards the weight rack. "Noted. I'll keep any grunting to myself."

Okay, the air conditioning was definitely on the fritz because Hanna was burning. Was Noah flirting with her? That definitely sounded like it and the flare of heat in his eyes looked flirtatious. But pursuing that line of thought was dangerous. She did not want to give Noah any new reasons not to trust her or risk losing her job. Responding to it was even more dangerous, so Hanna resumed stretching, surreptitiously watching Noah out of the corner of her eye.

And if the next group of stretches happened to show off how flexible she was and display some of her assets to their best advantage? Well, that was purely a coincidence. Each time she twisted, Hanna looked over her shoulder and caught the quick flicker of Noah's lashes as he looked away. She felt a smug satisfaction bloom in her chest at the thought that his slight flush was caused by her, not the exertion of his weightlifting.

In the opposite corner, Noah sat on a bench, lifting and pressing dumbbells in a series of movements that Hanna did not know the name for but looked impressive. The bottom of his shirt rose when his arms reached overhead, a sliver of Noah's toned stomach peeking out beneath the fabric. Momentarily transfixed by the tan skin exposed over gray shorts, Hanna forgot what she was doing and watched Noah's muscles flex in fluid motions.

"See something you like?" Smirking, Noah raised one eyebrow in Hanna's direction.

Caught, Hanna's heart pounded in her chest as tension froze her body. How did he want her to respond? With a lie to preserve their boundaries or the truth that would bring them to uncharted territory? Potential responses pinged through Hanna's brain, frantically searching for the correct one. Then she realized that Noah did not want the perfectly composed answer. He wanted *her* answer, whatever it might be.

Lowering her shoulders from where they hiked up to her ears, Hanna faced him directly. "Please. Don't act like you are not purposely showing off to impress me."

His smile stretched across his face. "So you are impressed," he said with a flex of his pecs. "Besides, you are no better with those 'stretches.'"

Hanna widened her eyes in mock-innocence. "These are completely legitimate stretches. You would know if you read the information I provided about the importance of stretching at the end of each day."

"Mmhmm." He cocked his head to the side and ran his eyes up and down her body. "Trust me, I would remember if any of the stretches you recommended were supposed to look like that."

She flushed with pleasure at his appraisal. Despite Noah's status as a tour guest, Hanna found him attractive. Not only was he incredibly handsome, with his thick hair, rugged jaw, and muscled body, but his dry wit and deep well of concern appealed to Hanna. Noah listened with an intensity that pulled her in, wanting to share all her worries and dreams so that he could keep them safe.

But Hanna did not trust that feeling. He was only in her life for two more weeks, then he would move on with his life and leave her behind. Just like everyone else. No one picked her to stay with. She was the vacation away from normal life, a rest stop on the way to the destination. It was better to keep things light and fun, that way it could not hurt her later.

Nearing the end of her workout, Hanna kneeled on the floor, bending to press her chest and arms flat while her hips rose into the air. Not an overly complicated position–Hanna was both impressed and terrified by yoga practitioners who could contort themselves into pretzels–the position released tension in her back, causing a low groan of satisfaction to slip past Hanna's lips. Immediately aware that the sound was louder than expected, Hanna squeezed her eyes shut, praying that Noah had his headphones in and missed the unintentionally sexual sound.

Her luck was never that good when it came to Noah.

A low grunt, like someone punched him, sounded from Noah's corner of the room. Whipping her head in that direction, Hanna saw Noah's eyes screwed shut and lips tightly pressed together. His arm hung limply at his side, hand open with the forgotten weight laying haphazardly on the floor.

"Are you okay?"

"Just dropped the weight on my foot," he ground out.

Hanna rose quickly, moving towards him before Noah put up a hand to stop her, twisting his hips away from her.

"It'll be fine, just grazed it really. I just...need a minute."

"Are you sure? I can get you some ice."

A thin circle of blue was visible around his enlarged pupils when Noah looked at her. "No, I can get it myself. I've already troubled you enough by interrupting your free time. Walking it off will probably help too."

Pulling her bottom lip between her teeth, Hanna nodded. "If you are sure. Pharmacy is closed by now, but I have aspirin if you need it. Just text me and I can bring it to you."

Noah stood and returned the dumbbell to the rack before moving towards the door.

"Thank you, but I'll manage. Enjoy the rest of your night."

Hanna knew she would not be able to enjoy the rest of the night, not while she worried about Noah's foot. Of course her attempts at light flirting would lead to an injury. Lesson learned. But as she watched him leave, closely monitoring for any signs that he might stumble, Hanna's concern melted into smug satisfaction.

Noah was not walking out the door like someone who injured his foot. No, Hanna suspected the grunt came from a pain a little further north.

# 7

## *Do Not Forget to Have Fun*

TEACHING a master class in the art of negotiation would be a walk in the park after Hanna arranged for a private painting class in Monet's Garden. Keeping with the artistic theme after their day in the Louvre, where she booked a private viewing of Mona Lisa, Hanna knew that their trip to Monet's Garden needed to be just as impressive. She had to call in multiple favors, promise additional ones, and sweet talk her way past assistants just to get a phone call with the foundation's director. It was only after mentioning that Mai Kato–a well known patron of the arts and chairwoman of a high-profile art museum in the United States–was on her tour that the director offered a private tour and painting lesson before the house and gardens opened to the public.

When she received the email a few weeks ago from the director welcoming them to the gardens and providing instructions for their arrival, Hanna felt a rush of dizzy glee at the satisfaction of securing the once in a lifetime opportunity for the group. Alone in her room at Sarah's house, Hanna leapt to her feet and unleashed her joy in a spontaneous dance.

Now, cradling a to-go mug of tea in Madeline's van, Hanna struggled to contain her excitement at the surprise. A patroness of the arts and a fan of Monet's work in particular, one item on Lillian's list of must-dos on the trip was visiting the famous water lily pond. Still in the first days of the tour, Hanna was trying to find common ground with Lillian to get the starchy woman to warm up to her, the need to have everyone like her agitated like a splinter under her skin. Hanna could not wait to see Lillian's face when she saw the easels set up along the walkway of the pond.

"You're fidgeting," Noah remarked in a flat voice from the seat behind her. Despite offering Noah the front seat so that he would have more legroom, he insisted on sitting in the back, directly behind her. Probably so that he could keep an eye on her and make sure she was not being sneaky. "What's wrong?"

Hanna turned as much as she could in the seat, keeping her voice soft to not disturb the rest of the group who were nodding to sleep in the back two rows.

"Jumping to conclusions again? Why does something have to be wrong? Maybe I just had too much coffee this morning."

Noah looked at her skeptically. "You don't fidget. "

"Maybe you do not know me as well as you think you do."

Leaning forward so that his elbows rested on his knees, Noah brought his face close enough that his breath stirred her hair. "No, but I do know that you always look calm and collected, even when everything is in chaos around you. The only giveaway is a slight flush across your nose and cheeks. Just like there is now."

Hanna's face flushed deeper, watching as Noah tracked the movement with his ice-blue eyes. She felt his gaze like a caress, the phantom touch tingling. She worked hard to mask any signs of distress or worry when on tour, the last thing Hanna wanted was her guests to pick up on her emotions and panic that something was wrong.

"If something is wrong," he continued, "tell me and I can help fix it. I know how much Mai and Lillian are looking forward to this trip."

Her flush at his close perusal blazed into indignation. Why did he continue to doubt her ability to lead this group and incorrectly assume that her excited shifting in her seat was a sign of agitation?

"I know they are excited." Hanna smiled over the bite of her words. "Which is why I planned a surprise for them. You mistook my excitement for fidgeting. Maybe instead of assuming something is wrong, you could trust me to take care of things and loop in the group when necessary."

"I wasn't–"

"Noah, are you pestering Hanna?" Hazel drawled sleepily, glancing between the pair with a twinkle in her eye.

"Not at all," Hanna responded. "He was just asking about our itinerary for the day. I let him know that I have everything taken care of." She flicked a sharp look in his direction. "Besides, I would not want to ruin the surprise."

Laughing at the exchange between Hanna and Noah, Hazel said, "She's keeping you on your toes. My grandson has never been a fan of surprises, but if anyone could convince him, it's you, Hanna."

"Did Hanna say she planned a surprise?" Daphne called out from the third row.

Hazel nodded, eager anticipation brightening her features. "Thank heavens we are close to Monet's house. I don't know if I could wait to find out what it is."

"I love surprises!" Daphne practically bounced in her seat. For someone who recently had a knee replacement, she was surprisingly nimble, probably owed to her years as a professional tennis player and physical therapy. "The last time someone surprised me was when Damon Sutherland invited me over for dinner and..."

After hearing Daphne's story, the group–minus one furiously blushing Noah–laughed so hard that they started crying. Madeline cheered on Daphne in French, calling her an honorary French-woman. Not one to be outdone, Hazel launched into her own escapade with a man she met at dance class.

Noah practically pitched himself out of the slow moving vehicle as they pulled in front of Monet's house.

"Please, mémé, I do not need to hear that." He pointed to Hanna's bag. "You would not happen to have something to wipe my memory in that endless purse, do you?"

Laughter danced through Hanna at his put-out expression. Hanna did not blame Noah. She would not want to hear about her family member's sexual exploits either, but his exaggerated pout seemed more like an attempt to soften the tension between them.

"Hush, you!" Hazel smacked Noah's arm as she stepped out of the van. "This is a girls' trip and we are going to talk about whatever we like. You can stay at the hotel if you do not like it."

Daphne came out next. "Maybe he's just grumpy because he has been single for too long. Hazel, how long did you say it was since his last girlfriend?"

"Two years."

"Please stop talking about me like I am not standing right here." Noah put on his sunglasses, hiding his eyes but not the adorable way his ears were turning red.

The women ignored him.

"Two years is too long." Mai rolled over to join them. "You are young, smart, and handsome. Your heart is too big to keep to yourself. The only downside is your surly attitude."

"Getting laid would fix that," Lillian chimed in.

A professional interrogation had nothing on these silver-haired septuagenarians. Once they latched onto the topic of Noah's dating life, they were not letting it go. Noah was flustered as the group continued to pepper him with questions about why he was single. Hanna watched with amusement from a safe distance away. It was fun watching the drama, not being in it.

"Hanna." Hazel's sharp eyes caught on her like a heat seeking missile. "You agree with us, right? There is no reason two young, attractive people like you and Noah should be single."

Crap. Hazel wove a magnificent web and Hanna was caught in her trap.

"Well..." She looked for a way to stall. There was no way she wanted to have this conversation with a grandmother set on match-making. "Oh, look, the docent is ready for us."

A well-dressed student in their early twenties opened the green door on the front walkway, descending the matching steps to greet the group.

"*Bonjour*, my name is Lou and I am delighted to show you around Monet's home and gardens today."

Hanna returned the greeting in French and introduced the rest of the group. When Lou was introduced to Mai, their eyes lit and they began rapidly asking her questions about the museum she worked for. The two became fast friends, and Hanna held back a smile at the way Lou insisted on helping Mai with her wheelchair, leading the group past the green shutters and pink stone walls of the building.

"Now will you tell me what this surprise is?" Noah slowed his steps to match Hanna's, bringing them shoulder to shoulder. Lou was ahead of them with the others, talking about Monet's background and history leading up to the purchase of the home.

"You really are impatient." Hanna shook her head before looking up at Noah. "Not a big fan of surprises, are you?"

"I like to be prepared."

Lou took them from room to room, their lilting voice enthusiastically answering Lillian and Mai's numerous questions. A few paces behind them, Hanna and Noah followed at a leisurely pace.

"Do you like surprises?" Noah leaned over to ask her.

They were more alike than either of them originally expected.

Hanna shook her head in response. "Giving surprises is fun, but I have never been fond of them myself."

For her, surprises were a vast unknown where any possibility lurked in the shadows. Whether it was the first time her parents announced the "surprise" that they were moving to another country, or the countless moves after, the surprise when each of her siblings went away for college and left her behind, or the countless other unexpected events in her life, they rarely ended well.

"Just like you, I like being prepared."

"Really, I never would have guessed." Noah bumped her arm with his.

She liked this side of him, a little bit playful.

When he stepped away again, Noah's expression turned somber. "This experience, and the other's you planned for us, I know you are good at your job. Amazing, really. When I asked about you fidgeting in the car, it was not meant to insult you, I was worried about you. You never ask for help, not with luggage or anything, and I just want you to know that I am here if you need help. You don't have to do everything on your own."

In her experience, people on vacation wanted an escape from their regular day, including chores and other mundane tasks that, when paying someone else to accomplish, preferred not to lift a hand. Not Noah, though. He helped her with the luggage and was always the first out of the car to open the doors for Hanna and the others. Maybe he was genuinely concerned for her and wanted to help. Hanna had said she would stop assuming the worst in what he said.

"Thank you. I am glad you are starting to appreciate my work, but I do not need help. I've got this covered. Since you've been so nice, I will let you in on the secret."

Beckoning Noah closer, Hanna whispered in his ear. The edge of her palm brushed against his stubble, the scratchy sensation delightfully pleasant. She wanted to linger, to see how it would feel to run her fingers up and down the rough surface. Instead, Hanna drew back, watching Noah's expression for what he thought of the surprise painting lesson.

Looking over at the group following Lou out into the garden, Noah brought his gaze back to Hanna.

"They are going to love it."

"And you?"

His response mattered more than she wanted to admit.

"If you planned it, I'm willing to give anything a chance."

As they stepped onto the path, the other's delighted laughter filled the air as they spotted the setup. Warmth spread through her chest and pulled her lips into a smile at the sight of their happy faces. There was no greater joy than seeing her guests happy. Lit by the bright glow of the morning sun, their wide smiles and eyes glistened, the white canvases stark against the colorful garden behind them.

Enjoying the expressions of gratitude and thanks at the opportunity to paint in one of the most famous locations for painters in the world, Lou launched into an explanation of how they would be emulating Monet's impressionist-style by creating a painting from whatever inspired them in the garden.

"Why are there only five easels?" Hazel turned to ask Lou.

Knowing that the docent would not have the answer, Hanna stepped up to reply. "This activity is just for your group. I will still be nearby if you need anything, but this time is for you to enjoy as a group."

"That's no fun," Hazel said with a small pout. "I wanted you as our tour guide because I enjoy spending time with you. Come paint with us. You are part of this group. Madeline, too, if she wants to join."

Hanna was touched by the gesture, the thoughtfulness of being included in their group chipping away at the shield protecting her heart. She did not want to get close to people again just to have them forget about her later, but it was so tempting to lean into this feeling of being wanted.

"It is really okay, I do not want to intrude–"

"I insist," Hazel interrupted, turning back towards Lou. "Are you able to get another easel and stool for Hanna? And Madeline?"

At the question, Hanna sent a quick text to her friend, inviting her to the painting lesson. Madeline replied with a polite declination and a sleepy emoji. Knowing that she was not a morning person, Hanna suspected Madeline was taking a quick nap in the car while the group was occupied. While Lou was retrieving the extra supplies, Hanna helped Mai get comfortable at the easel designed to accommodate her wheelchair, the others settling onto stools around them. Conveniently, when Lou returned, the only place for them to set up the additional easel and stool was the empty space beside Noah. From the sly looks and poorly concealed giggles coming from her left, Hanna knew it was no coincidence.

These women were on a mission, determined to stick Hanna and Noah together at every opportunity.

In the patient voice of a teacher, Lou explained how impressionist artists created their work, encouraging them to take time to find a view that spoke to their soul, one they wanted to capture on canvas, before they left the group. As the sun rose higher on the horizon, rays of light caught on the rippling water, the sound of brushstrokes and birds chattering the soundtrack to their morning.

Keeping a close eye on the group, Hanna saw Lillian and Hazel's faces scrunched in concentration, Mai's serene, and Daphne's full of humor as they worked on their art. On her own canvas, Hanna was attempting to paint the waterlily pond. After all, when in Rome, or Monet's Garden as it were.

Next to her, Noah leaned in his seat to peek around Hanna's canvas.

"Hey!" She tried to maneuver her body to block his view. "Focus on your own painting."

"I just want to make sure I'm doing it right."

"Lou said there is no right way to create a painting, art comes from your heart."

"Really? Is that why you look like you could set your canvas on fire with how hard you are glaring at it?"

"I am not glaring!" She absolutely was. "I am focusing."

"I thought it did not have to be perfect."

She snorted. This is why Hanna preferred to stay away from drawing. Everyone said it did not need to be perfect, but when they saw the lopsided blobs that were Hanna's attempts at flowers, their lips tightened like they were holding in laughter. There were many things Hanna was not good at, and she knew it was unrealistic to be good at everything, at least if no one else saw it she could pretend to have an adequate painting.

Turning back in her chair, Hanna tried to ignore Noah and focus on the canvas in front of her. Out of the corner of her eye, she saw Noah do the same. They continued painting in silence, the gentle sounds of the water lapping in the pond and the breeze rustling the trees creating a serene atmosphere.

Noah sighed. Glancing at him, Hanna saw him dipping his brush onto the palette before raising it to the canvas with a precision that looked painful. The others were smiling and laughing as their brush-strokes captured the beauty before them while Noah looked like he was under penalty of death if his paint moved outside whatever imaginary line he saw on the page.

A pang of hurt for him resonated through Hanna's heart. Painting might not be her favorite activity, but at least she found joy being outside. She did not want Noah to be miserable. Thinking of ways to draw him into a lighter mood, Hanna grabbed her easel and turned it so that her painting was facing Noah.

"You do not have to keep painting if you hate it."

"I do not hate it." He smiled at her skeptical look. "Okay, it is definitely not my favorite activity, but I do not hate it. I just did not think it would be this hard. Or that I would be so bad at it."

"Want to know a secret?" Hanna leaned forward and Noah followed suit, meeting in the middle.

"Always," his whispered confession carried on the wind into her ears, tickling the skin of her neck and sending a shiver down her spine.

"That's why I tried to politely decline participating. I hate the idea of showing my guests that there is something I am not good at. They expect excellence from me, perfection even. The last thing I want is them wondering that if I am not the best at everything, then how can I be the best at anything?"

Noah nodded. "It's exhausting, always trying to be perfect. Sometimes, I feel like there are dozens of people waiting for me to make a mistake, ready to take my place. People see mistakes as a weakness, when in reality they are the only way we grow and improve. "

He understood her in a way few others had. Confidence was currency in Hanna's line of work, with people more than willing to find another tour company the moment she made a mistake. It sounded like Noah experienced the same feeling, a constant pressure to excel at everything, building a solid wall so that no one could find your soft spots.

There by Monet's lily pond, Hanna realized that she and Noah were finally seeing eye to eye. Their previous truce was replaced by understanding, accomplished by revealing small parts of themselves for inspection and being validated instead of found wanting. A tendril of warmth curled beneath her chest, a feeling Hanna did not want to give word to taking root. With their faces an arm's length apart, Hanna could see the faint freckles on Noah's cheekbones, drawn out by the sun's rays, and the darker shades of blue that cracked through the lighter shade of his irises. Falling into those endless pools, Hanna saw someone who felt just as deeply as she did, but who learned to hide it to protect themselves. If she looked long enough, what else would she find in their depths?

A duck landing on the surface of the pond, quacking in delight and splattering water as it flapped its wings, broke the stillness. Hanna straightened with a sharp inhale, trying to convince herself that her heart was only racing because she moved too fast.

"Your painting cannot be that terrible." She took a drink of water to clear her dry throat. "Not compared to mine at least."

Noah looked at her painting and gave her a lopsided smile. "You think that is bad?" He turned his easel to face hers. "Take a look at this."

Swirls of multi-hued paint mixed together on the canvas. What could generously be described as water looked more like a black hole surrounded by green planets.

"It certainly is...unique." Hanna would never laugh at someone else's attempt at art, not when her own was abysmal. "The purpose of art is to put your own flair on it."

"I thought impressionism was all about creating a realistic portrayal of what you see."

"Well," she said and smirked, "who can say that what you put here is not what you are seeing?"

Noah threw back his head to laugh at her sarcastic quip. "Where was this version of you hiding before? I like it."

"Not quite the prim and proper robot you thought I was before, am I?" Hanna teased.

"Eh." He rocked his hand side to side. "The jury is still out. You are still polished on the outside, not that I mind."

Feeling mischievous, Hanna reached for her paintbrush. "Yeah? How's this for polished?"

With a flick of her wrist, Hanna sent paint flying at Noah, droplets speckling his face alongside the freckles. A few dots of blue landed on the exposed portions of his shirt, the rest falling harmlessly on the apron meant to protect his clothes.

Blinking in surprise, Noah wiped a hand across his face, smearing lines of blue along his skin before looking at his paint covered fingers and clothes. He was silent for a moment and Hanna worried that she went too far. All she wanted was for Noah to have some fun.

Instead of getting angry, Noah's eyes flashed with delight, a wicked grin curving his lips. "Oh, you will pay for that."

Noah lunged, hand reaching for Hanna's face to smear matching paint along her cheeks. She shrieked at the feel of the cool paint contrasting with the warm brush of Noah's fingers. Twisting out of his reach, Hanna stood from her chair, paintbrush dangling from her fingers.

She danced around the chair as Noah pivoted on his heels to grab her again. Weaving between their two easels, Hanna sought to put distance between them, flicking the paintbrush in Noah's direction in an attempt to slow him down. Undeterred by the paint launched his way, Noah swiped his fingers through her abandoned palette, quickly swallowing the ground between them with his long legs.

Their laughter as they chased each other around the pond and pathways spilled through the air, infusing the day with happiness. Hanna could not remember a time when she laughed this hard or felt so free to enjoy a moment. Her brain emptied of all thoughts beyond how to avoid Noah while simultaneously getting more paint on him. She was not thinking about the mess, how long it would take to clean the paint from her hair, or who might see them acting like two kids with their first crush.

Noah's shoulders stretched the fabric covering his torso as he spread his arms wide, wiggling his fingers in a harmlessly threatening gesture. Trapped on the narrow stretch of path with trees behind her and Noah in front, Hanna breathed heavily. There was nowhere else to run. Knowing she was all-but-caught, Noah moved forward, his measured steps drawing out the suspense. Black swallowed the blue of his eyes, his chest moving rapidly with his breath. Hanna was helpless under his gaze, pinned in place.

She took one step back, the hard bark of the tree biting into her back and shoulders. Arms raised with her paintbrush in one hand, Hanna held her body steady as Noah reached her. He raised one hand and brushed his index finger down the slope of her nose. Hanna forgot how to breathe. Even if she remembered, it would be a mistake to draw air into her lungs because it would push her chest closer to Noah's.

Eye's flashing with heat at the expression on her face, Noah reached forward again. His hand hovered in the air, angling for her jaw as he looked into her eyes for permission. Swallowing thickly, Hanna nodded.

Her skin prickled with awareness as she waited to feel the brush of his finger against her. Closing her eyes, Hanna held still, sensing the warmth of his hand moving closer.

"Ms. Poole?" Lou called her name, notes of amusement and chastisement mingling in their tone. "Your group is more than welcome to continue exploring the gardens, but the museum is opening to the public soon and I need to clean up the area."

"Oh, Lou," Hazel chided as Hanna ducked underneath Noah's arm to hide her guilty expression. "We need to have a chat about timing. They were just getting to the good part. Now we might have to start all over again."

# 8
# *Always Plan for the Weather*

WEATHER WAS one element of travel that could trip up even the best tour guides in the world, and Hanna counted herself amongst those select few. She checked the weather apps the week before and again on the day of an excursion. She knew weather apps did their best to predict something innately out of human control, but Hanna enjoyed the challenge of controlling what she could. Travel-sized sunscreen lived in her crossbody bag along with a tin of spare hair ties and bobby-pins, a compact first-aid kit, makeup for touch-ups, tissues, and a whole array of other essentials the group might need. Sure, she tried to keep it to a manageable weight, but there was a reason she stretched sore shoulders every night. People on vacation want to cast away their cares and not worry about the little details, like where to get a Band-Aid when their cute new shoes, purchased specifically for vacation, gave them a blister. Yet, the more she planned for contingencies, the more she realized there were some things she simply couldn't prepare for.

Like spring storms and Noah Eversham.

"Shouldn't you have one of those?" Noah pointed to a large group of tourists, their guide holding aloft what appeared to be a selfie stick with a laminated card dangling off the end. The group was finished with their tour of Versailles and were now strolling through the gardens. Above them, the sun peeked around grey clouds, the dark color and a bite of chill in the breeze threatening rain that was not in the forecast when Hanna checked the weather that morning.

She sent him a playful glare once assuring that the rest of the group was fixated on the opulence of Versailles. "Those are to help keep groups together. Five people, adults no less, are within my capacity to manage without losing someone. But–" Her voice was sweet once more. "–if you think you'll have difficulty keeping up with us, I'm sure I can find you a child leash so you don't wander off."

To her surprise, instead of replying with a witty retort, Noah tipped his head back with a laugh, stunning her momentarily speechless. Sunlight caressed his face, highlighting the sharp angles of his cheekbones and the flex of his neck. Tiny lines appeared at the corners of his eyes, and without his usual frown, Noah looked younger.

A man who could make her laugh was attractive. A man who knew how to laugh at himself was dangerous to her heart.

Just as she suspected, when Noah smiled, it lit up his face, the bright white of his teeth contrasting with the dark hair of his beard. "Not my thing, but if I ever feel like trying something new–" Noah had the audacity to wink at her. "–you'll be the first to know."

It was not Hanna's thing either, but there was a certain appeal to having a man like Noah yield to her bidding. After their adventure with paint at Monet's Garden, the set of his shoulders and the way he looked at her had relaxed, making her think that Noah might actually trust her.

Hanna responded to Noah's comment with a noncommittal, "Hmm." There was no reason to open up the Pandora's Box of Noah's sexual preferences. As much as Hanna was trying to uphold her end of the bargain, there was still a line for how much of her real personality Hanna was willing to show Noah. Not when their truce felt so precarious, and there was too much at stake to jump in headfirst.

Several feet away, Daphne waved to get their attention,

beckoning them towards the Latona Fountain. "Hanna, come take a picture with us!"

"Of course." Hanna arranged the group and then held out her hand for the phone.

Daphne gave Hanna a puzzled look as she tucked the phone back towards her torso. "Get in here with us! We want you in the photo, too. Noah can take the photo."

"Are you sure? This is your tri–" Hanna was cut off as a surprisingly strong grip yanked her forward, squishing Hanna between Daphne and Lillian. The group shuffled to create more room and Hanna quickly smoothed out her skirt and blouse, patting her hair to make sure it was falling into place.

Reaching around, Hazel clasped the hand Hanna had resting on her thigh. "This trip would not have happened without you and it's just the first of many. You're part of the group now. Better get used to it because you are stuck with us."

Hanna's throat felt tight with emotion and her gaze flicked to Noah to see his reaction. With how protective he was over Hazel, Hanna could not imagine that he was happy with her open offer of connection to the group. As expected, Noah watched her closely, and while Hanna previously took the assessing gaze as proof he was trying to find fault with her, she found herself looking closer. Eyes that once looked cold and unfeeling were fixated on Hanna's face, spearing into her as if they could tunnel to the core of her being.

Whatever he saw had Noah's face softening, his head tipped slightly to the side as if he found something in Hanna's gaze that was unexpected and perhaps...relatable. Could he see how much she wanted to accept Hazel's offer? How she longed to trust others with her heart and yearned for someone to keep it safe? Her circle of close friends was small, kept that way to protect her bruised heart.

"Well, we are paying her." Lillian's voice interrupted Hanna's thoughts.

"Technically." Noah's voice was firm as his mouth settled back into a frown. "Mémé owns the company that pays me. Does that disqualify me from being part of the group too?"

Hanna wished Noah was holding up the phone to capture the look on Lillian's face, like she had swallowed one of the lemons from the orangery.

"Well...no, but..." Lillian struggled to find her point after Noah decimated her argument.

"But nothing, Lillian," Mai said. "Hanna is part of our group and that is that. Now, smile for the camera. I want to explore the gardens, not sit here all day."

Noah took several photos, even turning to stretch the phone out in front of him to capture a selfie of the entire group, minus Madeline who chose to remain with the car. After the first batch of photos, Hanna stood and took the phone from Noah, taking candid pictures of the friends. While they were coordinating how to pose so that it looked like they were kissing one of the fountain's gold frogs, Hanna felt something hit her forehead. Brushing it away with the back of her hand, another raindrop caught her gaze as it splashed on the phone's screen.

So much for the weather forecast. Giving the rain a resigned sigh, Hanna motioned for the group to stand and calmly explained that the rain was likely to get worse before it got better and that they would find somewhere dry to wait. Employees were standing at the doors, directing guests to head in their direction, so that was where Hanna led the group. There was no point getting soaked by trying to make it back to the car.

"Wait!" Lillian cried. "My bag. It's Balenciaga."

Glancing back, Hanna saw the brown leather purse on the lower rim of the fountain. Far enough away that they could not retrieve the bag and still make it indoors before the worst of the rain started. Knowing that she had seconds to decide, Hanna faced the group.

"Keep going and get inside. Leave the bag to me."

Concerned for Mai with the slippery conditions, Hazel and the others followed Hanna's directions without question. Satisfied that her guests were taken care of, Hanna started for the purse, only for a strong hand to clasp around her arm and pull her back towards the door. Pivoting so that the momentum brought them under one of the arched windows lining the exterior of the building, Hanna scowled at Noah.

Noah's face was as stormy as the clouds rolling above them. "Forget the purse. It's not worth risking your safety."

"I don't have time for this, Noah." Already, fat drops of rain were descending, splashing against Hanna's body. The inset design of the window offered some coverage, but that would only last until the weather got worse. "It's just a little water. The more time you waste the longer I am out here."

"We can go back for the purse once the rain stops," he insisted, starting to turn away.

Hanna held her ground and resisted the tug on her arm. Noah whipped around and glared at her.

Taking a step forward, Hanna poked a finger into his chest. "Just because you are paying for my services does not give you the right to boss me around. You might get to make the choices when it comes to this trip, but not for me."

Noah matched her step with one of his own. "*I'm* not paying you or trying to take your choices away. I'm trying to keep you safe."

Wind joined the rain, tousling the ends of Noah's hair. Pieces of her own hair flew into Hanna's face. "Then stop wasting my time and let me go. I would have been back by now if you had not stopped me."

She poked his chest again and Noah caught the offending digit in his free hand.

"And I keep trying to tell you that a damn purse is not worth your safety."

The wind was picking up speed, howling around them and making it difficult to hear. Or, at least that was the excuse Hanna later gave herself for why she took that final step between them, toe-to-toe with Noah. Frustration made her breath come faster, her chest rising and brushing against Noah's with every inhale. Heat pumped through her veins at his proximity, warming the skin that was getting damp by rain.

"You're so stubborn," she yelled to be heard over the wind. With both hands trapped by Noah, she could not swipe at the hair trailing across her face and Hanna tried in vain to toss her head to dislodge the wet strands.

Releasing her hands, Noah pushed back her hair, keeping it contained with his palms settled along the sides of her head.

"Stubborn? Pot, meet kettle. You are the most stubborn woman I've ever met. You tell the rest of us to head indoors, trying to keep us safe and warm while you venture out into a literal storm. You could roll your ankle, or worse, get struck by lightning. Is a purse really more important than you?" His chest was heaving now, the grip on her head tightening protectively.

They were not drenched yet, but that would quickly change if they remained at a standoff. Hanna knew that Noah had a point, that even if she had immediately gone to get the purse, it still would have gotten wet. At this point, the damage was already done. But this went deeper than retrieving a bag. Hanna was unwilling to let this go because she thought that it would prove to Lillian and the others, prove to Noah and prove to her family that she could do this job. Getting this purse somehow became proof that she helped people in her job, and that would make it worthy to her parents and siblings, something to be proud of.

"Well, it's my–"

"Job? Yeah, I get that." Noah leaned down to stare directly in her eyes, his voice matching the rumble in the sky. "But, no, it isn't. Your job was to plan this trip, guide the group, and provide information along the way. And you're damn good at it, phenomenal even. Going above and beyond shows your dedication and passion for the work you do, but this is a step too far."

He ran a hand through his damp hair, the perfectly styled locks now sticking out in random directions. It made him look softer and less imposing as he continued. "You got us here and gave us the unique experience promised, job complete. Fetching a grown-ass adult's belongings is not part of your job. Lillian can afford to buy another purse. Hell, I'll buy one for her, if it means you won't risk breaking your neck. You might help out when you can, because it is the kind thing to do, but you are not being kind to yourself. Your job is not to work yourself so hard that you get injured."

Hanna forgot how to breathe. The intensity of Noah's gaze eliminated all other thoughts. So close to her own, Hanna could see every emotion crossing Noah's face. Frustration, empathy, and fear. When she licked away a drop of water that slid from Noah's finger to her lips, Hanna saw how he tracked the movement, pupils dilating with desire.

"Your job–" The words were puffs of air against her mouth. "–is not to put everyone first but yourself."

Hanna could not feel the chill in the air because Noah's body was radiating heat. Even when angry with her, Noah protected her, shielding her body with his own from the worst of the gathering rain.

She needed space, needed to think without Noah distracting her. Fighting back her own attraction, Hanna's voice was less firm than she intended. "Yeah, well your job isn't to take care of me. Just enjoy your vacation. I can take care of myself."

Would he take the bait, choose the easy path and leave Hanna behind, like everyone else did?

"Maybe it's time you let someone else take care of you."

Hanna sucked in a shaky lungful of air. She wanted that. Wanted a partner who she could lean on, share her worries, and take care of too. But it seemed impossible with Noah. He had a life and home to return to. Hanna wandered the globe and had no place to call home. And that did not even begin to cover the complication that he was a guest on one of her tours.

That was all difficult to remember as their chests moved in synchrony, a deep breath enough to bring their lips together. It was just a kiss, it did not need to be life changing, and yet she felt a bolt of electricity stronger than lightning shoot through her.

Another thunderous roar broke through the air, jolting Hanna and Noah apart. Hanna pushed Noah back further and slipped away. Rushing out into the rain, Hanna only dared to glance over her shoulder once, but Noah was no longer in front of the window. His arm brushed hers as he sprinted past her, scooping the purse under his arm before pivoting and running back to Hanna. A burst of laughter escaped her at the way his face scrunched to prevent rain dripping into his eyes, breaking the tension between them as they ran for the door.

Hazel yanked them both inside, patting them down and chastizing them both for being foolish enough to run about in the rain like children playing in puddles. Noah tried to remind her that they were not outside for fun, but Hazel was having none of it. Despite its somewhat sodden appearance, Lillian reached for the purse with a sob, clutching it to her chest and thanking Noah profusely.

"It was Hanna who got it," Noah said.

To her surprise, Lillian hugged Hanna, thanking her for saving the purse that was a gift from her mother. Over her shoulders, Hanna arched her brow at Noah, trying to communicate that rescuing the purse was the correct choice. In response, Noah passed her a small towel that one of the employees handed him, leaving his own hair wet against his head as he watched her dry off.

Sweeping sheets of rain poured down in front of them, pooling and darkening the sand pathways. Outside the arched windows, guests dashed towards coverage, holding jackets or umbrellas over their heads, not that it protected them from the onslaught of water. Employees rushed around the interior, focused on keeping dripping guests away from the priceless artwork while ensuring their safety. Hanna was glad they made it inside with minimal damage. Their damp hair and clothing would dry off soon enough.

She was more concerned with the damage to the walls around her heart. Noah's words made a crack and now Hanna was worried that he would take it apart piece by piece, leaving her defenseless when it was time for him to go home.

# 9

## *Only Buy What You Can Carry*

FLEA MARKET DAY was one of Hanna's favorites to organize in Paris. Some of her favorite outfits, vintage dresses with flared skirts and shirts with wide collars, came from Le Marché aux Puces de Saint-Ouen. When Mai asked Hanna where she got her camel colored high-waisted skirt and fitted white blouse, Hanna told her, which promptly sparked the group's enthusiasm for visiting the famous market. Noah was markedly less enthusiastic, but Hanna caught him hiding a grin as he watched the elderly women gush over what gems they might find while shopping.

It was also one of the few excursions where Madeline would join the group. She loved hunting for the perfect trinkets for her numerous family members. Hanna recalled a particular instance where Madeline and a merchant were engaged in a loud and heated argument over the price of a pocket watch–an exchange Hanna thought would result in one of them getting arrested or Madeline leaving without her prize–but the tenacious Frenchwoman had the final word. With a flippant gesture, Madeline was turning to leave the stall when the vendor called out one last price. Madeline pivoted immediately and briskly shook the merchant's hand.

The iconic green-metal and glass roof of the Marché Dauphine reflected the shining sun, light winking back at visitors capturing images of the two-story building. Navigating the grey cobblestones was tricky with hundreds of tourists streaming in and out of the building, stopping with no warning to look at an item that caught their eye in a stall. Undeterred by the onslaught of sights around them, sparkling jewelry and fibrant fabrics fought for their attention, Hazel, Daphne, Mai, and Lillian charged into the market like generals leading a troop into battle.

They stopped at nearly every stall, browsing through the tightly packed displays of books, clothing, antiques, and art. Hanna stepped in to converse with the merchants in French, giving them no room to think they could charge higher prices just because the older women sounded American. She also had to step in–quite literally in the case of one pickpocket who hobbled away with a dent in his shoe from Hanna's heel–to protect them from thieves.

A stall selling antique furniture was too narrow for Mai's wheelchair to pass through, so Hanna waited with her in the breezeway, watching as the others picked up items to show them from the open entryway. Madeline acted as their translator inside as Noah trailed behind them. Hanna smothered a laugh when Noah picked up a metal shoe horn in the shape of a slug, the eye stalks bent to fit around the shoe and assist with pulling it off, and looked at the price tag. His eyebrows shot to his hairline as he turned the slug over in his hand in befuddlement, critically examining it as if to discover some hidden detail that would validate the price.

"Are you having fun?" Mai turned to talk to Hanna.

Hanna did not need to polish her answer before replying. "I am. Visiting the flea market is one of my favorite things in Paris."

"I can see why. The energy of this place is incredible. All these objects with their stories and history intertwining with the rush of the present, connecting people together and giving new life to old things." Mai watched a middle-aged couple walk past, holding hands and carrying a set of porcelain vases in their free hands. "Maybe those vases were owned by nobility, or just a person who loved beautiful things, now getting a second chance to liven up a space and bring joy to a new household."

Mai understood Hanna's love of antiques perfectly. It was the possibility of everyday items that captured her interest. Her own lack of possessions notwithstanding, Hanna loved the idea of a home filled with personal touches, mementos, and memories lining the walls and shelves, illustrating a life well lived and full of love.

"That is what drew me to flea markets in the first place, creating stories for the unique things that I find, imaging where they came from, who their family was, who loved them. I know it is silly to personify objects, but for a brief moment in time, they might hold a memory, transporting their owner back to a feeling or period of time in their life."

Hanna gestured to her clothing. "Maybe this dress was worn by a woman on her first day of college, or it was this dress she was wearing when she first met her spouse." Hanna glanced away from Mai and landed on Noah. He had his hand on Hazel's back, leaning over to listen to what she was saying, but when he stood his eyes met Hanna's and her breath caught in her lungs. "Here, anything seems possible."

"They become part of our stories," Mai agreed. "Why did you return that necklace you were admiring?"

At one of the shops selling jewelry, Hanna found a cameo necklace with a birdhouse etched into the cream shell set into a powder-blue background. A halo of lace-patterned gold surrounded the pendant, the braided chain warming against her skin. It reminded her of the wristwatch from her father.

Hanna shook her head. "I move around too much to collect a lot of possessions. For me, just enjoying the experience of seeing beautiful things is enough."

Mai looked at her with an expression Hanna had trouble placing. It was not pity, but something closer to sympathy. "That must be very difficult for you."

"Oh, no, I am used to it. How many people get to say that they love their job? Not having a place of my own seems like a small price to pay for getting to travel the world."

Even though her heart stung a little at the thought. She had no regrets with her job, but lately Hanna felt a dull ache when a tour was over, the gap between tours bringing a sense of limbo when she had nowhere to go. Hanna rationalized not owning a home or apartment as a way to save money for the business, but the utilitarian aspect of most of the hotels or shared apartments she rented when not living with Sarah were starting to feel...empty.

"Something can be difficult and you can still love it. That's life, dear. Take it from a woman who has lived long enough to make many, many mistakes. Loving your job is wonderful, and you are right that many people do not experience that, but if you do not have a life outside your work, that is not living. And when you have someone to share it with, even in a platonic sense, your joy is amplified. It does not have to be all at once, but maybe start with something small. Like a beautiful necklace, or a handsome man."

Hanna did not know how to respond. Had she been so immersed in her job that she started living her life for other people, stepping into their stories for the time she was with them, that she stopped living for herself? Maybe it was time to open herself back up to the possibility of building a community around herself again. Reveal more pieces of herself to others, like Sarah and Will, Noah and this group of women, and trust that they would still like her.

Mai let her suggestion sink in, observing the flow of people around them while Hanna processed her words. Snippets of conversations flowed around them, some of them in languages Hanna knew, but they sounded discordant to her. A sensation built in Hanna with a feeling she had not felt in a long time.

Lost.

She was confident in her ability to navigate practically anywhere around the world, but when it came to building a home? There was no map or GPS to help her with that.

"All done?" Mai said to others as they approached, startling

Hanna and pulling her attention back to their surroundings. Hanna mentally chided herself for getting so lost in thought in a busy area.

"For now." Daphne lifted her handful of bags. "Give me a cup of coffee and one of those giant croissants with chocolate and I will be ready to keep going."

Hanna reached for the bags, informing the group that she was going to store their purchases in the car while the others grabbed a bite to eat.

"I hope everything fits," Hazel remarked. "We still have so many shops to visit and I would hate for us to run out of room in the car."

Reassuring her that they would find a way to transport all their purchases, Hanna took her time getting to the car and back. She needed time to process what Mai said before she could put on the mask of tour guide again.

When the group finished for the day, Hanna and Madeline stood together, staring at the car. Bags and boxes stacked on top of each other threatened to escape the confines of the trunk, and there were more bags sitting beside them on the curb. Mai was settled comfortably in the car with the others, joking that they could start their own store with everything they purchased.

Hanna wished she was exaggerating.

Blowing air out of her mouth so that it ruffled her bangs, Madeline crossed her arms and frowned at the situation in front of them. They were out of usable space if everyone was going to fit in the car. Who even needed this much stuff?

"I could drop them off at the hotel and then come back to pick up the rest?"

They were exchanging solutions in French so that none of her guests worried. No one wanted to know how sausage was made, just that it tasted delicious.

"I would have to stay here, too. With my seat free, would that give us enough space to fit the rest of the bags? I could catch a taxi or take the metro."

"It would help, but even with your seat, there still is not enough room. Besides, I do not like the idea of leaving you alone at night."

Hanna rolled her eyes. She used to live in this city and knew which places to avoid and how to keep safe. Besides, the sun was still out, and she had a few hours before it set.

"Is everything okay?" Noah slid out of the car, walking over to join them.

Pushing aside her initial reaction to hide the problem from Noah, Hanna trusted that he would not overreact. If anything, with each small problem that arose, Noah proved he did not hold it against Hanna, letting go of his belief that she wanted to steal his grandmother's money.

"There is no way to fit everyone and the bags in the car," Hanna said, pointing at the merchandise. "Madeline could make two trips, but traffic at this time means that could take hours. I just offered to take the metro back to make more space for the bags, but Madeline said even that would not be enough."

Glancing between the remaining bags and the car, Noah frowned. Brows furrowed in thought, he rubbed a hand along his jaw before turning back towards Madeline.

"What if I went with Hanna? That would free up two seats and we could carry whatever bags did not fit. And I don't like the idea of you travelling alone at night." He directed the last statement at Hanna.

Madeline shot Hanna a look, switching back to French to quickly say, "He likes you."

Noah's eyebrow twitched.

Hanna was glad that Noah did not speak French or else she would be more embarrassed than she already was.

Hanna hefted a few bags into her arms. "Might as well give it a try before we think of something else."

The three of them filled the available space, tucking a few bags between each seat for good measure. It was snug, but they got it all to fit.

"Do you mind if we walk back?" Noah asked as they watched the van pull away. "It's nice out and I'd rather enjoy the view on foot than stuck in traffic or crammed in a metro car."

"It's a long walk back," Hanna warned. "I would not want your feet to hurt."

He glanced at her feet. "I'll be fine. Unless your feet hurt?"

Bumping against him playfully, Hanna scoffed. "Me? I am used to it. At this point I am more surprised when my feet do not hurt."

"Seriously?"

"A hazard of the job. You try walking as much as I do and see how your feet feel. I still prefer walking as much as I can though, it helps me familiarize myself with the city."

They walked in companionable silence for a while, strolling through quiet neighborhoods and areas buzzing with activity. With his long legs, Noah easily kept up with the quick pace Hanna set, an uncommon occurrence. When they came across places she recognized, Hanna pointed them out to Noah, sharing a few of the stories from when she lived in the city.

Her purse started vibrating when they were walking along Pont Alexandre III bridge. Hanna glanced at her phone, silencing it when she saw who it was. The photo of her parents, taken when a tour to Greece coincided with their mission location, smiled at her before blinking away into a black screen. Moments later, a notification pinged, and Hanna quickly scanned the message, shoving her phone back into her purse forcefully when she saw the attached job application.

To his credit, Noah did not pry when she let out an angry huff, giving her a sympathetic look. Was this what unconditional support felt like? Hanna was unfamiliar with the sensations it provoked. She wanted to confide in him, give him a glimpse of the imperfect hurts and truths lurking behind the facade she projected to the world. Could she trust him to take what she said and keep it safe? There was only one way to find out.

"My mom just sent me another job application. Neither of my

parents understand why I picked this career," she said, feeling a bit like she was taking a step onto an invisible bridge over a canyon. "They both work for a medical non-profit, providing aid to those most in need, and taught my siblings and me that giving back to the community is the highest priority. I was a surprise child. There is a ten year gap between me and the twins, Samuel and Nathaniel. Adriana and I are fourteen years apart. Considering that my mother is a doctor, you think they would have been more proactive with birth control." Hanna's joke sounded forced to her ears. "They were happy when they found out they were pregnant, but I do not think they ever quite knew what to do with me. For the first few years, they were given special consideration for missions in the United States where they had family who could help take care of me while they worked, but once I was old enough, they began taking missions farther away. I cried for weeks the first time we moved, not knowing why I had to say goodbye to my friends and family no matter how much my parents tried to explain that people needed their help."

Hanna's oldest memories were of tents and medical facilities in remote areas. Switching schools with each new town, and sometimes country, was too erratic and complicated, so her parents home-schooled her with the help of whatever colleagues had time or their own children to teach. She remembered the boredom of sitting still, feeling out of place among her siblings.

"Looking back on it, they should have realized that I was different from my sister and brothers. They loved working alongside my parents, asking questions about medical conditions and treatment plans. My questions were always about the people. Where did they come from? What was their home like? Could we go visit? I lived in all these new, exciting places, but I never got to experience it. You know what I mean?"

Beside her, Noah hummed in agreement.

"Because my siblings were older, and my parents were so busy, they were often expected to take care of me. You can imagine how well that went over. No teenager wants to take care of their baby sister. We had nothing in common."

"I can imagine. Are you close with them now?"

"Not particularly, but out of the three of them I stay in contact with my sister, Adriana, the most. She's the only stationary one out of the bunch. She got tired of moving around our whole lives and stayed in New York after finishing college. Adriana and her wife, Cal, adopted a little girl, Nina. She just learned to read and loves getting postcards from around the world, so I try to write to her as often as I can. Makes me think that I can pull off being the 'cool' aunt." Hanna gave a self-deprecating laugh.

"Eh, with how much you geeked out over how many replicas of the Eiffel Tower there are in the world, I don't see you winning any awards for how cool you are," Noah teased while bumping his shoulder against hers.

"Wow. Thanks for your vote of confidence. If I remember correctly–" Hanna bumped him back "–you were pretty excited over that fact yourself."

The moment of levity dissipated some of the tension that was tightening in Hanna's chest. She felt close to Noah, like they were connecting on a level where he truly understood where she was coming from. Like he felt the same loneliness creep in and dull happy moments with its gloom, sewing seeds of doubt that even if you tried to let people get close to you, they would still leave you.

"I do not resent her for not wanting to hang out with me when we were kids, but sometimes I wonder if we would have been better friends if we were closer in age. Nathaniel and Sam were always together, like two sides of a magnet. By the time I was old enough to be interesting, they were getting ready for college. Then it was just me and my parents. Any friends I made were temporary, we moved every year or so, which made it difficult to get close enough to anyone. Because I was a minor, we were always sent on missions to safer areas of the world, which meant I was usually so close to all the places I wanted to explore, but with no way to get there on my own, I felt…"

"Trapped?" Noah supplied.

"I don't mean to sound ungrateful, we helped a lot of people and I ended up with a more robust education than most people my age."

Noah shook his head, his sunglasses hiding his expression. "Just because you wish that things were different does not make you ungrateful. You were a child who could not control the experiences you were thrust into, and as an adult you have to process the impact it had on you. Acknowledging the bad that comes with the good does not mean you are selfish, it means you are human."

His words settled into Hanna's skin, sinking down into her blood-stream to flow into unhealed cuts and bruises. Was she holding onto unnecessary blame, judging herself harshly for having mixed emotions about her past?

"I thought it was in poor taste to complain about volunteering."

"You were a teenager. Of course, you were going to complain about it."

Mirth bubbled up inside her, bursting out in a peel of laughter.

"The first time I asked for money to take the train into the city with some of the other girls from the town, I thought my parents were going to ground me. Asking for money for doing the chores that were supposed to be volunteer hours felt so wrong."

"And did they?"

"No, but I did get a lecture on the importance of giving back. Since I technically could not get paid from the organization, my parents established a system where some of my volunteer hours counted towards an allowance. I think that they thought if they let me explore with other kids my age, it would slake my desire to see the world. Like it was a passing interest before I settled back into valuable work."

As if a cloud were passing in front of the sun, Hanna's good mood vanished at the reminder of her parent's opinion on her career.

"Little did they know that once I started seeing the world, all I wanted was to see more. I saved so that I could visit new places as often as I could, leaving on the first train and returning on the last.

When I was in secondary school, I would go with classmates, sometimes for school trips, but mostly for fun. It was on one of those trips that I ran into the tour guide who ultimately introduced me to Stephanie. My parents thought it was just a summer job, but when I told them that I was deferring going to university, they tried to change my mind. They even got Adriana and the twins involved, calling out of the blue to wax poetic on the value of university and the doors it would open for me. But my mind was made up. When my parents left for their next mission, I stayed in Europe and started working full time for Stephanie."

Beside her, Noah paused along the walkway. Hanna turned and went towards him, heart dropping at the sight of the frown on his face. So, she had found the line that marked the boundary of how much of her real personality Noah wanted to see. Now that he heard her story and listened to her failures, he found her lacking. She never went to university, not like Noah had, and had two parents who wanted what was best for her, nothing worth complaining about. He must think that she was so unappreciative of her life. Hanna fixed a bright smile on her face and started to open her mouth to give a blasé remark to course correct the conversation.

"That must have been difficult for you, wanting to pursue something that was at odds with what your family thought was best for you," Noah said solemnly. "Choosing to forge your own path when it would have been easier to go along with what they wanted. That takes courage and conviction, far more than I had at that age."

Hanna's heart skipped a beat, thudding back to life as Noah's words penetrated. Her smile fell from her face in awe, eyes wide to take all of him in. Was it really that easy? That he could look at the exposed and wounded parts of her and value them just as much as the happy, easygoing parts? She wanted to offer Noah more pieces of herself, see if he would hold onto them while she worked on welding them back together. Not fixing her, but giving her the unconditional support to heal herself.

"It wasn't easy," Hanna admitted, taking a step closer to him.

Around them, tourists snapped photos and walked past them, rushing like the river beneath the bridge. Noah paid them no mind, angling his taller frame to protect Hanna from getting jostled.

"And now you run your own business." Noah's sentence hung in the space between them, the unasked question like an echo. *Does your family understand now?*

"They still think that I am playing around, wasting my time trotting around the globe when I could have a worthwhile career. Something to be proud of, something that gives back. No matter how many times I explain that I am happy and have enough to take care of myself, not that wealth equals success," she was quick to add, "but it's never enough for them."

Hanna took a ragged breath, tipping her head up to the sky to keep the tears at bay. "*I* am never enough."

Eyes closed so that she could not see the pitying look that was surely on Noah's face, a shadow darkened the back of her eyelids and Hanna felt a presence move closer to her.

"Hanna." Noah's breath fanned over her cheek, one warm finger trailing along her jaw to draw her attention. "Look at me."

She blinked slowly, focusing on the startling blue of his gaze behind his glasses. This close, she could faintly see flecks of darker blue and gold highlighting the lighter tones.

"Whether you fit into their mold of what you should or should not be. You. Are. Enough. If they cannot see that, then that is a flaw in them, not you. Anyone who spends even five minutes with you can see what a gift you have. You've shown me that this job is more than just trip planning. You take away the stress and headache of planning and replace it with relaxation and pleasure, and do it so seamlessly that people forget their worries and burdens for a few days. You find what people love, what makes them unique, and somehow give them an experience tailored specifically to them. That is something very few people can do and you should be proud of it."

Hanna's heart cracked, not in the way caused by heartbreak, but in a way that broke away the damaged parts, creating paths for her fragile edges to knit back together. Hearing Noah validate her choices and earnestly praise her healed something in Hanna that she did not know was injured. From her time with him, Hanna knew that Noah did not give out praise thoughtlessly. He meant every word he said, carefully considering each one before he gave it voice. Noah saw her, past the perfect facade to the insecure parts she tried to hide, and instead of feeling scared, Hanna felt safe. Valued not just for what she had to offer others, but for herself.

Words caught in her throat, fading away before she could get them out. Staring at her reflection in Noah's sunglasses, Hanna reached up to push them on top of his head. She needed to see him, to peer into his soul and know that she was not alone in feeling this way. His gaze was unwavering, opening himself up to her so Hanna could see the truth behind his words.

Her fingers lingered by his brow, grazing the strands of his hair as they waved on the breeze.

"Thank you," she whispered.

Noah's gaze softened in understanding, as if he knew exactly how much his words meant to her. Wordlessly, Noah brought his hands up to capture hers, frowning when he felt how cold they were. Bringing them to his mouth, Noah breathed warm air against her cool skin before lowering them to her side.

"Come on," he said. "Let's get you back to the hotel before you turn into a popsicle."

Hanna laughed at the idea, turning to walk alongside Noah once more. With the memory of Noah's words and touch warming her, Hanna thought she would never be cold again.

# 10

## A Little Relaxation Goes a Long Way

FIRST IT WAS THE RAIN, then it was the wind that destroyed Hanna's carefully laid plans. Riding in a hot air balloon was simply *impossible*, the long-suffering Frenchman tried to explain to Hanna over the phone. Rationally, she understood why he was cancelling their trip, but the high-speed train currently hurtling through her brain to come up with an alternative solution was threatening to jump the rails. Plans changed, reservations were cancelled, it was the reality of working tours.

Usually, Hanna was able to replace the activity with an equivalent one. There was no replacing a hot air balloon ride. Apparently, when wind took one of them out of commission, it took them all. Running a hand through her hair in frustration, Hanna replied to the man on the other end of the phone that of course she understood that he could not risk his crew's safety, and of course she appreciated the offer of a credit to rebook the trip, but unless the wind was going to allow them to fly later in the day, a credit was pointless.

Typing a quick message to several of her contacts throughout Paris, all while listening to apologetic French through her earbuds, Hanna scrambled to find something else for the group to do during the day. They had wine tasting later in the evening. She just needed to fill the empty hours until then.

Several messages pinged while she paced the floor of her hotel room.

*Nothing available on short notice, bonne chance!*

*Sorry, all booked today.*

*Maybe next week. Keep me in mind.*

Clenching her jaw in frustration as she replied with pleasantries–every opportunity was one to build professional relationships–Hanna prayed for patience as the negative responses came through. She had dealt with this before, but the idea of letting down Hazel and the others made it feel like a thousand bees were in her stomach.

Drawing a calming breath through her nose, Hanna finished putting on her makeup and touching up her ruffled hair while she called a few more contacts. Yes, it was an incredibly last minute request. Yes, she understood that she was asking a lot. Yes, Hanna would consider using their company in the future.

Heart beating rapidly in her chest, Hanna smiled broadly when a spa agreed to host their group with a private room and any services they requested. It was a relatively new location on the spa scene, something Hanna could commiserate with, but their focus on sustainable products, quality services, and giving back to the community were all values that Hanna sought in her partnerships. Their willingness to work with her on short notice–and their shrewd request for exclusivity going forward–impressed Hanna. Add in the fact that they were the only contact to get back to her with availability, Hanna was relieved to finally have an option to present to her group.

"There has been a slight change of plans," Hanna informed the group when they gathered in the lobby. "We cannot go on the hot air balloon because of high-altitude winds." As expected, this statement was met with a round of disappointed sighs and Hanna rushed to continue. "But, I was able to book you a day at a wellness spa. We've packed a lot into the last few days, so I thought that a day of pampering and relaxation was just the thing to rejuvenate you."

"A spa day," Daphne said dreamily, "we have not had one of those in ages."

"Speak for yourself," Lillian said. "I have a recurring appointment for a massage and facial every month."

Daphne rolled her eyes at her friend. "Okay, beauty queen. What I meant is that we have not gone to the spa as a group in...how long has it been?"

Hazel pursed her lips. "Longer than it should be if we have to count. This is just what we need. Excellent job, Hanna."

Preening at the praise, Hanna gave them a rundown of everything the spa offered, making notes of what they each expressed preferences on so that she could let the spa know.

"It sounds heavenly," Mai agreed. "After all this sightseeing, these old bones need a good soak."

Hazel laughed. "And we don't even do this every day. If anyone deserves a day at the spa, it's Hanna." She turned to address Hanna. "You are coming with us, right?"

Looking up from her notebook, Hanna gave a reassuring smile to the five sets of eyes staring at her. "I can if you want me to. Otherwise I will go to check you in, get you settled, and then pick you back up in time for dinner. Either way is fine with me."

"You deserve pampering, too." Hazel looped her arm through Hanna's. "I insist. We will make a girl's day out of it. Noah?" She gestured for him to shoo. "Find somewhere else to be today."

"As you wish." Noah winked at Hanna as he quoted the famous line. "Maybe I'll buy a face mask and have my own spa day here."

The thought of Noah with a goopy mix of product covering his face should not be attractive, but imagining him in an open robe, the lines of his face relaxed in bliss, was working for Hanna. He certainly could use something to relax the lines forming from all the frowning he did...though, that was a less common occurrence each day. Sure, Noah still looked like he was watching for something to go wrong, but more often than not Hanna saw him relax and enjoy the moment, keeping true to his word to trust her to plan the trip.

"I can recommend some activities–" Hanna started to say.

"I'm alright, Hanna. Go relax. My grandmother is right, you

deserve to enjoy yourself too. Somehow I found a way to entertain myself before you came along with your spreadsheets. I can manage scheduling one afternoon's worth of time on my own." He said it with a note of pride and admiration, no judgement in his playful tone.

"Well," Hanna teased, "if you think it is that easy, do not forget to turn on your location sharing so that I can find you when you get lost."

His gaze sparked with delight. "Worried about me? All you had to do was ask if you wanted my location so badly. I'll share mine if you share yours."

Was it hotter in the lobby than she remembered? Heat sizzled up her body at Noah's flirtatious tone. The urge to respond in kind was too strong and Hanna found her body and mouth moving without conscious thought.

Tossing her hair over one shoulder playfully, Hanna spun around. "I only share my location with friends when I am going on a date, or with family, and since you are neither..." She gave him a quick once over. "I guess you will just have to live with the mystery of where I am."

She was proud of her ability to leave Noah speechless. And was it her imagination or was he fighting back a smile? Even as these thoughts ran through her mind, Hanna forgot to look where she was going and nearly barreled into Hazel when she turned around. Four heads with varying degrees of gray hair were turned towards Hanna and Noah, watching their exchange like it was the Olympic tennis finals. Which, for Daphne, was ironic since she actually had participated in that competition.

Mai, Hazel, and Daphne did not attempt to hide the expectant looks on their faces, smug with satisfaction that their machinations were playing out the way they wanted. Hanna half expected them to retract their invitation for her to join them and insist that she tour Noah around the city, or invite Noah along and conveniently disappear so that they were alone together. Lillian was ignoring them, scrolling through something on her phone.

"Oh, look!" Lillian shoved her phone into her friends' faces. "The spa offers a CBD massage. They say it's good for arthritis."

Mai grabbed the phone from Lililan and held it at arm's length, peering down at the screen. "Hmm, sounds less fun and more expensive than getting high. I have some gummies in my bag that I can get."

"You've been holding out on us, Mai," Hazel jokingly scolded her. "Some friend you are."

Ushering the group outside with a goodbye to Noah, who hid a laugh behind a cough at Hanna's flicker of panic over the aforementioned gummies, Hanna commented on some of the other services the spa offered. Like a lavender steam room that was also good for joint pain relief.

The spa was everything the website and online photos promised it would be. Their shoes clacked against the smooth floor, the polished tiles gleaming in the soft overhead lighting. To the left of the doors were two cream loveseats, inviting guests to sink into their plush comfort while they filled out the waiver and service interest forms. A few steps in was a long white desk, a clear vase with vibrantly hued dahlias adding a splash of color against the sand colored walls. An older Frenchwoman greeted them and Hanna recognized her voice from the phone call earlier.

Sophie owned the spa with her sister, a fact that ignited a round of questions from the group of female entrepreneurs. Skin glowing without an ounce of makeup, she appeared years younger than the wrinkles and abundance of gray hair suggested. Settling the group onto the couches with cups of herbal tea, Sophie explained the variety of services available to them.

"Oh, we should do the group facials," Daphne said as she looked at the others for agreement. Their enthusiasm was infectious and Hanna found herself smiling and nodding along with whatever services they picked.

The ethereal music floating through the air around them, combined with the aromatic oils, teased her senses into a state of relaxation that almost had her missing the mention of group seaweed wraps. Hanna had to draw the line at being around her guests naked.

*You are forgetting the one guest you would very much like to see naked,* her brain supplied unhelpfully. Flashes of Noah's shirtless arms and glimpses of his chest through a partially unbuttoned shirt scrolled through her mind like a personal dating app.

Swipe right for pectorals, left for biceps.

Hanna switched from tea to sparkling water in an attempt to cool off. A laughable attempt since they were heading into the steam room first, but Hanna needed to banish thoughts of Noah if she was going to spend the day with his grandmother.

"So, Hanna, you live near Los Angeles, right? You and Noah should get dinner together when we return." Hazel's voice carried over the door from her changing room.

Hanna was in the middle of putting on her black, one-piece swimsuit and stumbled, bracing against the bamboo locker to stop from sprawling onto the floor.

Mai laughed. "Subtle, Hazel. Do you already have their wedding colors picked out too?"

"Burgundy and sage. Somewhere outdoors, nothing too formal." She said it so matter of fact that Hanna was nearly convinced the wedding was happening.

Face the same shade as the color Hazel picked out for her imaginary wedding, Hanna busied herself grabbing towels for the group as they made their way into the steam room. Lavender scented clouds filled the room, obscuring their vision, moisture beading along their skin like dew. Hanna was grateful the lack of visibility hid the growing panic at having her personal life be the focal point of their conversation.

Lillian, of all people, took pity on her. "They are young, Hazel. Let them figure it out on their own." Hanna sighed in relief. "Besides, you did not even ask if she was single."

Her relief was short-lived. Dating–not that she and Noah were dating–was difficult enough without an audience. Living away from her own family for so long, Hanna forgot how many "nice, single men" were conveniently thrown in her path like they were produce at a market. It was nice, though, to have people who cared enough to invest actively, if not obtrusively, in her life.

Inquiring eyes turned towards Hanna. Guests asked her this question all the time, usually followed with a line of inquiry on other aspects of her personal life. They spent so much time with her, it was expected that guests would eventually ask about the person sharing glimpses of the world with them. For the most part, she kept the information surface level, preferring to steer the focus back on her guests, learning about their lives and interests. It kept her heart safe from getting too attached when she had to say goodbye at the end of the tour.

"No," she answered the question honestly. "I am not dating anyone right now. With as much travel as I do, it is difficult finding someone willing to work around my schedule. I also want to focus on my business right now, getting it off the ground and operating smoothly so that I can dedicate more time to a partner when I do find one."

Daphne hummed in agreement. "Smart woman. Focusing on yourself is important, it gives you time to build a life for yourself so that you are never dependent on someone else for your security. I remember the waves I caused when I announced that I was not quitting tennis after getting married. Everyone expected me to slow down and focus on popping out babies, and I almost let them convince me that was my path in life. But, everyone's path is different, and you have to figure it out on your own." Daphne gave Hanna a nod.

"Despite the progress women have made, there are still people who want to tear us down and keep us under their boots," she continued. "We might make comments about you and Noah, Lord knows the two of you would be adorable together, but what we really want is for you to be happy. Even before we met you, I felt like we knew you based on Hazel's stories. You remind me of a younger version of us, driven, passionate, and so damn smart that I look forward to seeing you trailblaze through the business world. When one woman succeeds, we all succeed."

"Straighten each other's crowns, right?" Mai settled her hand over Hanna's on the bench.

The humid air was only a small reason why Hanna was glowing from the inside out. Tours were often isolating, she worked alone, planned alone, and rarely heard from guests again unless they specifically requested her for another tour. Maybe it was because this was Hanna's first tour with her own company, maybe it was the size of the group that lent an air of connection, or maybe it was just who these women were that gave Hanna a sense of community for the first time in years. These highly successful women treated her as an equal, welcoming her into their group as if their age difference was just a number. Meddlesome as they were, Hanna knew that their questions came from a place of genuine support and care. It made her feel like she could open up to them, show them pieces of the real Hanna, just like she was doing with Noah, and that they would still accept her.

Hazel's age-worn hand settled over Hanna's free hand. "I keep pushing you and my grandson together because I want you to find happiness outside your work, and I think you and Noah could give each other that. You are an amazing woman: tenacious, spirited, and can do anything you set your mind to. I know you can be happy on your own, but the right person helps you flourish and supports your interests outside the relationship, growing together. My own marriage was arranged by our families, but we learned to care for each other and Marcel became my loudest champion when I opened the business. I do not think there is anything wrong with wanting the same for two of my favorite people."

Misty eyed, Hanna beamed at each of the women. "Thank you. There are not a lot of people who find value in what I do, they treat this job like I get an endless vacation. Meddling aside..." She gave Hazel a sidelong glance, to which the older woman shrugged. "It means a lot to know that you care enough to want success for both my professional and personal lives."

"Good," Hazel said definitively. "Though I have known you long enough that I am a little insulted you did not reach out to me for advice when you were putting together your business plan."

Chagrined, Hanna gave a self-deprecating laugh. "I thought it would be inappropriate to reach out looking for free advice."

"It is called networking."

Something Hanna still found uncomfortable and made her skin itch. The very thought of reaching out to people because she needed something made Hanna want to crawl into a hole and disappear. Talk to a group of strangers for days on end, no problem. Reach out and ask them for help, hives.

"What else were you too afraid to ask?" Mai hit the nail on the head with her question. One of the main reasons Hanna did not reach out to Hazel was the fear that she would laugh at her ideas or call them impossible. "You have a captive audience now, so ask away."

An hour passed by quickly as the group shared their successes and failures as business owners, and as they were called into individual treatment rooms, Hanna's head was full of ideas for marketing her business. Relaxed from a deep-tissue massage, Hanna rejoined the group for their facials.

"So, what's the worst group you have ever given a tour to?" Hazel asked, the words sounding like they were rolling over marbles before exiting her thin lips.

Hanna fought back a laugh at Hazel's attempt to talk without moving her mouth. Their faces were covered in a tingling face mask designed to combat aging, and their esthetician warned them against moving too much to allow the ingredients to settle properly. That was apparently too much to ask this group of women, who had scarcely lasted two minutes before breaking the silence.

There were so many ways she wanted to answer Hazel's question. She could tell them about the time a guest ignored her suggestions to swap alcohol for water on a river cruise and projectile vomited all over the deck and several other guests. The worst part was when they demanded a refund since they did not enjoy the experience.

Hanna shuddered at the memory.

Then there were the countless groups who demanded special treatment, snapping their fingers to summon Hanna like a trained pet. She deserved an award for the restraint she showed, especially when they got to the end of the trip and told her that they did not believe in tipping. Her satisfaction at a job well done was reward enough apparently. She briefly considered asking them if that was a valid form of payment for bills.

She would never share that with other guests though. Complaining was a recipe for disaster in the service industry. It left the group wondering what mean things were said about them behind their backs. Plus, you never knew who someone was connected with, and negative talk had a way of coming back to bite you later.

So, Hanna kept as close to the truth as she could. "Every tour has its own challenges, but I consider them learning opportunities. I would not say any of them were the worst."

"You are not fooling anyone with that PR-approved answer," Hazel said with a chuckle. "Believe me, I understand how women must be extra-cautious of our reputations. We get called bitches for the same attitude men are praised for, but this is a safe space. We will not judge you for calling out people who deserve it, their bad behavior is not a reflection of you."

Daphne agreed. "Mmhmm. I still remember my first television interview, nothing too big, but I was still nervous and pacing the dressing room so much I worried I was wearing a hole in the carpet. That's how one of the assistants found me, pacing back and forth, reciting my talking points. He took one look at me and said, 'You would be prettier if you smiled.'"

Outraged exclamations drowned out the ambient harp music. Despite their difference in age, there were some experiences that were sadly universal for all women. Ask any woman and she would recall a moment where someone told her a version of that phrase.

Unsolicited. As if hearing it unlocked a mystery of the universe the woman was missing in her life.

"That is terrible, Daphne. I hope you did not let that ruin your big moment."

Daphne snorted. "I was a black woman in a predominantly white, male space. So, I did what I was raised to do, smile politely and thank him for the advice. Then I 'accidentally' stepped on his foot with my heel as I left the room."

Hanna could picture it in her mind. Beautiful and strong, head held high, smiling like an angel as she crushed the man's toes. Laughter burst out of Hanna, and the others joined in.

When her laughter died down, Hanna felt comfortable enough to share her own story. "I wish I could say nothing that horrible happened on my tours, but we all know that is a lie. When I was starting out, there was a boy my age on tour, Antonio. He sat next to me at every meal and invited me out every night. I thought we were falling madly in love, reckless and passionate as only young love is, believing that we could overcome any obstacle. Unfortunately, he did not feel the same."

Hanna heard a sharp inhale, but she was too ashamed to look them in the eyes to tell this story. Of all the tours she could have shared with them, this one popped up as the first choice. Like dipping her toes into water to find out how cold it was before jumping in, Hanna wondered if her subconscious chose this memory as a test. Hazel said that she wanted Hanna and Noah to date, but maybe she would change her mind once she knew how disastrous it ended for Hanna before.

"His father caught us together one night. Called me some pretty horrible names and threatened to get me fired. I thought that Antonio would defend me, explain that we were in love. But he said nothing, just stood off to the side while his father yelled at me. I almost lost my job and all I could think about was my broken heart."

Shame resurfaced at the memory. Hanna felt so exposed and small in that hotel room, betrayed and alone as she clutched the sheets to her naked body. Never before had she felt so ugly and unwanted, and it took Hanna years to shake off the experience. She still cared what people thought about her, but Hanna no longer placed her personal value on other's opinions.

"What a spineless worm," Daphne spat out.

Hazel swore in Dutch.

"We should cancel him," Mai stated firmly.

Lillian rolled her eyes. "I do not think you used that phrase correctly, but I agree. As long as there was nothing against a relationship in the company's policies, inadvisable as it was, you did nothing wrong. How typical to blame you when his son was also a consenting adult in the relationship. I hope your boss stood up for you."

Their quick defense of something that happened to her a decade ago healed a wound that had scarred over her heart.

Hanna nodded. "She did. Stephanie was a fantastic boss and earned every bit of her early retirement. When she found out what he said to me, Stephanie got him blacklisted from all the major tour companies and encouraged me to report him for harassment. Last I checked, he was in a lawsuit against several of his employees for allegations of harassment in the workplace."

"Serves him right," Mai said with a nod. "Too many people get away with that kind of behavior."

Daphne agreed. "It's a sad reality that what happened to you is still so common. No one should have to go through that."

"I feel the same way." Hanna allowed some of the righteous anger to fill her voice. "Once I can hire employees, I still plan on being hands-on with planning tours, keeping an eye out to make sure no one is treated poorly. I never want anyone who works for or with me to feel unsafe or unsupported."

It was Hanna's impetus to establish policies against unacceptable behaviour that were clearly outlined in her contracts. If those policies are violated, the tour immediately stops. Without a refund.

"Anyone would be lucky to have you as their boss," Hazel said as she turned in her chair to look at Hanna. "When do you plan on expanding your business? You'd better let us know how we can help." It was a demand.

Something must run through the Eversham family blood to offer help at every turn. But Hazel asked the million dollar question—-and yes, Hanna meant that literally. Luxury travel was a lucrative business. With the rate of itinerary-only trips Hanna was booking, along with several promising private tour inquiries, the plan was to hire an assistant within six months. A second guide after a year. But that relied on maintaining a steady stream of business.

Hanna had it detailed in her business model, but uncertainty and fear lurked over her shoulders like silent sentinels. Whispering words of doubt to her in voices that sounded suspiciously like her family. *Tours are not a stable career choice. You need a backup plan.*

If one piece of her business plan failed…Hanna did not want to think about Trips Ahoy's employment offer waiting in a sealed envelope at Sarah's place.

"Well…" she hedged.

A sliver of light sliced across the room as the door opened, the esthetician slipping into the room on silent feet. He gasped as his eyes bounced from each of their faces.

"I told you not to move!" He tsked as he pressed a damp towel to Hanna's face, wiping off the mask. "How do you expect these to work if you do not listen to directions? You're lucky your skin is already flawless. I cannot work miracles."

He continued muttering about his wasted time as Hanna and the others giggled.

WHEN THE REST of the group retired for the evening, Hanna went to her room to shower and change into more comfortable clothing. Used to working long hours, her mind was still buzzing with content ideas for social media, especially after exchanging ideas at the spa, and a small thread of anxiety she could only quell by checking her business site and responding to any outstanding emails. She knew it would take time for any referrals from Hazel and her group to kick in, but Hanna suspected that she would worry until her depleted finances were replenished and her tour calendar was fully booked.

The hotel's business suite was comfortable, in the minimalist, beige way that was the en vogue aesthetic. Small desks lined one wall, low partitions providing privacy and a semblance of seclusion in the open space, leather desk chairs at each cubby. Along one side was a printer and other office supplies, the opposite wall hosting a loveseat with textured throw pillows. Hanna settled into one of the desk chairs, turning on her laptop with a hum before getting lost in the methodical rhythm of answering client questions and inquiring with potential vendors.

Hanna stood, pushing a strand of hair back into the bun on top of her head as she stretched, rolling her head to work out a few knots. Bending backwards with her hands linked over her head, Hanna heard the door open. This late at night, Hanna did not expect to see another person, let alone one of the guests that she was leading on an early morning tour the next day, but Noah was not like other people.

Of course, Noah had to find her like this, no makeup, dressed in stretchy pants, a tank top and cardigan, hair likely a mess. Noah should be sleeping, not walking into the business center looking soft and welcoming in a pair of gray sweatpants and a black T-shirt. He looked recently showered, the ends of his hair curling against the nape of his neck, no hint of the product that usually kept it sweeping back off his face.

Her thoughts tumbled like a tower of stacking blocks when a lock of hair fell onto Noah's forehead. She wanted to run her hands through the damp strands and mess them up more. Like their time in Monet's Garden, seeing Noah in casual dress made him touchable.

Trying to direct her thoughts back into the professional realm to prevent crossing a line, Hanna pulled her cardigan tighter across her chest, clutching the fabric together with one hand. "Is everything okay? Can I get you anything?"

Noah blinked quickly, as if waking from a dream and clearing his eyes to make sure what he saw was real. "Yes, and no." He tipped his chin in the direction of her open laptop. "I came to get some work done. Looks like we had the same idea."

"Guess that makes another thing we have in common."

He laughed, the lines around his eyes softening his usually stern features. Millions of euphoric bubbles burst in Hanna's chest at the sound, feeling like she won a prize at a carnival game. She had to work for it, missing the target time after time, but the reward was worth it.

For a moment, their eyes met and held, looking at each other without any artifice. She could see questions swimming in his eyes and only hoped that hers were answering correctly. *This is me, as I am. Do you like it?* His eyes seemed to ask.

The ping of a new email broke the moment, and Hanna tore her gaze away, choosing to stare at a framed picture of the Arc de Triomphe that hung on the wall as if it was the most impressive piece of art she had ever seen.

Noah leaned against the door frame, neither in the room nor out. Hanging somewhere in the balance, much like Hanna's feelings towards him.

"Was the wifi in your room not working?" This was a safer question, something Hanna could solve and distract her from the emotions swirling in her chest.

"You just cannot stop helping people, can you?" Shaking his head with a sigh, Noah stepped towards her. As he came closer, Hanna caught a whiff of his soap, the scent of clean laundry and sunshine. "The wifi is fine. I just don't like working in the same room as I sleep. When I started working from home more often, I thought it was important to keep my work space and relaxing space separate. That way I can pretend that I have work-life balance."

Hanna watched as the tips of his ears turned pink. Apparently she was not the only workaholic on the trip.

"Me, too. I guess that means we have two more things in common."

"Good. I like having things in common with you." Noah's voice was faint, like the admission slipped past his lips without his permission. But they were standing so close now, if one of them stepped forward they would touch. Hanna heard every word as if he shouted them.

This was dangerous. Knowing that she liked him was one thing, Hanna could control this one-sided attraction. Probably. But knowing he liked her too? The urge to reach out and touch him possessed her. Practically no effort was required. Just a few inches forward and her hand would brush his. She could feel the heat radiating off him and swayed toward it like a flower reaching for the sun.

But reaching for the sun was a surefire way to get burned.

Turning away, Hanna started packing up her laptop, hands trembling with the repressed urge to touch Noah. "You can have the room now. I was just finishing up. Let me know if there is anything you need while you are working."

Lightning sizzled across her skin as Noah's hand touched her arm to get her attention. Her breath caught in her throat at the intensity of his gaze.

"Who takes care of you while you are busy taking care of everyone else?"

"Me, I guess. Someone else would just get it wrong."

His blue eyes were whirlpools, pulling her into their depths. But instead of turbulent water, Hanna knew that if she let herself fall into him, the water would protect her, wrapping around her like a cocoon.

"If you gave me a chance, I would like to get it right."

# 11

# There is Always Time for a Cabaret

ONE OF THE benefits of travelling with a smaller group meant that Hanna could structure the itinerary around unique group requests, not just large tourist hotspots. The average age of the group and wealth meant that they also lacked the hectic rush of college students trying to frantically squeeze every drop of time out of the trip so that they would not miss anything. As someone who stayed in enough hostels, packed their own food, and crammed days off with endless hours of exploration to make the most of the time she had, Hanna could appreciate the relaxed days Hazel and her friends enjoyed.

Choosing to breakfast in their suite most mornings, Hazel, Lillian, Mai, and Daphne were in no rush to leave early, which worked in their favor since most places in the city did not open until at least 9 a.m. Since his grandmother and her friends ate in their room, Hanna was surprised to find Noah in the hotel dining room each morning. They ate together and the conversation flowed easily, primarily focused on stories of their work and travel, learning more about each other's preferences and habits..

After the art-focused first days of their trip, Hanna scheduled something that was unique to Daphne's interests. They spent the day learning how to make macarons at a patisserie operated by the same family for over two hundred years. Relaxing after the sugar-high, the group was now preparing for one of the most anticipated activities on their agenda.

"A kiss on the hand might be quite continental," Mai sang as she wheeled over to where Hanna was waiting in the lobby.

"But diamonds are a girl's best friend," the other three sang in unison, their giddy laughter jumbling the words together happily. All four women were dressed up for the evening, wearing knee length dresses that swayed against their legs and caught the light as they danced in place. Perhaps they were already tipsy, but if there was any place to arrive inebriated, it was the cabaret.

With a jacket folded over one arm, Noah shook his head in amusement as he walked toward them, shoes clacking against the tiled floor. He looked especially dashing in a shirt the same color as his eyes and a charcoal vest. "You know we are not going to the Moulin Rouge from the movie, right?"

Hazel waved him off. "Don't be a spoilsport. We've been looking forward to this for months."

"I wouldn't dream of it, mémé. Not when you all look so lovely." He gestured to the group.

Daphne blushed like a schoolgirl. "You flatterer. Why, if I was–"

"Don't even think about finishing that sentence, Daphne," Hazel snapped.

"What?" Daphne laughed. "He might be your grandson, but he is a handsome devil."

Hazel puffed up proudly. "Of course he is. He inherited all my family's good genes. Especially the beautiful blue eyes."

Funny that Hazel would choose to compliment a feature that was a mirror image of her own sparkling eyes. Hanna stifled a laugh as the women playfully bickered over Noah's inherited looks.

Mai's gaze swung to her, a mischievous tilt to her lips. "Honestly, you two are as bad as children sometimes. We need an unbiased opinion. Hanna, what do you think? Is Noah a handsome devil?"

Sneaky, meddlesome woman. Wasn't it enough that Hanna had to hear her own mother and grandmothers bemoan the fact that she was single, traipsing around the globe with no sign of settling down in sight? Now she had to contend with matchmaking guests as well. All eyes were on her, Mai looking downright smug at putting her on the spot, Daphne had a grin from ear to ear, and Lillian was affronted at the notion that Hanna would weigh in on the matter. Hazel's lack of surprise (and was that satisfaction lurking behind her forced nonchalance?) made Hanna immediately suspicious that perhaps Hazel put Mai up to this line of questioning. Or, worse yet, that they dreamed up another scheme together.

For his part, Noah was unreadable. His face stripped bare of any emotion that Hanna could easily convince herself that he did not care at all. Except...except for the clench of his hand and unwavering focus. He watched her carefully, as if his next movement, even his next breath, depended on her answer. There was no playful flirtation in Noah's gaze like in the garden, just a raw desire for her honesty.

Hanna only had eyes for him, wishing it were just the two of them in the room as she replied. "Not a devil, no."

Amusement danced behind Noah's gaze. "Ah, just handsome then."

"I did not say that."

"You didn't not say it either." He stepped closer.

A shiver swept down her body at the rough tone of Noah's voice. "Please, I am not going to inflate your ego. If you want a compliment, you have to earn it."

"Is that a challenge?"

"Yes." Hanna was surprised at the raspy quality of her own voice. There was something about Noah that made Hanna want to challenge him, pull him outside his comfort zone and have him do the same for her. She wanted him to be the exception to the rule and prove that something could happen between them without the world falling apart. With his chest moving faster, Hanna thought that Noah might want that too.

"As sweet as this moment is..." Lillian's voice was dripping with sarcasm. "We are paying you to give us a tour, not flirt, and we have someplace to be." She pointedly looked at the slender watch on her wrist.

Noah stiffened next to her, thunder clouding his expression.

Hazel smacked her friend in the arm, her tone reprimanding. "Lillian! Don't be rude."

"I was being honest," Lillian replied. "She's here to do a job."

For their part, Mai and Daphne both looked embarrassed at Lillian's comments and angry on Hanna's behalf. A fight was brewing within the group and if Hanna did not carefully diffuse the tension, it would ruin an evening that the women had talked about for weeks before it even got started. Stepping away from Noah, Hanna held out her hands in a placating gesture.

"Let's focus on all the fun you are going to have tonight." Hanna saw Madeline pull up to the curb and gave a sweeping gesture. "Montmartre awaits and I planned a surprise at the show that I know you will enjoy."

"Not until Lillian apologizes." Hazel resolutely stood in place, blocking Lillian from walking away.

Looking like she was going to argue again, Lillian huffed in frustration when Daphne and Mai flanked Hazel, three unmoving statues.

"Fine." Lillian turned to Hanna with an exasperated flap of her hands.

"And mean it," Hazel prodded.

Clenching her jaw, Lillian stared at Hanna for a moment. Staring back, Hanna was not going to give her the easy way out by breaking the silence first. She ran through the rain to get this woman's purse, the least she could do was admit when she was in the wrong.

As if she realized that herself, the fire in Lillian's eyes burnt out, her shoulders deflating. "I am sorry, Hanna. That was disrespectful of me and I should not have said it. You have been nothing but professional and courteous to this group and I hope you can forgive me."

Taken aback by the sincerity in her tone, Hanna accepted the apology, despite the urge to reject it on principle. While she doubted that she and Lillian would bond like she had with the rest of the group, hopefully the scathing remarks would stop.

Sending one last quelling glare at Lillian, Hazel led the group towards the car, needling Hanna to give them a hint about the surprise. While Madeline got Mai and the others situated in the car, Hanna hovered near the front bumper, taking a moment to douse her anger. The implication that Hanna did not know how to do her job raised her hackles and set her on the defensive. As the youngest child of four, Hanna grew up feeling like she had to prove herself worthy compared to her more traditionally accomplished siblings, and she feared not being good enough. Lillian's reminder that Hanna only had value to the group for the job she did added a disappointed, hollow-feeling on top of it all.

Breathing in the cool night air, which was marred by the pungent burn of smoke and car exhaust, Hanna released the bitter feelings and tried to focus on the night ahead.

"Are you okay?" Noah's presence was reassuring instead of suffocating, his broad frame sheltering her from any peering eyes inside the car.

Tilting her head back to look at his face, Hanna expected to see guilt and regret in his expression after getting called out for flirting with the help. Maybe he was starting to resent her unprofessional behavior.

Instead, Noah lifted a hand toward her face, then lowered it with a wrinkle in his brow. "Lillian shouldn't have said that. I am sorry."

Hanna shrugged, trying to look like it didn't bother her. "She was right, though. It was unprofessional to flirt with you."

"Don't." Noah shook his head. "Don't dismiss it like that. No one should talk to you like that, regardless of their reason. Job or not, you are a person, and everyone deserves to be talked to with respect. Besides, I liked you flirting with me, and if I didn't, I should be the one to tell you, not Lillian."

His voice was thick with vehemence, passionate in his defense, and it warmed Hanna's heart. A lot of people thought that they could treat workers however they wanted, as if accepting condescending and oftentimes discriminatory comments were part of their job.

Letting her pleasure at his comment show in the smile spreading across her face, Hanna rested a hand on Noah's arm. "Thank you for saying that. I've gotten so used to people saying comments like that that I try not to take it personally, but it still hurts. I appreciate you checking on me, though." The door slid shut behind them, signaling it was time for them to get in. "For the record, I like flirting with you, too."

During the ride, Hanna tried to loosen the remaining tension in the group by sharing the history of the Moulin Rouge and cabaret in Paris. With some of the more provocative tales, the women started laughing and joking around with one another. By the time Madeline was dropping them off in front of the iconic landmark, the group was in good spirits again, though Noah's frosty demeanor towards Lillian suggested that not all the trouble was gone.

Hanna found her contact, a small, round-faced girl named Colette and began checking them in for the show, listening to the excited hum of energy around them. In the red light of the marquee, Noah was taking photos of his grandmother and her friends, patiently waiting for them to rotate through a series of poses before dutifully capturing the image from multiple angles. Watching him present the phone to them for review and listen to their feedback without a hint of exasperation was endearing, and Hanna felt another smile creep onto her face. An expression that was becoming commonplace whenever Noah was around.

"*We have everything arranged for your party just as you requested, Anna,*" Colette spoke softly in French. "*The performers know where your group is seated to meet them after the show. A table for four directly in front of the stage.*"

"*Four?*" Hanna responded in French. Unless math changed recently, there was one seat missing at that table, since neither she or Madeline were going. "*It should be five.*"

Colette frowned down at her tablet, re-reading what was listed for the reservation. *"I'm sorry, but the reservation is listed for four."*

Worry pumped through Hanna's veins, quickening the blood and causing her heart and lungs to fill rapidly. *"No, I confirmed the reservation earlier this week. For five guests."*

"Is something the matter, dear?" Great, now Hazel was here to witness the mistake. She must have heard the worry in Hanna's voice and come over to check on her. The tour was going so well, just under a week in, with few mishaps, but Hanna knew it only took one major mistake to lose any referrals.

Trying to be helpful, Colette switched to English and said, "Just a minor issue with the reservation. Let me speak to the manager about adjusting the table to five instead of four. It should not be a problem."

Noah stepped around his grandmother. "No, four is correct. Only my grandmother and her friends are attending. I called yesterday to change the reservation."

"You did?" Hanna looked at him in shock, the stress of the situation cracking her voice.

"You aren't the only one who knows how to make plans." He smirked like she should be proud of what he did.

She wasn't. Hanna was furious.

But she would wait until the others were gone before she unleashed that fury on Noah.

The others were fussing over Noah, asking what he planned on doing with his evening if he was not joining them. He mentioned something about grabbing drinks with a business contact, but Hanna was only half-heartedly listening.

"Well." Hanna brought her hands together quietly. "We do not want to delay you getting into the show any further. Madeline and I will be here to pick you up when it is over."

Colette stepped forward and ushered them into the theater, leaving Hanna alone with Noah.

"I cannot believe you did that." She turned on him so quickly that Noah took a step back.

"Did what?"

"Went behind my back and changed the reservation." She poked a finger in his chest. "You had no right to do that."

He raised his hands in a defensive gesture. "I thought it was helpful. Cabaret is not my thing, so I thought I would save you the trouble and cancel the ticket myself. You are doing everything else for us, I did not want to add one more thing to your schedule."

That snuffed some of her fire, but not all of it. "Though I appreciate you wanting to help me, deciding what I need help with is not your decision to make. This is not just a job for me, Noah. Everything that happens on this tour reflects on me and impacts my reputation as a qualified guide and planner, something that took years to build credibility. Which is now more important than ever. Do you know how difficult it is to build a business?" Tears welled with the rise of her emotions. "To put everything–your heart, soul, reputation, and funds–on the line for other people to judge and deem you worthy?"

Her breath was coming faster as the swell of emotions took over. It was such a small thing, Noah changing the reservation, so why was it impacting her so strongly? Was it the long hours and lack of sleep? Or, maybe it was the stress of having to take care of everyone finally coming to a peak, her heart instinctively knowing that she could fall apart in front of Noah and not worry about having to pick herself back up.

"Hanna," he exhaled her name as if it pained him.

Reaching out and pulling Hanna into the circle of his arms, one hand banding around her waist to secure her tightly to his torso, the other cradling her head to the crook of his shoulder, Noah held her steady. Around them, people hustled to get into the theater, cars honking as they were cut off, and tourists dashing across the street to pose for a photo with the bright lights illuminating the night. Within Noah's embrace, Hanna felt cocooned in an intimate bubble, uncaring about the world around them.

She was tired. So very tired of having to be perfect all the time. But with Noah, the relief of having one person with whom she could be herself was a salve. At this moment, she did not care if it was a mistake to unload on a guest, she just needed someone in her corner. The pressure of this job, how much was at stake, never left her mind. Slowly building like a pressure cooker, Noah acted as a release valve, allowing Hanna to vent against the calm wall of his support.

Low enough that Hanna knew the words were meant for her ears only, Noah said, "I do know what that is like. The constant fear that whatever you do will never be enough. I am so sorry that I had any part in making you feel that way and I promise that I will not over-step in the future and check with you first before making any changes. Should you want or need help, you only have to ask and I will give it."

He tipped up her chin so that she was staring directly into the deep pools of his eyes, crystal clear with their honest intensity. "You are one of the most capable people I know. You are brilliant, creative, and so giving of your time and energy. It's inspiring, and a little terri-fying, how much you can accomplish. And I am grateful that I get to witness just part of what you can do."

If the lights were not already painting her face in rouge, the heat that filled Hanna at Noah's words certainly would have done the trick.

"Thank you," she replied before resting her cheek back against his shirt. Beneath the fabric, she could hear the pounding of his heart, a match to her own beat. For several long moments, they stood on the sidewalk, needing nothing more than the comfort of each other's embrace.

Pressed as she was against Noah, Hanna heard and felt a small grumble. Laughing, she stepped back to find Noah sheepishly looking away, embarrassed that she caught his stomach's protest at a lack of food.

"Come on." She reached for his hand. "Let's get you some food before your stomach mounts a revolution."

IN THE HEART of the district known for its artisans and thriving nightlife, people flowed through the streets, laughing with friends, popping in and out of shops, or stopping to enjoy a street performance. Above it all, Sacré-Cœur loomed, a beacon of white against the darkened sky. Empty plates and a nearly finished bottle of wine cluttered the tiny, wrought-iron table where Hanna and Noah dined, the cool night air deterring few from the outdoor patio. The low timbre of a cello carried through the night air, the song relaxing the table's occupants and creating a buffer to the din of restaurant chatter around them.

Swirling the contents of her wine glass before taking a sip, Hanna pursed her lips and lowered her brows at Noah as he began to pour the remaining wine in her glass. "And here I thought you disapproved of me drinking."

"What?" He paused what he was doing to look at her. "Why would you think that?"

Hanna made a flippant gesture with one hand. "You were so judgy on the plane, glaring at me when the flight attendant offered me champagne."

Noah's eyes widened in surprise. "That? No, I was definitely not glaring at you, and certainly not over free champagne on a flight. It's just..." He ran a hand through his hair with a sigh. "You had not even finished settling into your seat, and when the flight attendant came over, you acted like you were inconveniencing her just by being there. I just wanted you to be comfortable, but I didn't know what to say, and by the time I figured it out the moment was over."

"Oh." Hanna felt guilty for jumping to conclusions. "Well, I am sorry for thinking the worst of you."

"I didn't give you the best first impression," Noah replied with a wince, finishing pouring their wine. "Plus, I've been told that I have severe RBF."

A laugh burst from Hanna's mouth. Noah was effortlessly funny with his dry sense of humor, so much so that Hanna was surprised how easy and often she was laughing with him. His laugh was more subdued, a wry chuckle or a sharp exhale punctuated with a quirk of his mouth the most Hanna would get from him. The glint of amusement in his eyes was all she needed to see to know that he was enjoying himself, though.

Deep into their second bottle of wine, Hanna reflected on how naturally the conversation progressed between them, almost as if it were a dance. Hanna learned that Noah was an only-child, loved reading cozy mysteries, and had a movie collection to rival a streaming service. His mother, Rachel and father, Leo, were high-school sweethearts and lived in a bungalow near San Diego. Leo was deployed overseas shortly after Noah was born, so Rachel and Noah moved in with her parents, Hazel and Marcel, for support.

"Is that why you and Hazel are so close?" Hanna knew many tight-knit families. Though her own was scattered, they still loved each other.

"Yeah," Noah answered quickly, then paused. Hanna waited patiently, giving him a moment to gather his thoughts.

"It was more stable for us to live with them while dad was on deployment, and even in the months when he was back, it just made sense to stay where we had a support system. With my mom working too, mémé was usually the one picking me up from school and helping me with homework. Dad was fortunate to get stationed in San Diego and mémé's house continued to be more of a second home than a place to visit for holidays."

Their conversation was put on hold as the waiter came to clear their dishes. Hanna smiled at Noah, feeling like some of his puzzle pieces were finally clicking into place. Of course he was protective of the woman who helped raise him.

"I really admire how you two care about each other. Though I still think you could have handled it better, I understand why you were hesitant to trust me. Protecting Hazel had to come first."

A shadow clouded Noah's downturned eyes, a solemn atmosphere settling over them as he swirled the remains of his wine. His abrupt change in attitude was unexpected, more bitter than sweet now. Maybe the bill gave him sticker shock, except it had not arrived yet. Something tugged at Hanna's core, urging her hand to reach across the table to drape over Noah's. She blamed the indulgence on wine, not her untethered emotions.

Beneath her palm, Noah's fingers curled into a tight ball. "Not always, unfortunately."

Frowning, Hanna watched shame twist Noah's features.

With a sigh, he leaned forward in his chair and locked eyes with Hanna. "Did my grandmother tell you that she started her own business after I was born?"

Hanna nodded. "Organic cleaning products, right?"

It was one of the reasons she admired Hazel so much. As a young mother, Hazel was appalled by the chemical cleaning agents favored by her neighbors. For years, Hazel made organic products in her home, and taught her daughter how to make them after she had Noah. When other children came over to play with Noah, parents commented on the organic ingredients and started buying them from Hazel. What started as a small, home-grown business was now nationally renowned. Her formal retirement in the last few years, and the passing of her husband, were catalysts for Hazel's travel-bug.

"Right," Noah continued. "I watched my grandmother make bottle after bottle of cleaning solution in her home, building the business with mom's help. And, selfishly, when I started college, I thought that I could make it better, find the magic solution to make it bigger so they could expand. Which is why I became a business major." He smiled ruefully. "I was so cocky, thinking that I knew better than them, and it made it that much easier to get manipulated."

Hanna remained silent, allowing him the time to work through how he wanted to proceed. She saw his pulse pounding against his neck as Noah breathed in the crisp, night air, averting his gaze for a moment.

"There was a professor, Finley, successful, brilliant, and persuasive. A pioneer in the investment world. His books were best-sellers and students practically worshiped the ground he walked on, and I was one of them. Any class he offered, I signed up to take, and when it came time for my MBA there was no other choice than him as my advisor. Naturally, in the hours spent together, I shared details about my grandmother's business and he offered advice and suggestions. I idolized him and he knew it. When he offered to invest my grandparents' savings, I was blown away. Here was a man who CEOs and CFOs came to for advice, and he was giving it for free to my family."

Noah's voice shook, cracking over the mention of his family. Squeezing her fingers over his, Hanna tried to send reassurance and warmth through their connection. Her heart broke over the obvious ending of the story and how much of the blame Noah was shouldering.

"He took it all, every penny my grandparents saved because *I* told them to give it to him. And when he first disappeared, I made excuses for him, saying that he must be travelling for work or busy with his next project. They lost *everything* because of me, and my grandfather never forgave me. I was the reason mémé could not retire earlier and had to wait to travel. After everything she gave me, I cannot have her lose it all again." His azure gaze implored her to understand.

Hanna wiggled her fingers between Noah's clenched digits, spreading them open to rub soothing circles in his palm. "Hazel would never blame you, Noah." She shook her head to emphasize the point when he tried to interrupt. "I cannot speak for your grandfather, but it does not give me a high opinion of him if he resented you. You were young and put your trust in the wrong person, but it was just a mistake, Noah. All the blame lies with Finley for manipulating you and taking advantage of your trust. People much older and wiser than you fall prey to people like that all the time, just look at the news."

A corner of his lips quirked at her playful tone regarding his intelligence.

"And you did better than most people. You *learned* from your mistake and worked hard to build back what was lost. I wish that never happened to you and your family, but your tenacity and perseverance built something that you and Hazel should be proud of. You said you thought I was impressive, but it takes one to know one."

Candlelight flared in his eyes, burning away whatever held Noah back before. With a sharp tug on her arm, Noah pulled her forward, leaning the majority of the way towards her so that table dug into his side, not hers, and giving her an opportunity to pull away if she wanted to.

Hanna didn't.

For all their push and pull, playful remarks and sizzling tension, their lips met softly, their heads tilting to find the right angle. Pressing more firmly into him, Hanna leaned forward, pulling away only centimeters before crushing their lips together again. Noah smelled like wine and soap, the cut of his trimmed beard scraping against her jaw as he opened his mouth against hers.

Intertwined on the table, their hands grasped and caressed each other, reminding them that they were connected by more than just their lips. With his free hand, Noah cupped Hanna's face, smoothing his thumb over her skin in distracting circles. Every nerve was firing with his touch, the hairs on her arm standing up as electricity pinged across her body.

Noah's eyes opened when she released a growl of frustration, the edge of the table digging into her ribs and preventing them from getting closer. She wanted the distance between them to disappear, to feel the warmth of his body next to hers and be able to touch him freely. Both of Noah's hands reached out to cup her face and neck, supporting Hanna as their lips met again.

This was a moment stretched in time that Hanna never wanted to forget. Here, they were just Noah and Hanna, two people enjoying a tender moment after a meal. There were no time zones separating them or work getting in the way. No tour guide and client separation.

As soon as the thought entered her head, awareness returned to

Hanna's brain, reminding her of everything she had to lose. Pulling out of his reach, she mourned the loss of his touch immediately, like discarding a warm blanket after a cozy stay on the couch. Noah's eyes blinked open slowly, two lines appearing between his brows in confusion.

Avoiding the question in his gaze, Hanna looked at her watch, the birds taunting her with their endless circuit around the face. Timeless as their evening felt, their time alone together was at an end.

Motioning for the check, Hanna said, "We need to leave soon to pick up Hazel and the others. This was a lovely evening, Noah, but it cannot happen again."

"Why not?" His downturned mouth matched the wash of disappointment that sank into her chest. "What you do in your free time is your business and I would never do anything to jeopardize your career."

With a sad smile, Hanna folded her hands onto her lap to prevent reaching for him again. "But that is just it, you *are* my business, at least while you are on tour with me. You are my client, and while you might not use that against me, there are plenty of others who would."

"I would never hurt you, Hanna, and I don't want to waste another minute pretending that I do not want you. You need to protect your company, I get that, so if that means I cannot be with you until this tour ends, then I will wait for you at the end of it. Just be honest with me. If you do not want me, fine, I can handle rejection and will never make a move on you again, but if you do want me, even for stolen moments, I will take whatever time I can get. You have said before that we are grown adults, capable of making our own decisions. So make the decision you want, not what you think everyone else wants you to make. And my grandmother is your client, not me."

"That is semantics at best, misconduct at worst. We cannot change the rules just to suit our desires. Being a tour guide means that the job never truly ends. I do not get nights off. If a client calls, I need to answer."

"Not past 10 p.m."

Now she was really confused. "What?"

Noah settled the bill and stood, offering a hand to help her stand. "Your contract stipulates that when on tour, the rate includes services until 10 at night. Anything after that is considered an emergency service and billed separately."

Hanna had completely forgotten about that. When reviewing the business proposal, Stephanie recommended the addition as a way for Hanna to set boundaries with her clients. Granted, this was her debut tour, but she had never needed to enforce the rule.

Was that why Noah looked perplexed when he saw her around the hotel after 10? Mentioning it now opened the door to possibility. Technically, if she was off the clock, did that mean Noah was no longer her guest? And would that change anything for her if it did?

Thoughts in a muddle, Hanna did not notice that they started walking back towards the Moulin Rouge. Content to walk in silence, it gave Hanna time to think, running through scenarios in her mind. As the bright lights came into view, Noah turned to face her.

"Just think about it, okay?" He brushed her hair behind one ear before lifting the back of her hand for a kiss.

Lights and sounds came back into focus as people poured out of the building. Right on time, Madeline pulled up with the car as their group arrived, bright faced and exuberantly sharing every detail about their evening. Hanna took advantage of the distraction they provided, listening as their voices wove around each other. Once they were all settled into the car, Hanna did what Noah asked, and thought.

# 12

# Your Tour Group is not Your Family

"REMIND me again why I thought calling you was a smart idea?" Hanna rolled her eyes as Will stuffed a falafel pita wrap into his mouth on the screen of her laptop.

"Because I am literally the only person you know who understands the situation you are in," he replied around a mouthful of food. Charming. "Spotting the difference between someone willing to engage in some vacation fun versus one who will cling on and get you in trouble is my specialty. If you came to me years ago, you never would have gotten into that situation with Antonio. Too self-absorbed for a good fling."

Grimacing at the memory of her ill-advised dalliance, Hanna brought the conversation back to the topic at hand.

"Noah is not Antonio. He is thoughtful and considerate, though he comes across as a bit of a grump at first." Hanna grew warm just thinking about him. "He steps in to help without getting in the way and he cares about what I think." Her thoughts wandered as she remembered their kiss from the night before, the way he listened to her and admitted when he was wrong.

Will cleared his throat and gave her a knowing look. "Do I need to go so you can be alone with your thoughts?"

Memories of how Hanna was alone with her thoughts the night

before brought color to her cheeks. Thank goodness for camera filters that hid her telling blush. There were some things even close friends did not need to know about.

"Nevermind, I'll call someone else to get their advice." She leaned forward and pretended to reach for the end call button.

With a lurch that was unsurprisingly graceful (Will was the reason Hanna knew yoga), he slid his feet off the cluttered desk and onto the floor, the pita wrap tucked onto a plate, and his face composed into an expression of rapt attention. "Wait, wait, wait. I'm sorry, I shouldn't tease. You never ask me, or anyone for that matter, for help, so I admit I'm more than a little surprised. Casual flings are my specialty, but the way you talk about Noah, it sounds like you want something more than physical."

"That's the problem," Hanna said and sighed. "I cannot have more than that. This trip is done in just over a week. Then he will return to the states and I will be...well, hopefully on another tour, but either way we will not see each other again."

Somewhere along the way, amongst the weekly phone calls with questions about her personal life and the trip, Hanna grew closer to Noah. Based on his admission the night before, so had he, and that scared her. Moving constantly as a child taught Hanna that she did not get to keep people. No matter how many promises were made to write to friends, time and distance slowly ate away at those precarious ties. Emotions were fickle things, and Hanna knew better than to let herself get attached to someone she would have to let go of. Other people stayed where they were, growing and burying roots to form communities. For Hanna, it was easier to remain a seed carried by the winds of change than have her roots ripped out again and again.

Sunlight crept over the horizon, pouring through the open window in Hanna's room. Perched on the cushioned desk chair, she watched the dawn break while she collected her thoughts, Will silent on the other end of the call. She called him with the intention of finding out how he managed to have no-strings-attached relationships, several of which were with guests, without it biting him in the ass. Casual was the best word to describe all of Will's relationships, yet this conversation spiraled into her revealing deeper feelings than Hanna was ready to admit.

"I don't know if I can let him get close, just to say goodbye at the end," she whispered, nose burning and tears stinging her eyes. Her fingers smoothed out a wrinkle in her sleeve, over and over.

Will's eyes melted with concern. As surface level as he kept physical relationships, Will was a fierce and loyal friend. Hanna knew that if he ever turned that dedication and commitment onto a partner, well, that woman would be lucky.

"Hey," he said in a soothing tone, "you don't have to do anything you aren't comfortable with. I just want you to be happy. Be honest with yourself about what you want, and then share that with Noah. Talk to him about this, not me. Only the two of you can figure out the right answer."

"But he's a client." She clung to the one line discouraging her from running to Noah.

"Does your service contract say you cannot be in a relationship with a client?" Hanna shook her head. Luxe Travel's employment contract stipulated that employees had to disclose any relationships to guests with human resources, but considering Hanna was the only employee and acting as HR, it was a moot point.

"Then he isn't your client. No, wait." Will held out a hand to stop her protest. "I know you are going to say that even if he isn't, it would still look bad if someone found out, but you already said his grandmother was shipping you two. If it really bothers you, talk to her too. Clear the air so there is nothing left unsettled and make sure your recreational activities do not impact your work."

His nonchalant and cavalier attitude meant people underestimated Will, but Hanna knew he was remarkably astute. Going to him for advice was the right choice. The only way forward was clarifying her own feelings and articulating them, accepting the risk to her reputation. If she was wrong about Noah's feelings...no, there was nothing gained from that line of thinking without talking to Noah first.

Not wanting to monopolize what little time they had to catch up, Hanna asked how Will was doing. He was back in Long Beach after a few weeks leading whitewater rafting trips in Colorado, preparing to leave for the summer to work at a ranch. The self-proclaimed "god of fun-der"–Will's resemblance to a certain superhero appealed to many guests–was a hot commodity for the ranch, returning year after year to assist with horseback riding and ziplining in the hills. Tales of a previous year's bachelorette party "roughing it" in the hills of Montana at the cowboy-themed retreat had Hanna wiping away tears of laughter.

"Oh, hey," Will added before they ended the call, "you got another letter from Trips Ahoy. Want me to leave it with your stuff in the garage?" It was strange that the letter was delivered to Sarah's house since Hanna had all her mail forwarded to a PO box while she was gone.

"Yeah, thanks. It's probably just another attempt to get me to work for them now that I'm competition."

"Those bastards," Will joked. "How dare they try to win back the best tour guide in the world."

"Stephanie only trained the best." Her golden standards were the reason Trips Ahoy rose to prominence and was viable to sell for an early retirement.

As they said their goodbyes, Hanna felt lighter after talking with her friend and developing a plan of action. Never one to remain idle for long, Hanna felt better knowing what her next step was, as daunting as talking about her feelings was. Standing with a stretch, Hanna looked at her watch and decided to head down to breakfast early. The group had nothing planned for the morning and early afternoon, the late night before necessitating sleeping in as long as possible, and the only item on their itinerary was dinner at a jazz club. Maybe Noah would join her for breakfast again and they could talk.

Smiling to herself as she walked out to the breakfast room, Hanna paused in an alcove when her phone chimed with an incoming text from her mom.

*Have you had a chance to look over the job application I sent you?*

Hanna's good mood evaporated and her stomach dropped. How many times did she need to tell her family that she was happy with her job? That she was fulfilled, driven, and accomplished even if there was no prefix or list of accolades attached to her email signature. When she first got the job with Stephanie at Trips Ahoy, they said having a job was good, but wouldn't working somewhere that looked good on university applications be better? The decision not to attend university was brushed aside with emailed internships and promises of referrals to whatever non-profit or NGO she wanted to meet with after her "gap year." Hanna typed her response quickly.

*I already have a job, but thank you for thinking of me.* 🙂

Three dots blinked on the screen, disappeared, then reappeared again. Knowing her mom was revising her response filled Hanna with dread. Nothing good would come from whatever the three dots turned into.

When the incoming message notification never chimed and the three dots did not reemerge, Hanna let out a cautious breath. Perhaps her mom would leave it alone this time.

The shrill sound of an incoming call proved otherwise.

"*Hola, Mamá.*" Hanna loved the rhythmic flow of Spanish, the nuance and accents as familiar as her mother's voice.

"*Mija.*" Camila reminded Hanna of summer, warm and full of energy, a winning combination for a doctor and mother of four. "*How are you? It's been too long since your father and I heard your voice.*"

*Not entirely my fault,* Hanna thought to herself. Telephones worked both ways and Hanna made a point to inform her whole family what time zone she was in. The mention of her father meant that he was on the call too.

"Hey, Duckie." Her father loved using her childhood nickname, born from her habit of following her older siblings around like a baby duck. Hanna smiled at the irony that now she had people following her on a daily basis and returned her father's greeting in English.

Her parents were the reason Hanna was fluent in multiple languages. They both spoke Spanish and English fluently, raising their children on the importance of knowing each language from their heritage. Hanna learned French while they lived in Canada, one of the first places the non-profit placed her parents while Hanna was young. From there, Hanna picked up phrases from each language of the countries they lived in, learning from the locals as well as the other doctors and staff working with her parents.

Dr. Camila and Rev. David Poole were humanitarians for a non-profit working to bring medical care to areas around the globe that lacked access. They met in graduate school on an aid trip and fell in love. After finishing school, they were hired by the non-profit as a doctor and nurse chaplain, respectively. When it came to their children, Camila and David raised them on the values of giving back to others and dedicating their lives to helping those in need. By Hanna's count, a seventy-five percent success rate was still a win.

Adriana, the oldest, founded and managed a non-profit with her wife, focused on educating girls and women in developing nations. They had one daughter and were currently in the process of adopting their second child. The twins, Sam and Nathaniel, were doctors and–not helping Hanna's perpetual feelings of inferiority–worked for the same NGO their parent's did. At least Nathaniel was still unmarried, distributing the push towards matrimony between two siblings instead of leaving Hanna alone. Sam had to go and marry a doctor the year prior. Hanna liked his wife, insofar as well as she knew her, but honestly, the amount of MDs, PhDs, and other titles in this family were getting a bit extreme.

*"You sound tired. Are you getting enough rest?"* Camila asked after her husband updated Hanna on their current mission trip.

"Well, getting a business started is difficult," Hanna said, defensive. "On top of managing the tours themselves, I have to run the accounting, marketing, social media, and coordination of future tours.

Sleep is a little low on the priority list right now, but I promise that I am eating healthy, drinking plenty of water, and exercising daily."

In the awkward silence that descended, Hanna heard the background noise of people walking somewhere behind her parents. Most likely other volunteers moving around whatever facility they were in. Work was constant and Hanna wondered if her parents were taking their own advice and resting.

"We just care about you and want what's best for you–" her father started.

"–and we worry about this business of yours." Her mother picked up the end of David's sentence in the way only people who spent years together could. "You are doing so much with no help at all. You need something with stability, to provide for your future. This job may be fun for now, getting to travel and meet new people all the time, but what if it doesn't work out? You need something permanent."

This coming from the people who uprooted Hanna every few years to move to a new place. Those disappearing text bubbles were coming back to haunt her, the unfinished thread of conversation not something her mother would drop easily. Hanna tightened her arms around her waist, feeling the weight of disappointment threaten to crush her. Her back pressed into the painted wall behind her, the sturdy surface keeping her upright.

"I need a *real* job, is what you mean." It stung, the entire family's disregard for her choices. Hanna's career was cute, fun, a diversion from the correct path in life. Never taken seriously or valued. They loved her, she knew they did, but they did not respect her. Despite years of knowing how they felt, like they were waiting for her to find her way back to the right career, Hanna thought that opening her own business would prove to them that this was a legitimate choice.

Static mixed with her father's voice as it came through the phone, like he was standing behind Camila where she held the phone. "That is not what we said."

No, but it was always what they meant. "You were such an

inquisitive child, always on the move, learning new things. Bouncing from one project to the next. You've done well for yourself over the years, but there is no harm in keeping your options open. Just in case."

In case she failed. They did not believe Luxe Travel would succeed. They did not believe in *her*.

Heart cracking, Hanna fought against the constriction of her throat, tipping her head against the wall to prevent hot tears from slipping down her cheeks. Her legs crumbled beneath her, swept out from under her with the realization that nothing she did was good enough for her parents. She could not keep going like this, dashing her fragile hope against the unyielding rocks of their expectations.

"Well, then." Her voice was thick with bitterness. "I guess I'll just keep on being a disappointment. This is the career that I chose, and it makes me happy. Until you can support that, I am not sure what type of relationship I want with you, but I know that I do not want one where you diminish what I do."

"Hanna–"

"*Ana–*"

Her parent's spoke at the same time, but however they planned on finishing their sentence, Hanna did not want to know.

Fighting to keep her voice steady, Hanna ended the call saying, "I have to go get ready for my tour. Be safe."

It felt like someone punched her in the chest, hollowing out the space where her heart sat, continuing to beat even though it was battered and bruised. Establishing boundaries was supposed to protect you from getting hurt, but Hanna was terrified the invisible line in the sand would separate her from her parents forever. Part of her wanted to call them back immediately and apologize, but the larger part of her, thanks to her therapist, knew that she had to stop hurting herself by allowing them to say things that hurt her.

They called her duckie because of the way she chased after her siblings, always striving to catch up with the much older children, mimicking their actions in the hope of being noticed. Of being enough. Here she was, years later, still trying to keep up with them. Going from place to place hoping to prove that she was just as good as them. Wanting to find someplace where she felt seen, valued, and loved exactly as she was.

How she felt when she was with Noah.

A cautious voice asked, "Hanna, darling, are you alright?"

Choking back a sob, Hanna wanted to laugh at how unfair it was that Hazel chose this particular morning to come downstairs for breakfast and use this exact hallway to get there.

Hyper-aware of how she probably looked, Hanna kept her face downturned and tried to discreetly wipe under her eyes to remove any smeared mascara. "If I say yes, is there any chance we can pretend this never happened?"

Hazel's tan loafers came into Hanna's line of sight. Then, the soft pressure of a hand pressed into the top of her head. "No." The firmness of Hazel's voice belied the gentle way she pat Hanna's head. "Now pick yourself off the floor and come with me. I suspect this conversation will go over smoother with a cup of tea and a croissant."

Grateful for the brief reprieve walking to the dining room gave her, and the decorative mirrors along the hall that revealed she did not have complete racoon-eyes, Hanna followed along after Hazel. Their server sat them at a table in the corner, at Hazel's insistence, away from other guests and with wing-back chairs that offered more privacy.

After placing their order, Hazel folded her hands on top of the table. "Now, tell me, did my grandson make you cry? Because he might be taller than me, but I can still give him a thrashing if needed."

The unexpected image of Hazel flicking Noah's ear or lecturing him while he stood over a foot taller than the silver-haired woman had laughter bubbling in Hanna's chest. She could picture Noah's chagrined face perfectly, ears tipped pink and shoulders slightly slumped.

"I'm sure you could, but there is no need. Noah had nothing to do with any of that." Hanna gestured vaguely in the direction of the hallway.

"Good." Hazel poured cream and sugar into their teacups. "Squabbles are normal for a couple, but they should never leave you crying in the hallway like a wilted flower."

Tea went down the wrong way and Hanna coughed. "C-couple? No-o...we..."

Hazel offered her a glass of water and settled her pale, wrinkled hand over Hanna's on the table. "I might be old, but I am not blind. Everyone can see the way you two look at each other." The mischievous twinkle in her eye suggested that Hazel was purposefully misconstruing the reason Hanna tried to inhale her tea.

Gulping down water served two purposes. One, it helped subdue her coughing fit. Two, it kept her mouth busy while Hanna thought of an appropriate answer. Since Hazel brought up the subject herself, it was as good a time as any to address the idea of entering a relationship with Noah while on the trip. Plus, resolving this item on her to-do list would relieve Hanna of some of the turbulent feelings disrupting her emotional peace.

Returning the glass to the table, Hanna lifted her gaze. "So, if Noah and I did start dating, you would not be upset?"

A broad smile split Hazel's lips, happiness beaming from her pores. "Upset? Hell no. You should know that by now. There is nothing I would love more. When I first met you, I knew you would be a great fit for him. You two have many things in common: your love for organization, food, and need to protect those closest to you. But you also have qualities that Noah needs in his life, your ability to take chances and live life to the fullest. Noah's kept himself closed off for too long, and I am beginning to suspect that you might have too."

Knowing that Hazel thought so fondly of her caused a new prickle behind Hanna's eyelids. "But you hired me. You do not think it would be...wrong for me to be with Noah?"

"Not when I've been trying to push you together. If you were being sneaky or secretive, I would have thought differently, but it speaks well of your professionalism that you came to me even though I was vocal in my support before. Plenty of people meet at their place of employment. You can't fight who you fall in love with, and I've lived long enough to know that when you find love, you need to grab hold of it with both hands and not take a moment for granted." The wistful look on her face made Hanna wonder if Hazel was remembering her husband, Marcel, or if it was memories of another love that danced behind her steely eyes.

Her heart pounded loudly in her chest, tugging as if on one end of a string trying to pull her towards the other end. "Don't you think it is a little premature to call it love?"

"Is it?" Hazel tossed back with a quirk of one silver eyebrow. "That's for you and Noah to decide. Life is what you make of it, and it's far too short to spend crying in hallways over a broken heart. Want to tell me about it?"

With a resigned sigh, Hanna recounted the conversation with her parents. Hazel only interrupted with a few clarifying questions, and Hanna found herself sharing more of her personal life than she ever had with a guest. Evershams must emit some sort of truth serum, it was the only explanation why Hanna opened up to them so easily. Although she did not share as many details as she had with Noah, Hanna talked about the pressure of growing up in a family of exceptional people, trying to find her place when she never measured up. Moving from place to place, always forced to leave, and not being a good enough reason to stay.

"So many people needed help, and I am so proud of my parents and siblings for dedicating their lives to helping others, but I feel like I got lost in the mix. My siblings were over a decade older than me and I was expected to follow along and keep up. I know I should be grateful that I was raised in some of the most beautiful parts of the world, with dozens of the smartest, compassionate, and inspiring people helping to raise me, but all I ever felt was..."

"Alone?" Hazel's face tightened with understanding. "You can be surrounded by hundreds of people, but that means nothing if they do not love and support you."

Relief and guilt waged war in Hanna's heart. "They do love me, I know they do. I just hoped that they would finally understand. See what I accomplished and be proud of me, not view my business as a distraction from what really matters in life."

Setting aside her fork, Hazel leaned against the curved arm of her chair. She regarded Hanna thoughtfully, taking in the defeated set of Hanna's shoulders, the tight draw of tension in the corners of her mouth. "You should be damn proud of what you created. Building a business from the ground up takes work, and you've put in years of effort to build your base and learn the ins and outs of the industry to create a solid plan. And as a woman, there are more than enough hurdles for you to get through without worrying about approval from people who don't deserve it."

If anyone knew how difficult it was, it was Hazel. Married when it was still legal to prevent a woman from owning her own bank account, Hazel lacked access to open her business until later in life.

"Have you talked to them about how you are feeling?"

"Not specifically. Whenever I bring up the business, the conversation pivots to how worried they are about me and all the stable options I have waiting for me. I just told them that I do not want to speak to them again until they can support my choices. That's when you found me."

"That must have been incredibly difficult for you. For what it's worth, I think you did the right thing. Relationships are never easy, but keeping your feelings hidden only lets them fester and wound deeper. Remember that you get to decide how much of your life they are part of, and if they are smart they will work to be part of it."

Brushing away the tears that escaped, Hanna gave Hazel a shaky smile. Now that she placed the boundary, Hanna needed to reinforce it. If her parents called again, Hanna knew that she needed to talk to them about how she was feeling so she could move past it. Hopefully, it would also help her parents understand and support her better, as long as they respected her boundaries.

Rubbing her thumbs against the tension gathered in her forehead, Hanna let out a resigned laugh at her predicament. Open communication about her feelings was shaping up to be the theme of the day. And she needed to talk to Noah.

As they leisurely finished their breakfast and tea, Hanna started to relax. Hazel talked about her life in Belgium before her family moved to the United States and her subsequent marriage to Marcel, a family friend. With a full belly and warm sunshine relaxing her, Hanna asked Hazel why she was up so early and not dining with her friends.

Hazel straightened as if remembering something. "Oh, I promised to meet Noah this morning. He has a few business meetings today with potential clients and such, and wanted to go over his pitch with me. Even though he runs the company now, I still like to keep a hand in things, and Noah indulges me, getting my opinion before any major deal."

For someone who's default facial expression was a frown, the man oozed sweetness. Knowing what she did now, Hanna's heart squeezed at the thought of him including Hazel, not only because he cared about her opinion, but also as an attempt to make up for his perceived mistakes. Looking at Hazel now, Hanna wished Noah could see what she could. That Hazel did not hold anything against Noah, the pride and love in her eyes making it clear that she trusted and believed in him. Noah's unwavering commitment and care to those he loved was obviously learned from the woman seated at the table.

Like one end of a magnet drawn toward another, Hanna saw movement out of the corner of her eye and turned, instinctively drawn to the presence in the dining room doorway. Dark hair contrasted the cream suit molded to the curves of his muscles. An olive green shirt popped against the lighter fabric and drew focus to the crystalline quality of his eyes. Noah looked powerful in his suit. Not in the way that signaled he would crush anyone in his path, but that he would do anything to protect those within his inner circle.

When he saw where they were seated, Noah strode towards them, eyes darkening and scowl deepening as he tracked Hanna's tear-stained face. He barely glanced in Hazel's direction as he approached the table, lowering himself to one knee so that he was face to face with Hanna.

Strong hands cradled her jaw, thumbs swiping at the now-dried tears. "What happened?" Noah's voice was a rasp. "Are you hurt?"

Cupping her hands around his, Hanna leaned into his hold. A muscle twitched in Noah's jaw, his body tense with anticipation, poised to jump to her aid. Knowing that if she asked for it, Noah would give whatever help she needed, reassured Hanna like the comfort of a weighted blanket. The desire to let him help shoulder her burdens was strong, but this was not the time for Hanna to talk to him. Not with his grandmother and who knows how many strangers watching them.

"I'll be okay." She squeezed his hand. "Just a rough phone call with my parents."

Noah peered into her eyes, watching every emotion that flickered across them, looking for signs of distress. "Can I help? Do you want to talk about it?"

"Later. We have some other things that we should talk about too."

Desire and what looked like hope flashed momentarily across the clear pools of his irises. "Let's talk now then."

"Noah," Hanna said and chuckled, as she sent a pointed look in Hazel's direction.

The older woman smirked, not attempting to hide the way she watched them like they were her favorite reality tv show. "Don't mind me. You two have your talk."

Mirth bolstered her spirits and Hanna gently pulled Noah's hands away from her face to rest against his chest. "You two have to talk business and I have things to take care of for tonight." A white lie. Their reservation for dinner was booked months ago, but Hanna needed an excuse to freshen up and decompress before she hopped back into tour guide mode.

"Fine," Noah grumbled, helping Hanna from her chair. "But we will talk."

"Later," Hanna promised before walking out of the room.

LATER ENDED up being the next day. Noah's business meetings ran late, one of the hotels he was working to secure a contract with offering to take him out for dinner and drinks after, something that Noah texted Hanna about, looking for an excuse not to go. She laughed at his impatience, reminding him that good business was built on relationships and he had to do something to counteract his grumpy attitude. He replied with a close up of his face, a pout pulling at his lips in a way that sent a rush of pleasure down her spine. Hanna nearly melted on the spot. Even stepping outside the jazz club and letting the breeze blow over her body did not cool the flush of her skin.

Hanna thought that sleep would relieve some of the need coursing through her, but her mind was so tangled up in visions of Noah that she dreamed about him. Vivid, technicolor dreams wove seamlessly together in a full-length feature film starring Noah and his soft lips. By the time Hanna woke, sheets twisted around her over-heated body, she knew she had to relieve some of the tension before she spontaneously combust when seeing him again.

Of course, Noah ruined her attempts to douse the desire raging in her blood by showing up to breakfast the next morning with his shirt-sleeves rolled up his forearms, dark hair curling against his skin. Hanna dug her fingers into her thigh to restrain herself from moving towards him, they did not need an audience for what she wanted to do to him.

Hazel, Lillian, Mai, and Daphne greeted Noah as he grabbed a plate and headed towards the sidebar set up with light refreshments and beverages. Given the early hour, the full kitchen was not open, and the hotel provided plates of pastries, sliced meats, and cheese for guests looking for something light to start the morning. Today, that included their entire group, the planned visit to Sainte-Chapelle necessitated an early departure so that they could make the sunrise reservation Hanna scheduled. It was the one time in the tour that Hanna insisted the group get up before the sun, since the unique experience of watching the first rays of sunlight spear through the stained glass was an ethereal moment that should not be missed.

Noah was the last one downstairs and there was a hint of dark shadows under his eyes. Had he not slept well the night before? Hanna knew he was out late for the meeting and worried that asking him to get up early was too much. A protective urge swept over her, wanting to bundle Noah up and give him time to rest. Most days, the group had time for a midafternoon nap, and Hanna would encourage Noah to take advantage of that time. Watching him bring back his plate and two steaming cups to the table, Hanna looked for any additional signs of strain.

Noah placed a cappuccino in front of Hazel, leaning down to kiss her cheek before moving around the other side of the table with the other cup in his hand. Picking at the fruit on her plate, Hanna watched him greet the rest of the table as he selected a tea bag and placed it in the steaming cup of water.

"Cream and one sugar?" He placed the cup of tea in front of Hanna, surprising her.

Looking up from her plate, Hanna's eyebrows drew together as she replied quizzically, "How did you know?"

"You make it the same way every day." Noah shrugged as if it was nothing and not one of the most thoughtful things someone had done for her. That noticing her preferences and saving her a trip to get a refill were insignificant. But for Hanna, those small gestures were everything.

"How thoughtful, Noah." Hazel took the words right out of Hanna's mouth.

Swallowing around the thick swell of emotions currently lodged in her throat, Hanna accepted the cup from Noah, their fingers brushing with a zap of energy. "Thank you."

While Noah finished his food, Hanna answered questions about the history of Sainte-Chapelle from Mai and Daphne, the two most alert members of the group. Two cups of coffee in and still only perfunctorily awake, Hazel and Lillian listened to the conversation without contributing much of their own input. While Hanna forced her brain and body to function at full capacity no matter the hour, her preference was to sleep in and take at least an hour, and one espresso, before she wanted to deal with the world. Compromising meant giving up the extra sleep and enjoying her espresso in her room before coming downstairs and switching to tea, a concession to her mother's worry about how the caffeine would impact her heart. For his part, Noah limited himself to one cup of coffee, though Hanna barely considered it coffee with the amount of milk and sugar he added in.

Sharing breakfast with Noah was quickly becoming Hanna's favorite part of the week. When Hazel stated that she and her friends would take breakfast together in their suite as a way to spend time together, Hanna thought nothing of it, but with each consecutive morning finding Noah alone at a table, she suspected matchmaking, not bonding time, was behind the decision. In the solid hour of uninterrupted time together, Hanna and Noah talked about everything and nothing.

At first, the comfortable silence surprised Hanna, expecting the impulsive need to fill the silence and dazzle Noah with her expertise to take over. Instead, the silence became an invitation for two people to lower their guards, show their truest selves, and learn to deeply understand and appreciate one another exactly as they are. A calm comfort settled over Hanna in those moments, like she knew that there was all the time in the world to learn every facet of this man.

Hanna felt a small kernel of resentment that their morning ritual was interrupted, which was unfair because Hazel and her friends deserved Hanna's attention just as much. But it meant that she could not talk to Noah like they usually did. Sighing internally, Hanna knew that she had to be patient. There would eventually be time to speak about their potential relationship. The promise of later could not come fast enough.

Tall pillars of stone greeted them in the gloomy morning light as Madeline pulled the car up to Sainte-Chapelle. Hanna ushered the small group under the arched doorways, sculpted figures tracking their movement into the sacred space. Footsteps echoed through the chapel, the limited number of visitors allowed in for this private viewing, whispering and snapping photos of the upper chapel while they waited for the sunrise. They gravitated towards the middle of the room, surrounded by all fifteen towering windows, the muted colors dull in the grey light of pre-dawn.

Having already suggested a few viewing locations based on what her group wanted to see, Hanna watched as the four women separated to wander on their own. They knew when and where to meet when it was time to leave, but otherwise Hanna gave them the freedom to explore on their own. A few other guides strolled through, maintaining a steady stream of conversation with their guests that Hanna found distracting. Places of worship or spirituality were the few locations Hanna refrained from giving a scripted tour, not wanting to detract from anyone's connection to something so deeply personal.

Sliding her phone out of her bag, Hanna angled the camera towards the painted floor tiles with one foot placed in front of the other as if she were mid-step, thinking of the perfect caption to go with the photo. Thank goodness for scheduled posts. They made it easier to maintain her social media presence while on tour.

"Do you have a secret job selling photos of your feet online?"

Laughing loudly would definitely not be appropriate and Hanna placed a hand over her mouth to muffle the sound that bubbled up her throat. Noah was full of unexpected comments and it delighted her. It was impossible to look at the mischievous twinkle in his eye and maintain a straight face, so Hanna turned her head to catch her breath. Once her laughter was under control, Hanna gave him what she hoped was a flirtatious wink. "Wouldn't you like to know?"

He returned her wink with one of his own, managing to look sexy and dorky at the same time. "Of course. I want to know everything about you. Especially if I need to be jealous that other people are paying to see your feet."

"You have a thing for feet you need to tell me about?"

Noah's smile flashed bright in the space. "No." He gave her a heated look. "But I have a thing for you."

Liquid heat melted Hanna from head to the very feet that started this conversation. A conversation that was slowly spiraling out of her control.

"So." Noah leaned over to look at her phone. "Why are you taking photos of your feet?"

"Because it's the opposite of what everyone else takes a photo of here. Obviously, looking up gives you a stunning view, but I want to remind people to pause and look at what is right in front of them. Millions of people walk across these floors every year, bringing their hopes and prayers, seeking connection to something beautiful and bigger than us, guided by the history of people who walked these floors before us. The steps we take in life determine where we go, who we become, the places we visit and the home we return to."

"And where is home for you?"

With that question, Hanna did look up, contemplating the vaulted ceiling. Searching, always searching, for the answer to that question. "I don't know," she said softly.

Noah was silent, moving to Hanna's side, his presence beside her like a steadfast soldier. Neither of them said anything. They did not have to. Though no part of them touched, Noah's proximity reassured Hanna, giving her the space and support to find the answer on her own. With Noah, not knowing what came next was okay. She was used to people trying to force her into a decision, Trips Ahoy with their relentless pursuit to get her to work for them, her parents and siblings to choose a new career. But not Noah. Never Noah.

When she thought of what home meant to her, Hanna pictured a place where she felt safe, welcomed, and loved unconditionally. Somewhere she could be herself, return to after a long day, and grow in the comforting embrace of people who supported her. She may not have that now, but it no longer seemed like an impossibility.

Together, they stood side by side, watching as tourists streamed back into the center of the room as the sunrise started.

"Isn't this view worth it?" If Hanna was a character in a romantic movie, this was the moment where she would look over at Noah and see him staring back at her. He would look at her fondly, lips lifted in a soft smile as he raised a hand to cup her face. Then, he would murmur something suitably cheesy, like "yes, it is," while maintaining eye contact to drive home the point that watching her was better than any view.

But her life was not a Netflix holiday special. Instead, she saw him gazing at the picturesque view in front of them, eyes fixed on the first rays of sunlight piercing through the stained glass. His face was divided into swatches of color. Red over his left eye, yellow along his forehead, green over one cheek and blue over the other like an abstract painting. Lips parted in awe, Noah watched as the room filled with color. A burst of longing struck Hanna, so intense she could almost reach out and touch it, wanting to freeze this moment and keep it with her forever.

A picture would never accurately capture the reverence in his gaze and like all beautiful things, it was fleeting and over in minutes. She had seen this view hundreds of times, but it felt brand new experiencing it with Noah. Just as Hanna was about to walk away, giving Noah a moment alone, she felt something warm and soft brush against her hand. Holding her breath, Hanna remained perfectly still and waited.

There it was again, a tentative brush against her pinkie finger. Looking down, Hanna was transfixed as Noah's fingers curled around hers, feeling the simple touch in every cell of her body. Drawing her gaze up from their joined hands, Hanna looked into Noah's eyes.

"It is," he whispered. "But this view might be my favorite."

# 13

# Stop and Smell the Roses

"WE ARE GOING to head back to the hotel to rest." Hazel hugged Noah with a pat on the shoulder and reassurances that they were just tired from waking up early to visit Sainte-Chapelle. "Hanna, take the day off and enjoy the beautiful weather with my grandson. It's too beautiful outside for you to stay inside with us old ladies all day."

"Are you sure? I can stay–" Hanna started.

"I am absolutely certain. After a week without a break, you need a day off. How you do this all year without your feet falling off is beyond me. The girls and I are going to lounge by the pool, nothing that requires either of you. We can fend for ourselves and I am sure the two of you can find something to occupy the time." With a blatant wink towards Hanna and Noah's flushed faces, Hazel slid into the car, Madeline closing the door behind her.

The tall blonde eyed the pair's shifting posture, standing so close that Hanna's hair brushed against Noah's arm with the breeze. Raising one slim eyebrow, Madeline asked, "Do you need me to pick you up later?"

Noah looked at Hanna for the response, always putting the power in her hands. "No," she answered firmly.

A broad smile covered Madeline's face as she switched to French. *"I want the whole story later. Preferably with a bottle of wine."*

*"Only if you're buying,"* a masculine voice replied in perfect French. Noah placed a warm hand on Hanna's lower back, as her mouth fell open in shock.

*"You speak French?"*

*"I never said I didn't,"* Noah replied. *"My grandmother is Belgian and helped raise me. Of course, I speak French."*

Damn if the light accent in his voice was not one of the sexiest things Hanna ever heard. And she had heard a lot of accents.

Laughing at Hanna's predicament, Madeline walked around the car with a wave. *"Keep this one. I like him. And you–"* She pointed at Noah from the open driver's door. *"Treat my girl right. The Seine has a history of making people disappear."*

Blanching, Noah waved the car off before whispering in Hanna's ear, "Remind me to stay away from the water."

Hanna bumped their hips together playfully. "You have nothing to worry about as long as you treat me right."

Suddenly nervous that she played her cards too soon, Hanna averted her gaze to her shoes. Sure, they had danced around the topic enough, and Noah said he wanted to be with her, but that did not mean he wanted a relationship. In a world of dating apps and post-pandemic situationships, Hanna found the ambiguity frustrating. Too many of her friends got played by people pretending to want a committed relationship when all they were after was a hookup.

In true Noah fashion, he tipped her jaw up with one hand, watching her as if working out a puzzle before his mouth ticked up on one side. "I'll have nothing to worry about then, for I plan to treat you very well."

Her legs threatened to collapse at the same moment her core tightened, everything in her midsection melting with desire. Those words. Uttered in his voice. Hanna shivered in delight, wondering what other things he might rasp into her ear and when she could get the chance to find out.

"Well, in that case..." Hanna ran a hand down Noah's arm, delighting in the way he shivered, before twining their fingers together. "We should find somewhere quieter and finally have that conversation."

Gesturing with one hand, Noah invited Hanna to lead the way, keeping the other firmly ensconced in his grip. They made their way along cobbled streets, sunlight warming their skin as they strolled alongside gawking tourists and focused locals alike. To any outsider, they were a typical couple, holding hands in the famed city of love. Despite the fact that they were not any other couple, they were not a couple at all.

Yet.

Grabbing a selection of pastries from a local boulangerie, they settled on a bench in the Square of Saint-Jacques Tower, listening to the noise of the crowds and street fade away in the small patch of nature created in the midst of urban development. From as far back as she could remember, Hanna loved being outside. So much of her childhood was spent indoors, homeschooled and assisting her parents in their makeshift offices and hospitals, that Hanna yearned to spend as much time outdoors experiencing the world as possible.

Their shared love of spending time in nature was something they learned on one of their many phone conversations. Noah grew up with his hands buried in the soil of Hazel's garden, learning how to grow the plants used for cooking and their organic cleaning products. Although he did not have space for a full garden, Noah admitted that his balcony was covered in pots and raised beds for herbs. Sunglasses protecting his pale eyes, Noah tipped his face back to absorb the sunshine filtered through the canopy of trees above them.

"So–" Noah leaned forward to wipe a crumb off her lips, bringing it to his mouth and momentarily distracting Hanna. "–are you going to keep me in suspense, or finally let me out of my misery?"

Hanna knew her decision, and Noah was right, it was finally time to get their feelings out in the open.

"I like you, Noah, more than I should." She pressed her fingers against his parting mouth to prevent an interruption. His warm lips pursed to press a kiss against her skin, a silent gesture to show he liked her too. "But I am scared of what that means. Scared that the thrill of a new place and allure of an exciting trip makes this feel bigger than it really is. Vacation has a way of covering everything in rose-tinted glasses, and I don't want to get hurt when you go back home and realize you don't have time for a relationship that you did not really want to begin with. And I will not risk my professional reputation for sex."

Hanna did not voice the secret thought that she worried Noah only liked her because she was temporary, good enough for a quick fling before he returned to his normal life. Not someone worth tying himself to long-term.

"So, I guess what I need to know is what you want this to be, Noah." Better to have her heart broken now, when she still had a chance at picking up the pieces, than after she gave it to him. If it was not too late already.

Sliding closer on the bench, Noah clasped her hands between his, tilting his head down so that eyes the color of the sky met with gold-brown. "I want this to be everything. When I first met you, I wanted you out of my life. Tried to push you away and scare you off to protect my grandmother. But, I think the one I was really trying to protect was myself. Somewhere deep down, after hearing countless stories about you from her, I think I knew that you were someone who would push me past my comfort zone. Break down the barriers I had and give me a reason to trust someone again."

He pressed his lips firmly against her hands, eyes squeezing shut with a huff of laughter. "But you weren't scared away. No, you pushed back and showed me your brilliant mind and generous heart. I want a relationship, to learn everything about you, take care of you, and let you take care of me. We'll have to figure out what that looks like, but I can work with your schedule. For you, I want to make it work."

Hanna's breath caught in her lungs and the world around her froze. Nothing outside of her and Noah mattered. Each of his words spun inside her, seeking out the bruised parts of her heart, settling over them like a salve. Gone was the guarded look Noah wore when they first met, a wall constructed to keep people out after having his trust broken, replaced with an open vulnerability. It was in the way the tension around his jaw and eyes relaxed, his sunglasses lifted so Hanna could view the soft, tender parts of himself that were worried about getting hurt again, but willing to risk it anyways.

"I want to make it work too," she whispered, the words breathed against his lips.

Noah sighed into her mouth, letting her press their lips together without making a move to push her further. They breathed together, chests moving in and out in synchrony. An infinite number of moments passed as they held each other before Hanna pulled Noah's head closer, her mouth opening over his. She felt his eyelashes brush against her cheekbone as they fluttered closed.

When she ran her tongue along the seam of Noah's lips, he groaned, plunging one hand into her hair while he gripped her waist with the other. Seated on a bench, their ability to move closer was limited by the unyielding metal, but Hanna tried her best to shift in every possible way in an effort to get closer, to remove every millimeter between them. Kissing Noah felt like coming home, the heady rush of excitement blending with the comfort of the familiar.

Hanna groaned in protest when Noah removed his lips, just to sigh in relief when he deepened the kiss by tilting his head to the perfect angle. She needed his next touch as much as she needed air to breathe. Finally Hanna knew what his hair felt like, running her fingers through the thick strands until they separated from the styling product and fell haphazardly. Noah looked just as good as she imagined, rumpled and disheveled from her hands, face flushed and eyes bright with desire.

Mouths met and separated between deep breaths, their chests heaving in the space separating them. Hanna accidentally shoved her knee into Noah's thigh in her impatience to remove any separation, her distant awareness that they were in a public park the only thing stopping her from climbing onto Noah's lap. The fingers fisted into the fabric at her waist squeezed, letting Hanna know she was not the only impatient one.

The next time their lips separated, Hanna opened hers to suggest they move somewhere private when Noah's face scrunched in pain.

"Shit," he bit out, jerking his body off the bench. A plump pigeon shuffled its wings in indignation at nearly being kicked. Noah leaned down to examine his ankle, pulling down his sock to look at the red mark forming where the pigeon pecked him. Glaring at the offending bird currently giving Noah the side-eye despite mistaking him for food, Noah muttered, "Wrong bird for a cockblock."

Checking for herself that Noah was not injured, Hanna let out an amused chuckle. "It must have thought I was trying to eat you and wanted to see what was so delicious." Recalling what they were doing moments before had Hanna covering her face with her hands in embarrassment. "I was practically mauling you. In public."

"Hey." Noah pulled her hands down, smiling brighter than the sun. "You'll get no complaints from me. In fact–" He pulled her into his chest and brushed his lips against her ear. "I cannot wait to do it again. Just in a more private place next time, yeah?"

"Yes, please," Hanna said in a husky voice.

"DO you ever think about wanting to do something else?" Noah asked her, a little bit later as they walked hand-in-hand through a used bookstore.

Hanna shook her head, soft curls rubbing where they rested against Noah's shoulder. She'd been having a wonderful time, as they took turns lifting cracked leather spines from their shelves and whispering passages of poetry into each others' ears. Several times, Hanna found herself grabbing a fistful of Noah's shirt, pulling him into a passionate kiss when he read something salacious in French. His ability to locate the dirtiest passages was an unique skill.

"No. Getting to meet new people and explore new places is all I ever wanted." Her lack of permanent address or solid community baffled many people, but frequent moving was all Hanna knew. "What about you?"

"More than I should," Noah confessed in a quiet voice. He looked at her with wide eyes, guilt churning in their depth. After everything he told her about the betrayal and subsequent work to build back his grandparent's savings and business, Hanna surmised that Noah had never told anyone that he imagined working somewhere else. His protective instincts would not let him.

The trust Noah placed in her by revealing that confession humbled Hanna and made her feel like she could fly. She would never betray that trust. Family was everything to him, something she respected and envied, her own distance from family like a bruise she forgot about until something pressed on it again.

"What would you pick, if you could do anything else?" Hanna leaned against a shelf, giving Noah her full attention. Light from the wall of windows at the front of the shop brushed his sharp cheekbones, highlighting the way his jaw clenched and relaxed while he thought.

He ran a hand over his hair, straightening some of the strands that Hanna set free as a nervous blush stole across his face. Quiet settled around them in the way that only an old bookstore could, the aging books and furniture storing the secrets of the historied clientele.

With a small shrug, Noah admitted, "Probably something similar to what I do now, just...more. Ever since I was little, I loved sitting in the garden with my grandmother. Working with the plants and mixing the product. But mémé needed more help running the business than she did making product, so I went and got a business degree. I don't regret the decision, I ended up really enjoying it, but I think I got stuck. Stuck in the same place, doing the same thing, because it was comfortable. Watching you this week, hearing about your business when we spoke on the phone, showed me how fearless you are. Leaving everything you knew and starting off on your own, I never had that kind of courage."

The tips of Noah's fingers traced the shell of Hanna's ear, down the slope of her jaw, before curling around the back of her neck. "You make me feel courageous. I want to be more involved in making the product. When we first started expanding internationally, I wanted us to partner with local vendors to get ingredients and create the products. Find ways to support the communities where we are selling the product. But it was risky, giving up control of creating the products ourselves. I feel brave enough to do it now, because of you."

Hanna's heart squeezed tightly. "That's wonderful, Noah. What you are trying to do will help so many people, and I know Hazel would support you. Just because you aren't making the products, does not mean the quality suffers. If you need some contacts, I can share mine with you. It might not be exactly what you are looking for, but I know several boutique hotels that partner with local business—"

Smiling lips sealed over hers, the warmth of Noah's body molding with hers as he pressed her into the shelf. When her eyes fluttered open, Hanna watched Noah's crinkle with mirth. "There you go, offering help without me even needing to ask. You are the most self-less, giving person I've ever met. Let me figure out this next step first, but I'll promise to ask for help as soon as I do."

She laughed into his shoulder. It was the unexpected joy of being with him that sent a wave of longing through her. Hanna wanted to keep them here, in this feeling, forever.

Noah pressed his lips onto her forehead before resting his cheek on the top of her head. "You don't think I'm being selfish? Asking for more when I've already been given so much."

"No." She nudged him back so that she could meet his eyes. "I think dreams should be bold and ambitious. The worst that can happen when you aim for the stars is that you land on the moon, and that's still better than only admiring them through a telescope."

It was something she reminded herself of daily. Her business might fail, but if it did, she would make damn sure that she did everything in her power to keep it going. No one could say that she failed because she did not work hard enough.

"And what are your big dreams, Hanna? What stars are you aiming for?"

Folding her arms around her waist, Hanna found the belled, elbow-length sleeve of her blouse and rubbed the fabric between her fingers in a nervous gesture. "Right now? Keeping my business going."

Some days, the black and red numbers on the spreadsheet mocked her, stress spinning tighter and tighter, faster and faster in her mind, causing her chest to restrict her breaths until it felt like there was no escape from the endless worry. "I have mostly been booking itinerary-only trips, ones where I am not with them. Which is still business," she rushed to say, "but I love leading the tours. Someday, I want Luxe Travel to be the premier name in tours and have the ability to hire employees to help me. Ideally take a vacation every once and a while."

Noah's hand found hers, spreading his palm beneath her fingers so that she was rubbing his skin instead of the fabric, the rhythmic motion and rough texture of his skin soothing her anxiety. Instead of trying to stop the nervous gesture, Noah helped her through it. Surrounded by his steady presence, Hanna felt protected. He was the lighthouse in a storm, guiding her to safety while giving her the freedom to get there on her own.

"You'll get there." He pressed another kiss to her forehead. "You are too damn stubborn and brilliant not to. Anyone who cannot see that does not deserve to stand near your spotlight."

The memory of her parent's lack of support dimmed the glow she felt in Noah's arms and he tightened the pressure of his fingers on hers. His eyebrows pinched together in concern, silently asking her if she wanted to talk about it.

A trio of teenage girls rounded the corner, their bright laughter and rapid conversation bursting through the bubble around Hanna and Noah. Still leaning against the bookshelf, Noah pressed further into Hanna, giving the girls space to pass behind them. They giggled and whispered behind their hands as they walked past, blatantly checking Noah out as they did.

Instead of politely continuing on their way and giving the couple privacy, the girls stopped a few shelves over and pretended to look at books while batting their eyelashes at Noah. There was no reason for Hanna to feel possessive when the teenagers had no chance with Noah, but jealousy was not a rational emotion. Staking her claim, Hanna slid her arms around Noah's waist, kissing him deeply before sending a smug glance at the teens. She felt his huff of amusement through their connected chests.

Tipping up her chin, Noah staked his own claim by kissing Hanna softly. "Want to get out of here?"

Mutely, Hanna nodded. A quick glance at her watch told her that they should be getting back to the hotel anyway to freshen up before dinner. Time had flown by, evident by the bluebirds' position on the watch face. They only had a few days left in France, and it was already slipping through her fingers faster than Hanna wanted.

# 14

## Hydrate

ONE OF THE problems with taking a day off in the middle of a tour was that it lulled Hanna's body into a false sense of relaxation. She was used to making the most of every hour of the day, responding to emails when she was not with the group or finishing other work, the minute she slowed down, Hanna's brain jumped at the chance to shut down for a few hours and unwind.

Her mind was sluggish after the high of spending an entire day with Noah. They did not stay out late, joining the others for an early dinner before they all retired for the evening, but Hanna had difficulty falling asleep. She kept replaying the day in her head, especially the moment he walked her back to her room, pressing her against the door in a kiss that left them both panting.

Thank goodness their private boat cruise along the Seine required minimal brain power on Hanna's part, because she had little to spare. Hanna was familiar with the captain and knew he liked to double as the tour guide on the boat, answering any questions the guests had and sharing his own version of Paris' history. Between him and several crew members staffed to help the group, Hanna had nothing to do during the four hour brunch-cruise.

For once, Hanna appreciated being redundant since it gave her more time to rest, the long days catching up to her.

Hanna blamed the fatigue for the way her ankle rolled as she got out of the car. Pain flared up her leg and Hanna stumbled, clenching her teeth. With the way she was positioned, Hanna was unable to stabilize herself, so she threw out her arms to catch herself before she fell. Her right leg was tucked awkwardly beneath her, left leg braced against the ground, and arms framing both sides of the door, Hanna knew she looked ridiculous. She would care more if she could focus on anything but the pain in her foot.

"Hanna." Noah rushed forward to help, eyes wide with fear as he grasped her by the waist and lifted her back onto the seat. "What happened?"

Turning at the commotion, Hazel and her friends hurried over to Hanna's side of the car.

"Are you alright?"

"What's going on?"

"Did you get hurt?"

"Do we need to call an ambulance, what's the number for emergency services here?" Their questions tumbled over each other.

It was sweet of them to worry over such a minor injury, but Hanna felt a little silly being fussed over. She held out both hands to stop them before they got an ambulance involved for no reason.

"I just slipped when getting out of the car, nothing major. The only thing injured is my ego."

"Are you sure? Ignoring an injury is never a smart choice," Daphne spoke from experience.

"Positive," Hanna said with a smile. "I grew up around doctors, so I know it's nothing serious."

Accepting her answer, the women continued making their way to the dock, one of the crewmembers greeting them with glasses of champagne. Noah watched her like a hawk as Hanna pressed forward to get out of the car. Careful of her ankle, she stepped down with her left leg first, then her right.

A small whine slipped past her clenched teeth when Hanna put weight on her injured ankle. Cursing, Noah bent in front of her, hooking one arm under her knees and the other behind her back to lift her against his chest.

"Noah," Hanna hissed, worried that the others would see. One of her stipulations to starting a relationship with Noah while on tour was no PDA during working hours. Supported by Hazel or not, Hanna had to maintain professional boundaries. "Put me down. I'll be fine, I just need to walk it off."

"No." His voice was unyielding as he deposited her into the rear passenger seat. "Walking on a rolled ankle will only make it worse. You know that. I'm not letting you put yourself in danger of a worse injury. You have two choices." Noah leaned into the car and braced himself on the armrests of Hanna's chair, his face close enough that each breath fanned across her face.

"One, you let me take you back to the hotel so that I can check your ankle and make sure you rest. Or–" he cut off her protest. "–I take you to the hospital and have a doctor check your ankle."

He met her defiant stare with steely resolve. They both knew he only threatened to take her to the hospital so that Hanna would let him take her back to the hotel. Unless the swelling and pain increased substantially, Hanna could treat the injury with ice, rest, and elevation. Noah was right that she would only make it worse by walking on it.

Noah arched his brow in question and Hanna let out a defeated sigh.

"Fine, you win. Take me back to the hotel."

Sneaking a kiss, Noah smiled. "When it comes to your safety, I'll always win."

While Noah jogged over to his grandmother to explain the change in plans, Madeline checked on Hanna, laughing at her sulking friend.

"Only you would complain over a handsome man playing nurse for you."

"T-that's not...we aren't...shut up." Hanna threw a balled up napkin at Madeline's head just as Noah reached the car.

He took one look at Hanna's red face and wisely chose to remain silent, picking up her legs and placing them in his lap for the ride.

THE DOOR to Noah's suite clicked shut behind them as he carried her into the room. From the moment they reached the hotel, Noah refused to set her down until they reached the bed covered in a decadent cream duvet and pillows. So intent on getting her comfortably settled, Noah brought her into the suite so quickly that Hanna was not able to enjoy the white and cream decorations or the stunning view of the Eiffel Tower outside the windows.

He left the room briefly to get ice and painkillers, bringing them back to Hanna with a glass of sparkling water. Watching her drink the entire glass, Noah rolled up the sleeves of his shirt.

"Lie back," he commanded. There was nothing salacious in the demand, the way he watched her ankle made it clear that Noah's primary concern was checking the injury.

Hanna settled against the mountain of pillows, handing one to Noah so he could place it under her ankle. Her shoes were already gone, since Noah removed both their footwear in the entryway. Gently, he lifted her right foot, checking the swelling before taking the wrapped towel filled with ice and placing it against her skin. Hanna winced at the initial bite of cold.

"Does it hurt?" Noah asked.

"Not too bad." Hanna sank further into the pillows as she shook her head.

"Can I check?"

Hanna nodded.

His touch was soft, feeling his way along her ankle with light pressure. Instead of feeling any dull pain from his touch, Hanna only felt streaks of pleasure. For the first time since they entered the room, it dawned on Hanna that she was in Noah's bed and they were alone. As Noah finished with his inspection, he rocked back on his heels, the worry in his gaze slowly replaced with desire as he took in the sight of Hanna draped across the cream fabric.

"Will I live?" Hanna tried to joke around the thick tension in the room.

"With the right treatment, you'll make a full recovery. But I should double check to be certain."

Hanna was about to ask what the treatment was when Noah kissed the top of her foot, his warm lips misting over the skin. He looked up at her through hooded eyes, sending her a questioning glance, as the rough pads of his fingers tightened on her calves. A gasp of air left Hanna's lungs. Just watching him kneeling before her turned Hanna on more than she thought possible. If he continued to touch her, it would destroy her crumbling resolve to keep their distance during the day.

"Noah." His name was a sigh on her lips. "We shouldn't be doing this."

"Why? I am just checking to make sure you are okay." His head cocked to the side in a gesture that would be endearing if not for the sensual smile on his face. The stubble on his chin grazed her leg and Hanna shuddered. Pinpricks of pleasure danced across her skin, dissolving rational thought.

"Because I cannot think straight when you touch me. We agreed not to touch each other while I'm working."

"Technically, you are not working right now. But, if it makes you feel better, I'll stop touching you."

His hands left her skin and Hanna had to clutch the covers to resist yanking them back. This was for the best. Despite how much she wanted to give in to the chemistry between them, she needed to stay strong. Looking at him invited naughty thoughts, so Hanna turned her head to look out the window and the gorgeous view that she struggled to focus on.

Something warm and soft pressed firmly against the inside of her ankle and Hanna turned her head so quickly she almost suffered from whiplash.

There was Noah. Kneeling on the floor, hands raised innocently. As she watched, his lips moved against her ankle, fluttering soft kisses along her calf.

"Noah," she groaned.

"What?" He buried his laugh against her leg. "I'm not touching you. You never said anything about tasting you."

"Semantics." Still, Hanna pressed her leg into Noah's cheek.

She felt his smile against her skin. "Do you want me to stop?"

To hell with her plans for professionalism, no one expected her to work after getting injured anyway.

"No," Hanna whispered, barely loud enough for him to hear. But Noah was watching her lips intently and saw the word leave her mouth. Desire blotted out the blue of his gaze, never wavering from her face as his sensual lips returned to her skin. The path his lips took was like a match dragging against flint, lighting Hanna up as a fire ignited under her skin.

Noah's dark hair was soft underneath her fingers as Hanna alternated between tugging the strands and smoothing them out. Each time she tried to encourage him forward, Noah nipped at her skin and told her to relax and let him take care of her. In control of everything else, accustomed to making decisions for everyone, Hanna did not know what to do with herself. This man possessed the ability to unravel the core of her being, encouraging her to forget anything but this moment.

When his lips crested her knee, Noah nudged Hanna's leg to the side with his lips, opening her to his hungry gaze.

"Where else does it hurt? Here?" Open mouthed kisses covered the surface of her knee.

Well, if she was going to pretend that what they were doing did not fall in the murky gray area, Hanna might as well go all in. She nodded.

Her inner thigh received a kiss.

"Here?"

Another kiss.

"Here?" The word whispered where the hem of her skirt had risen.

Another nod.

His nose nudged her skirt, rubbing along her inner thigh.

"In order for me to keep my promise, I am going to need you to help me," Noah said with a caress of his lips. True to his word, Noah kept his hands to himself, bracing against the bed as he leaned forward, clenching the duvet when breathy sighs left her lips.

Fisting her hands in his hair one more time, Hanna let the smooth strands glide through her fingers. She followed the curve of his jaw, the scrape of his stubble rough against the pads of her fingers. Tracing the outline of Noah's lips, the back of Hanna's hand brushed against the fabric of her skirt, teasing the skin beneath. Her breath hitched when Noah followed the motion, nuzzling the newly exposed skin. Sunlight streamed through the gauzy curtains, catching on the sheen along her inner thigh left by Noah's tongue.

"More," Noah groaned the word into her skin, biting down where the hem of her skirt lay.

Hanna tipped her head back on a moan. Need swirled beneath her skin, urging her to speed up and remove the remaining barriers between them. The warm press of his lips, and teeth, and tongue against her skin were explosions of light, the fireworks at Versailles a dull comparison to the bursts of color where Noah sucked her skin.

Her skirt lifted another centimeter.

Another.

Higher and higher the fabric slid up her skin, bunching where her thigh met her hip. Each scratch of Noah's facial hair against her sensitive skin sent a shiver through Hanna's body. There was no helping the wrinkles that were forming in the skirt from the flex and release of her fingers.

Noah's breath fanned over the remaining cotton covering Hanna.

She squirmed closer, letting her thighs fall open around Noah's broad shoulders as he stretched over her.

"More?" This time the word was a question roughened by the gravel of Noah's voice. His body was taught, muscles straining against his shirt with the effort to refrain from touching Hanna.

"Please," Hanna pleaded as she released her skirt to touch Noah. When she was with him, everything else faded away. Any thought beyond what they were doing, where he would kiss her, disappeared, and Hanna loved it. She knew that she could leave the details to him and Noah would take care of her.

Her pleas morphed into a whine when Noah passed over her core and nipped at her other thigh.

"I know," Noah soothed as he caressed her skin. "Waiting is so hard, but I promise I will make it good for you. Just let me taste you a little longer. You drive me wild, watching you in this skirt, knowing that you are mine but that I cannot touch you. Seeing you hurt yourself by trying to walk on an injured ankle, wanting to take care of you. Will you let me take care of you?"

Longing shone in the dark pools of his gaze, reflecting a matching need in Hanna's soul. Most of her life felt like walking on a tightrope, each step precise, always aware her job was to dazzle others with impossible feats, while inside she panicked that one misstep would send her toppling. Every day with Noah showed her that he was there to catch her, boosting her confidence that she could walk the rope on her own, but providing a safe place for her to land. Leaping off the rope and into his arms was nothing like Hanna thought falling would feel like. Instead of her stomach dropping and terror gripping her heart, Hanna felt lighter, as if she could do anything, maybe even fly.

She was tired of taking care of everything herself so it felt good to let Noah take the lead. Still, Hanna could not let him think she capitulated too easily.

With a cocky grin, she tossed the skirt back over Noah's head, laughing at the glimpse of surprise she caught on his face before the fabric covered him. Noah's head was nothing more than an outline under the fabric, shifting as he laughed.

"So you want to play, huh? I can play."

Hanna shrieked with delight as Noah hummed against her legs, finding places she never knew were ticklish. Tears leaked from her eyes as she laughed, gasping in lungfuls of air as Noah continued his playful assault. Her ribs hurt from laughing so hard and Hanna reached out to pull his head away.

Laughter flushed his cheeks and widened Noah's smile. "Do you surrender?" He looked carefree as he stared at her, contentment relaxing his features.

"Never," Hanna wheezed in her attempt to replenish the oxygen in her lungs.

Noah nodded as if that was the answer he expected. Then he dipped down for her skirt and stole Hanna's breath again as he took the fabric between his teeth and pulled.

She slid forward on the bed with a gasp, the movement allowing him to lean forward enough to flip the material so that it landed on her chest. Exposed from the waist down, Hanna held her breath as Noah pressed his nose against her center and inhaled.

This time, when he hummed, it did not tickle.

Hanna moaned as the vibration traveled through her core. She was impatient, greedy for more as her hips rocked against Noah's face. The wet heat of his mouth covered her, teasing her through the layer of cotton separating Hanna from the contact she craved.

Hooking her fingers around the waistband, Hanna shimmied her underwear down as far as she could reach. Noah took them between his teeth and slid them off the rest of the way before settling between her open thighs.

The first slow swipe of his tongue over her had Hanna arching off the bed with a cry.

"Noah!"

There was no part of her that Noah did not lavish with attention, never staying in the same place for long. He alternated between each side, gliding his tongue up and down, nipping at her tender flesh with his teeth, and sucking her between his lips to learn what she liked.

"You taste incredible." He thrust his tongue inside her, following the motion of her rolling hips. "I could live right here. Let me hear how good you feel while I make you come."

As if she could deny him anything while he was wreaking havoc on her body. Hanna was nothing but sensation, her thoughts obliterated by the curl and twist of Noah's mouth. His name jumbled together with moans and incoherent words asking for more. Harder. Faster.

Higher and higher she rose on a current of pleasure. She was so close, yet never wanted it to stop.

"That's it," Noah said seductively. "Let go for me."

Her head tipped back against the pillows as Noah honed in on the bundle of nerves desperate for attention. With languid flicks of his tongue, Noah brought her pleasure to a fever pitch, her hands pulling him closer.

Legs shaking, Hanna pumped her hips, straining for that final push over the edge.

She shouted when Noah closed his mouth around her, biting softly. Shockwaves of bliss pulsed under her skin as Hanna rode out the high. She collapsed under Noah, satiated and relaxed, nerves tingling with pleasant energy.

Noah rested his head against her sweat-covered skin, pressing kisses on her thighs. He looked pleased with himself, a smug smile on his face as he watched her through fond eyes.

Too tired to move, Hanna flopped back onto the bed after trying to get up. There was an amused glint in Noah's eyes as he watched her.

"Going somewhere?"

"I wanted water, but someone turned my bones to jelly." Not that Hanna was complaining. She felt more relaxed than she had in months.

Laughing, Noah got up and brought her some water, adjusting the bulge in his pants as he sat on the bed beside her.

"Well," he said as he handed her the glass, "now I know the secret to keeping you off your feet when you're injured."

"Oh, yeah? And what's the secret?"

"Orgasms."

Hanna sipped the water to cool off her rapidly heating body. One word from Noah and Hanna was ready to go again. She eyed the hard length of him pressing against the zipper of his slacks. With one leg bent near her chest and the other propped on the ground to support him, Noah's thighs were spread, open to her perusal. She wanted, needed, to see what he looked like. To touch him and bring him pleasure.

Leaning onto her side, Hanna placed her hand on Noah's thigh, following the seam of his pants up. His muscle tensed beneath her and Noah inhaled sharply as her fingers trained along the shape of him.

The balance needed to reach him had Hanna tipping too far on her right side, forgetting about her tender ankle until it throbbed in pain.

Noah lifted her hand from his lap, kissing each of Hanna's fingers before setting their joined hands on the bed.

"Believe me." Noah kissed the pout off Hanna's lips. "I want you. But the last thing I want is you hurting yourself more. I can wait."

She knew Noah would not change his mind, so Hanna tugged on his shirt to pull him fully onto the bed. If she could not have him the way she wanted, at least they could cuddle while her ankle healed. Resting against Noah's chest, Hanna dozed off and on while they watched a movie. They ate in his room, Hanna's foot elevated on Noah's lap at the table, while they watched the lights of the city slowly come to life as the orange rays of sunset faded in the sky. At her request, Noah carried Hanna back to her own room for the night, kissing her forehead and making her promise to elevate her ankle with ice.

# 15

# Pack a Cocktail Dress, Just in Case

"ARE you sure your ankle is alright, Hanna?" Hazel eyed her warily as they stepped out of the elevator into the club.

Live music pumped through the space at a moderate volume, the band on the stage playing covers of popular songs from several decades prior. It was tricky finding a nightclub that catered to the senior crowd in the vivacious city, but with Madeline's help, Hanna believed the location satisfied the group's desire to go dancing without Noah having a heart attack worrying over his grandmother, and Hanna's, safety.

Since the incident with her ankle, Noah hovered protectively at her side, offering his elbow every time she got in and out of the car. Hanna's annoyance was tempered by the excuse to touch him, keeping her self-imposed rule to keep their hands off each other during the day more difficult than she imagined. Every time she grazed his skin, Hanna felt a riot of emotions flare to life and she longed for more.

At a perfume shop the day before, they found ways to "accidentally" brush against each other as they examined bottles. When Hanna offered a sample for Noah to smell, he took the scented paper between his fingers and dragged it along her neck. Hanna nearly combusted when he leaned in, following the scented trail with his nose in a tantalizing almost-touch. If Lillian had not sneezed at that exact moment, reminding Hanna that they were not alone in the shop, she might have shoved Noah onto the nearest surface–horizontal, vertical, who cared as long as it was sturdy–and taken him into her mouth.

"–Hanna? She does look a bit flushed." Daphne stepped in front of Hanna, bending to look in her eyes. "Is your ankle hurting? Noah, maybe you should–"

"I'm fine. See?" Hanna rushed to show them, rolling her ankle in both directions in the slender heels Madeline lent her. "Just a little warm in here. Once I get some water I will be okay."

She hoped that was true. The way Noah looked tonight was not helping cool her libido. Pants tailored so perfectly they looked painted on, the dark mauve shirt that flowed along his chest, and his tousled hair made Noah look good enough to eat. When Hanna lifted her lust-filled gaze to his, energy crackled between them, rooting her in place.

Satisfied with her answer, the rest of the group was moving toward their private booth, leaving Hanna to trail after them once her legs remembered how to move.

Hanna felt Noah's heat at her back. Her body would recognize his anywhere. Shivering when his hand skimmed over the exposed skin of her back, Hanna knew that she needed to get him alone.

Soon.

Before she did something drastic.

"Thirsty?" His voice was a low hum in her blood.

Glad that the muted light of the club hid the way her chest peaked beneath the satin fabric of her dress, Hanna rocked back into Noah, the open, cape-like sleeves caressing Noah's thighs. Pretending that she lost her footing, Hanna used the motion to rub against him, feeling the hard press of him against her.

Air hissed through Noah's clenched teeth.

Two could play this game.

"Very," Hanna said in a low tone.

When Noah angled to pull her more firmly against him, Hanna twirled out of his grasp, her twinkling laugh surrounding them. She wanted him, but Hanna also wanted to enjoy one of her last evenings with the group. These women were special to her for many reasons: they were Luxe Travel's first booking; they rooted for her success; they brought her to Noah; and they believed in her.

Flutes of champagne and bottles of sparkling water waited for them at the table. Madeline was already pouring them sizable portions, lifting her glass to Hanna with a wink. Sipping her water first, Hanna let herself relax against the leather couch.

"What was each of your favorite parts of the trip?" Hanna asked the group at large as Noah slid into the empty space beside her.

Hazel rested her forearms on the table. "Definitely the cabaret. Meeting the performers at the end was a wonderful surprise, they even taught us some of their moves. Maybe I will take a dance class when I get home."

"I'll join you," Daphne said while tapping their glasses together. "Start up a cabaret of our own at the senior center. Wouldn't that be a riot."

"Just be careful that you don't break a hip or give someone a heart attack," Lillian teased. "Personally, I loved visiting Monet's Garden. It was a nice touch to arrange the private painting, Hanna, well done."

Time with her friends had softened the blonde's prickly attitude significantly, though she was still a little frosty towards Hanna. Hanna suspected it had less to do with her personally and more with the fact she was a similar age to the woman Lillian's husband left her for.

"Tell us your secrets, Hanna." Mai plied her with more champagne after sharing that her favorite memory was the private showing of Mona Lisa. "How did you make it all happen?"

Hanna laughed at Mai's serious tone, feeling as effervescent as the bubbles popping on her tongue. "It's not rocket science. Just persistence and knowing who to talk to. Once you have those two things, nothing is impossible. I've met a lot of people over the years, and since I keep bringing them business, they usually treat me well. Being courteous goes a long way, too."

"Ain't that the truth." Daphne toasted Hanna with her glass.

The band started the next song and Mai shouted with joy. "This is our song! Come on, girls. Let's dance!"

They scooted out of the booth, Madeline trailing behind them with a half-hearted excuse. "Someone needs to make sure they don't break anything."

Hanna was not sure if Madeline meant themselves or something around the club with the way they moved around the dancefloor.

Alone in the booth, Noah slid closer, until they touched from hip to knee. He draped his arm along the back of the booth, fingertips floating across the side of her arm. Hanna leaned into him, resting her head against his shoulder, listening to the music while the alcohol buzzed through her system.

"You don't even realize how impressive you are," Noah said.

Hanna lifted her head to look at him.

"I know I'm good at my job."

"Good is too simple a word for you. I hate that you think so little of yourself. Do you think just anyone could do your job? Deal with the stressful situations and shitty people with half the grace you do? You're running circles around the rest of us, solving problems we don't even see coming, all with a smile on your face."

He nodded towards the pack of seniors tearing up the dance floor. "Look how happy you made them. How happy you make me."

His eyes glistened with emotion and Hanna had difficulty swallowing around the sudden tightness in her throat.

"I was against you from day one and you knocked me on my ass. Put me in my place with a smile on your face and still made sure I enjoyed the trip. I wish you could see yourself the way I see you. Because the woman I see? She may not be a rocket scientist, but she brought the magic of the stars down to Earth. She can do *anything* she puts her mind to. And I am humbled that you decided to take me along for the ride."

Speechless, Hanna flung her arms around Noah, burrowing into his neck. His words meant everything to her, giving voice to the secret longings of her heart. Though she was proud of her work, there was a part of herself that Hanna tried to bury, a little voice whispering that she was not enough, that her job would always be the opener, never the main act. It would not disappear immediately, but Noah's voice was louder than any whisper, giving her the power to vanquish her self-doubt.

"Thank you," she whispered into his skin.

No response was necessary. Noah rubbed her back, holding her tight for as long as she needed.

When the band changed to a romantic ballad, Hanna knew what she needed.

"Dance with me?"

Noah pulled her out of the booth, leading them onto the dance floor where they swayed in each other's arms until the late hours of the night.

# 16

# *Don't Be Afraid to Ask for What You are Worth*

WITH ONLY A FEW days left of the tour, Hanna struggled to manage the worry over what would happen to her and Noah once he returned home. Combined with the melancholy at not wanting to end her time with Hazel and the others, Hanna found herself struggling to sleep, leading to another evening in the business center, distracting herself with more work.

A text from Noah interrupted her as she read an email. *Where are you?*

Hanna glanced away from her laptop as she typed her response. *The business center, why?*

Hanna waited for the three dots to appear, indicating that Noah was typing, but they never appeared. Glancing back at her message, she saw the words 'Read at 10:02 p.m.' but no new message appeared beneath hers. She waited for a minute.

Two.

The blue light of the screen mocked her. She set aside her phone with a sigh, disappointed and confused. Why would Noah ask where she was and then not reply? Did he need something?

Frowning at the lack of answers coming from the device, Hanna turned back to her laptop. A referral from an unknown source, the

Delgado family booked a tour with Hanna for a few days after Hazel's group ended. Almost too convenient, they were travelling through France and wanted Hanna to accompany them through Paris. Despite the last minute nature of the request, Hanna was able to reuse the majority of the itinerary from this trip for the Deglados and they sent the final payment weeks ago.

Her stomach dropped when she saw the email from Patricia Degaldo, cancelling the trip. Patricia's message was brief, letting Hanna know that due to unforeseen circumstances, their family would no longer need Luxe Travel's services. Perplexed, Hanna wondered what caused the change so close to the trip. The cancellation impacted her own travel arrangements. Hanna planned on staying in France between the trips, but now that would be a waste. Without another trip lined up, the responsible thing was to ask Sarah if her room was still available and return to California while she worked on booking more trips.

Drafting a to-do list, heart heavy with worry, Hanna jolted when the door to the business center slid open with a whoosh. There, holding onto the door frame with one hand, was Noah. Slightly flushed and blue eyes blazing, he watched her from the doorway like a predator locked onto its prey. Pulse ratcheting up at his heated gaze, Hanna swallowed, worry pushed aside by desire.

"Are you okay?" Her voice was thick and honey-sweet.

"You weren't in your room," Noah bit out as he prowled towards her.

Sitting up straight in her chair, Hanna tipped her head back to stare at him defiantly. "So?"

"It's 10 p.m."

The low rumble of his voice set her on fire, his voice and heated look caressing her skin like he had never touched her before. She wanted him to touch her like they had all the time in the world, with nothing to interrupt them.

"And? If you needed something from me, you could have messaged me. Oh, that's right, you didn't." She pulled her hair over one shoulder to bring cool air to her flushed skin. The intent behind the gesture was not flirtatious, but the way Noah tracked the movement and parted his lips had Hanna making a mental note to do it again later. On purpose.

Noah's arms braced on either side of the chair, leaning forward so that their mouths were a breath apart. "I needed to see you."

Pointedly looking up and down his body, Hanna followed the lines of his muscles, coiled tightly under the fabric of his dress shirt and pants. Always so dressed up and put together. How she loved to make him disheveled.

"Why," she teased.

"It's after 10 p.m.," he growled with a nip to her ear.

Hanna moaned, forcing herself not to arch her back to chase his mouth. It was exquisite torment, this back and forth between them. Not giving in, prolonging the suspense was its own kind of foreplay. "You already said that. What does 10 p.m. have to do with it?"

"Because you are off the clock now. Now, you're mine." Noah punctuated the statement by closing the distance between them and molding their lips together.

The dam between them opened and they frantically pulled each other closer. Together they managed to lift Hanna into an upright position, Noah's hands grasping her waist and Hanna's clenching around his shoulders. She felt the soft strands of his hair under her fingers as she gripped his neck.

Noah groaned into her mouth and fisted Hanna's hair in his hands, tugging gently, causing Hanna to moan in response. She felt feverish, head foggy and vision tunneled so that Noah was all she saw. Their chests brushed against each other with every breath, sending tingles through Hanna with every pass.

With his hands in her hair, Noah separated their lips and kept Hanna's head still when she tried to turn and recapture them. Her whimper of disappointment transformed into a moan as the warm press of his lips traced a path across her jaw. Licking and biting his way down one side of her neck, along her collarbone, and up the opposite side. A shiver went down Hanna's spine when Noah discovered the sensitive skin over her pulse.

He lingered on the spot, massaging it with the wet pull of his mouth. Knees weakened by the onslaught of pleasure, Hanna's one functioning brain cell reminded her that she wanted to drive Noah out of his mind with pleasure too. Leaning into him, Hanna wrapped her arms around him and lightly dragged her nails down his back. Noah's body tightened and his hips thrust forward.

Encouraged by his response, Hanna repeated the motion, dragging her hands up and down, up and down while he panted in her ear. She could feel the thick length of him against her stomach and she arched against it.

"Hanna," he moaned into her ear. "If you do not want me to bend you over this desk and take you where anyone could walk in, I suggest we go somewhere private."

It took Hanna a moment to drift out of her brain fog and remember where they were. The sharp ping of an email pulled her attention back to the computer and the work that waited for her.

With a gentle tug on her hair, Noah brought her dilated eyes back to him. "If you need to stay and finish." He gestured with his head to the laptop. "I can wait. But when I finally get you alone, I don't plan on sharing. My entire focus will be on you and your pleasure, and I want you right there with me. No work, no distractions. Just you and me."

"I have a hard time closing all the tabs in my brain and focusing on one thing," Hanna admitted.

"I can help with that." Noah trailed a hand down her side, brushing against the side of her breast and wiping any thoughts from her brain. "Anytime you start getting distracted, I'll give you something to focus on. Just tell me what you want."

There was a brief debate in her mind over the choice to continue working or leave with Noah. Practically humming with her need for him, the decision was an easy one. Nothing major would get accomplished by continuing to work, all the tasks could wait, but her yearning for Noah? That could not wait. The fabric of her being felt like it was unraveling with the intense desire to be close to him in any way possible.

And the attractive proposition Noah presented, added to the realization that she liked the firm way he directed her, had Hanna decisively reaching out to click the laptop shut, never breaking eye contact.

"Good girl."

Her brain short-circuited at his words as her legs clenched together at the rush of desire.

Well, apparently there were still things Hanna could learn about herself.

Scooping up the laptop with one hand, the other so low on her back that his fingers grazed the top of her pants, Noah guided Hanna out of the room. His fingers were the only part of his body touching hers, and while Hanna craved more, she appreciated his thoughtfulness when they passed other hotel guests in the hallway and elevator.

"Which floor?" A middle-aged man with silver streaked hair stood by the buttons. Noah looked at Hanna for the answer, leaving the choice with her.

She gave her floor number.

Noah's hand rubbed circles on her lower back, each rotation slower and stretching a wider path. Teasing the space where her shirt tucked into her pants, slipping under to graze her skin before pulling back up. Each brush of skin on skin sent a zap of pleasure up her spine until every cell was vibrating with unquenched need.

When the panel lit with her floor number, Hanna and Noah rushed out of the elevator with a brisk, "*Bonne nuit*" to the gentleman. In front of her door, Hanna fumbled to pull the keycard out her pocket. Her fingers shook with excitement. This was it.

They were finally alone without any injuries or work to interrupt them.

Noah pressed into her back, holding her hand steady as they

brought the key to the lock. He paused just before the plastic touched the pad.

"Only if you're sure."

Twisting in his arms, Hanna drowned in his blue stare. "Yes, no regrets." The lock chirped with the blink of a green light. "Now get in here and keep your promise."

They fell through the door, Noah tangling their legs as he fused their lips together and stepped into the room. Hanna tugged his shirt free as Noah kicked the door shut. Trapped between Noah and the wall, his weight pressing into her, Hanna felt delirious. Every place they touched burned for more and she hooked one leg around his, seeking friction.

Noah ground against her, using his free hand to lift her knee higher, spreading her as wide as the cotton fabric allowed, notching his hips between hers. Hanna threw her head back with a moan, the glide of fabric between her legs heightening the pleasure.

"Noah." She pressed kisses to his collarbone. "Please."

"Tell me what you need."

Stretching on her toes to try and fit their hips closer, Hanna sighed. "You. More."

Pinching his eyes shut as he absorbed the words, Noah bent his knees, curling his arm under her legs to scoop her into the air. Hanna clung to him as he crossed to the bed, touching the soft strands of his hair before Noah set her down. Her body slid along his, pulling the rest of her shirt free and teasing the skin of her stomach.

Watching the fabric flutter back into place, Noah slid one hand under the shirt to trace the line of her hips before grabbing the hem. When his attempt to pull it over her head was thwarted by the hand still holding Hanna's laptop, Noah stepped back.

"Don't move," he said when Hanna reached for the edge of her shirt. "I want to undress you."

Another alert pinged while Noah walked toward the desk. Arching his brow in question, Noah opened the lid to turn off the device, placing his wallet and phone on top of it in a small pile.

Hanna watched the flex of his muscles as Noah bent to remove his shoes. When he caught her gaze, Noah smirked and began unrolling his sleeves and unbuttoning his shirt, playing up the motions for her watchful eyes. Lamplight highlighted the dark hair between his pectorals, dusting along his stomach before narrowing below his pants. Hanna felt like a computer creating a 3-D model, scanning every inch of his naked chest, greedily absorbing the sight of his toned flesh.

Obeying Noah's request, her feet were rooted to the floor despite the curiosity over what he tasted like and how soon his pants would join the shirt on her floor. She ached for his touch, her bra chafing against her heaving chest. Yet, he remained frustratingly composed. Slowly drawing out his belt, rolling it into a coil that sent Hanna's heart pounding. The slide of metal as he undid the snap and zipper of his slacks was sharp in the quiet of the room.

Finally, clothing a heap on the floor, Noah was nearly naked. Tight black briefs hid nothing, the fabric stretched over every hard part of him. Taking mercy on her, Noah cleared the distance between them with two long strides. Close enough to nuzzle into his chest, Hanna took advantage of their proximity by trailing her fingers through the coarse hair there. Noah sucked in a breath when her hands followed the hair down, fingers tapping over his stomach. Groaning, Noah pressed an open-mouth kiss to her lips, sucking her lower lip between his.

In a flash, Hanna's shirt was over her head, the blurry stripes momentarily blocking her view of Noah's glowing skin. Once her vision cleared, Hanna blinked to process the image of Noah on his knees before her, curving his long fingers into the waistband of her pants.

Looking up at her under thick lashes, Noah leaned forward. "I've dreamed about these legs." He ran his tongue along her hip bone. "Watching you walk around in those skirts swirling around your thighs, imagining inching the fabric up until I found you bare and ready for me. Remembering the way you tasted."

His tongue left a damp trail from one hip to the other, pausing to suck on the skin above the button his fingers were currently sliding free. Hanna's head was too heavy for her neck, overcome with the need to watch his every movement, her hands restless in his hair, drawing the strands through her fingers. She pulled in a sharp breath when Noah lowered the zipper, skimming one knuckle along the newly exposed fabric.

"Teasing you until there was no thought in your head except for me." The slow, methodical cadence of his voice matched the motions of his fingers freeing her legs from each pant leg. "My touch. Bringing you to climax over and over again before finally pressing inside you. Once wasn't enough. I want to make you come until we are both too exhausted to move. Until I don't know where I stop and you begin."

"Please." Hanna swayed forward on unsteady legs, Noah's grip firm on her thighs.

"You like the idea of that, *Anna*?" It was the first time he used the French pronunciation of her name, marking the occasion as something special, unique to them in this moment. With his soft accent, her name sounded sexier than it ever had before. Hanna felt her blood rushing faster through her body, needing to be touched, to ease some of the pressure building inside her from their prolonged foreplay.

Kissing his way up her thigh, paying special attention to the curves of her hips and only grazing the lace still covering her, Noah squeezed her bottom between his hands.

"Condom?" he asked, and Hanna was glad he thought of it before they were drowning in pleasure and could still make rational decisions.

"I bought some earlier." Hanna gestured to the bathroom.

Noah smiled at her with undisguised pride. "Always prepared. I adore that about you." He pressed a kiss on her covered mound. "I bought some too. Just in case we run out of yours."

Standing, Noah went to retrieve the strip of condoms from his pocket before walking into the bathroom.

Without his touch to distract her, Hanna's thoughts wandered. *Was she supposed to stay in place again, or would it look better for her to lie down on the bed? Her pants would wrinkle if they stayed on the floor and she would rather get one more wear out of them before having to wash and iron them again. Should she take off her bra, or would Noah do that?*

From the open door to the bathroom, Hanna could see Noah looking at the box she purchased. *Were they the right size? What if he was having second thoughts?*

Thoughts swirling like a stormcloud, Hanna missed Noah's return. He was only gone for a minute or two, but Hanna's brain was wired to think five steps ahead, using any pause between activities to strategize, plan, and run through her never ending to-do list. The sound of plastic packets hitting the soft duvet reached Hanna's ears before she registered Noah's proximity, his hands cradling her face and tilting it up to look at him.

"Where did you go?" Black eclipsed blue as he examined her.

"Sorry." Hanna kissed him softly. "Just got lost in thought for a moment. I still want this–want you. My brain is just having a hard time turning off."

"You didn't do anything wrong. It just means that I need to do a better job of keeping your focus on feeling, not thinking. You spend all your time thinking of how you can take care of everyone else." He rubbed his thumbs across her cheeks, looking lost in thought himself for a beat.

Hanna knew the exact moment an idea came to him, eyes landing on something behind her and brightening. "Do you trust me?"

"Yes."

"Good girl." His words reignited the heat in her belly. Noah coaxed her lips open against his, thrusting his tongue inside her mouth. His hands gripped her waist and hips, massaging their way up her torso.

When the pads of his fingers skated along the undersides of her breasts, Hanna moaned, arching forward for more contact. Teasing her, Noah continued the featherlight touches along the lower band of her bra, occasionally dipping underneath before switching to the edge of the cups. Her groans of frustration were met with the curve of his smile against her lips.

He enjoyed drawing out each touch, keeping her on edge. In retaliation, Hanna pulled his lower lip between her teeth, satisfied with the tortured groan that fell from his mouth. They lost themselves in the kiss, lips and tongues and teeth provoking each other further. Finally, after an eternity where Hanna felt like her breasts were so sensitive they would burst free of their confines, Noah unsnapped her bra, done with his slow torture as he ripped the fabric away and tossed it across the room. Hanna knew she would need to search for it later, but that thought was quickly wiped from her mind as Noah sucked on one peaked tip.

"Yes!" Hanna gripped Noah's head, holding him prisoner against her.

As he nipped and soothed one side, his hand crept up to tease the other, pulling and twisting as he learned what she liked best. With his free arm, Noah supported her back, leaning into Hanna until she felt gravity tip her onto the bed. Kicking herself up the fabric, Hanna used Noah's biceps as leverage to pull him up with her, letting his hips settle between hers.

Their mouths met and separated, kissing along jaws, necks, and the upper contours of chests. Hanna wrapped her legs around Noah's hips, squirming with unmet need.

Noah reached for something over her head, the pull of his chest and arm muscles distracting her. Something soft touched Hanna's forehead and Noah's fingers fanned along the sides of her head. Trying to tilt her head up to see what it was, Hanna stopped when Noah spoke.

"You know what I think, Hanna?" His voice was thick with need.

"What?"

"To get you to stop thinking, I need you to focus on feeling." Fabric lowered over Hanna's eyes, the familiar weight and texture of her sleep mask casting the room into darkness. "Without sight, I want you to focus on my touch. How I make you feel. Can you do that for me?"

His words were punctuated by featherlight brushes against her skin. One sweep against her inner arms. Another along her soft stomach. The back of Hanna's eyelids swirled with bright pulses of color, each touch bringing a gasp of surprise to her lips. Her focus honed in on Noah, sharpening the sensations of touch and sound as she tried to predict where he was.

"Noah," she pleaded for more.

She could hear the smile in his voice. "I need you to say it, Hanna."

"Touch me. Please. I need to feel you. Make me forget anything but you."

No part of their bodies were touching and Hanna twisted on the bed to try and find him. Her pulse pounded in her ears and she felt like a live wire. Surely they would burn the place to the ground when they came together, if this was what it felt like when they separated.

Acclimating to the lack of one sense, Hanna swore she could tell when Noah opened his mouth to speak again. That she could feel his inhale as he kneeled between her legs.

"Good. Girl." His tongue ran up the seam of her lace underwear, creating such a sharp bolt of pleasure that Hanna screamed.

A series of slow licks followed the creases where her thighs met her hips, ending above her mound. Hanna arched her hips, trying to direct Noah where she wanted him. Continuing his slow torture, Noah hooked his fingers under the band of her underwear, dragging it down her legs. Picking up one foot, Noah kissed her ankle before setting it over his shoulder. The skin was soft beneath her calf and Hanna hinged her leg back and forth to drag against him.

He surprised her with each touch, kissing a path along her skin before lifting away from her and moving to another patch of bare skin. Getting closer, ever closer, to her core. Warm air blew across her center, and Hanna pressed against Noah's shoulder, using leverage to bring herself closer.

"Do you need something, Hanna?" Noah's tongue skimmed the outer rim of her core. Sparks danced behind Hanna's mask. She was already so close, tiptoeing closer to the peak with every brush of skin.

Tired of waiting, Hanna grasped the soft strands of Noah's hair and tried to yank him closer. "No more teasing."

A chuckle vibrated against her inner thigh. "Never let it be said that I denied you anything you wanted."

Wet heat engulfed her. Hanna moaned at the pleasant sensation and cried out Noah's name. He focused his attention on stoking the fire in her, no longer switching targets to keep her attention. There was nothing else on her mind besides Noah, beyond them, together. He knew what she liked, focusing on the pace and friction that earned him moans with every exhale.

Close, so very close.

Fingers gripped her thighs open, one hand tracing a path lower to ease a finger inside her, while he continued to consume her. Hanna threw her head back on the pillow, opening her mouth to pant.

A second finger joined the first and Hanna erupted.

Noah groaned as Hanna came down from the high, thighs quaking around his head.

Tugging the sleep mask off her face, Hanna gave Noah a satisfied smile. Her limbs felt like melted butter, soft and malleable. Coming around Noah's fingers and mouth took the edge off, but she wanted more. Wanted to feel his body on top of hers, inside her, moving together.

Noah fluttered his fingers inside her when she clenched around them. "Again?"

Her grin split her face. "Only if you join me this time."

Noah reflexively clenched her thighs, kissing the top of her mound before drawing his lips up her stomach. "It feels like I've waited forever for you."

Pulling down his briefs as he prowled up the bed, Noah kicked off the black fabric. Hanna watched as he sprang free, jutting forward with a slight curve, the ruddy base covered in wiry, trimmed hair. She wanted to touch him, but he was out of reach.

Noah kissed above her heart. "You drive me insane, working yourself to exhaustion, taunting me with your wit, and mesmerizing me with your brilliance. Every thought is consumed by you. When awake, I watch how you are always three steps ahead of me, dizzy to catch up, in charge wherever you go." He softly bit a path up her neck. "At night, you haunt me. Chasing your laugh and flirtatious glances. I've imagined you in every way. Over me, under me, against those desks you spend hours at. Laying down in a bed so I can worship every inch of you. Just as you are now."

Large thighs settled between hers and Hanna widened her legs to accommodate him. Reaching above her, Noah grabbed a pillow and wedged it beneath her hips.

"Tell me how you want me, Hanna. Tender." A kiss to her jaw. "Rough." A bite to her lower lip. "Anything you want."

Hanna felt the hot press of him against her core. He was solid, pulsing against her. Core clenching in want, Hanna dragged her fingernails down Noah's back. "I want everything. All of you. Don't hold back."

"Your wish is my command."

Ripping open the condom packet, Noah slid it over his length, gripping at the base to nudge her opening. Hanna tilted her hips to find the angle that allowed her body to accept him more easily. They groaned together as Noah slid inside her centimeter by centimeter, Hanna's body greedily pulling him in. Her nerves sang with each stroke.

Their bodies moved together, retreating and coming back together again and again, finding patterns that sent their heartbeats racing. Taking cues from the increased pitch of her moans and the frantic way she pulled at his shoulders, Noah snapped his hips forward before slowly pulling out. Hanna watched his face twist with pleasure, eyes darkening as they fixated on her face. Trying to get closer, Hanna hooked her knees around Noah's waist, flexing to help push him deeper.

"More." Hanna pulled him down for a kiss, opening her mouth so that she could stroke his tongue with her own.

Noah groaned as his control snapped. With one arm banded around her shoulder to hold her steady, Noah stretched to grip the headboard with the other, balancing himself against the furniture. Flexing above her, Hanna watched as the muscles of his arm tightened as he pushed them closer to the edge of desire.

Watching him was nearly enough to set off her own orgasm, the tight planes of his chest and stomach hypnotically sexual as they flexed. Next time, Hanna promised herself she would touch and kiss those muscles. For now, she was too close to spiraling into the haze of pleasure to stop and pay those muscles the attention they deserved.

"Hanna," Noah said her name like a plea. "Tell me you're close. I need you to come with me."

"I'm close," she cried out. "So close. Just...a little...*yes.*"

Her body pulled in on itself just before she came, spooling tighter and tighter before releasing. Energy burst like starlight under her skin, pulsing in time with her heartbeat as she came. Noah moaned as he felt her come around him, rocking his hips into her twice more before groaning into her open mouth and joining her in the fall over the cliff.

*La petite mort,* indeed.

Tucking her against his chest, Noah rolled them onto their sides, burrowing his face in Hanna's hair. Drawing in deep lungfuls of air, Hanna smiled to herself at how adorable Noah was after sex. He clung to her like a vine, wrapping their legs together and keeping their naked bodies pressed as close as they could get.

He pressed a kiss to her forehead. "That was incredible. Just like I knew we would be."

"That confident, huh?" Hanna gently bit his collarbone.

He twitched against her hip. Giving Hanna another squeeze, Noah got up from the bed and went into the bathroom. The sound of running water reached Hanna, so relaxed that she refused to lift her head to see what Noah was doing. Probably disposing of the condom. On his way back, Noah turned off the overhead lights, illuminating the room in the golden glow of the bedside lamps.

The bed dipped when Noah kneeled on it. "Open for me, sweetheart." He tapped her thigh.

"Ready for round two already?" Hanna mumbled into the pillow. Her bones were still pleasantly jellied, but after Noah's last performance, a few strategic touches could motivate her to find the energy for more.

A slap to her ass sent a pleasant zing up her body.

"As much as I like your attitude, I need more time to recover. We'll get to round two later. For now, just let me take care of you."

Noah used a warm washcloth to clean her off, pulling the covers over them when he came back to the bed. Facing each other on the pillows, Hanna struggled to suppress a yawn. She would not have pegged Noah as a snuggler after sex, but he continued stroking his fingers along her arms and hips as they lay together. .

Her eyelids drooped lower and Hanna wanted to give in to the urge to sleep, but she had not brushed her teeth yet. How much time was appropriate to wait until she could go clean off her makeup?

One side of his mouth ticked up as Noah watched her face. He reached up to tuck Hanna's hair behind her ear. "What's going on in that beautiful brain of yours?"

"That obvious?"

She did not realize that she was that easy to read. Before Noah, no one paid close enough attention to notice the small idiosyncrasies in her expressions. As happy as it made her that he noticed, Hanna was nervous to ask how long he planned on staying. It would devastate her if he wanted to leave.

"I was just thinking about brushing my teeth and washing off my makeup. You don't have to stay if you will be bored. It's a rather involved process."

"Trying to get rid of me already." Noah's tone was joking, but she could see the hidden worry in his eyes.

Maybe she was not the only one dancing around what she really wanted to say in order to protect the fragile parts of herself that feared rejection. Another piece of the armor around her heart broke off at the vulnerable look on Noah's face. She did not want him to worry about her interest in him. For him, she could be the brave one.

"I don't ever want to get rid of you. I want to fall asleep next to you and wake up beside you. For as long as you'll have me. I just didn't want you to feel pressured to stay if you don't want to. You have your own room, so I understand if you want to sleep there." Her fingers twined around the dusting of hair on his chest to settle the nervous fluttering in her stomach.

"Wherever you are is where I want to be." Noah lifted her hands and kissed the tip of each finger. "If I didn't think it was too soon and would scare you off, I would move my stuff into your room, or bring yours to mine."

Hanna's heart thudded against her chest. Another protective layer of her guard melted with Noah's earnest statement. It terrified Hanna how happy it made her, cautiously opening herself up to the possibility of getting to keep Noah. Worry whispered into her ear like smoke. Sure, Noah wanted to stay with her now, but what about when the relationship was tested with distance? In Hanna's experience, people lost interest when more effort was required to maintain the relationship.

"Hey." Noah rubbed at the furrow in Hanna's brow. "Where did you go?"

She did not want to worry him with her concerns, not when their relationship was so new. Giving him a small smile, Hanna stretched up to kiss Noah's jaw. "Just wondering if I had a spare toothbrush for you."

He saw through the blatant distraction technique and let Hanna get away with it. "Let's go find out."

Using the packaged toothbrush from the hotel, Noah brushed his teeth with Hanna before returning to the bed while she washed her face. Hanna climbed into bed naked. Honestly, what was the point of pajamas when they limited her access to Noah? Noah waited until she turned off her side lamp before curling an arm around her waist to pull her flush against him. He buried his face into her hair and Hanna threaded her fingers through his.

Her back moved in cadence with Noah's chest, slowing as they drifted into sleep.

# 17
# Don't Prolong Your Goodbye

THE FINAL DAY of most tours was bittersweet. Exhausted, feet sore, and emotionally drained from constant social interaction meant that both guests and guide alike were ready to say farewell and return to the comforts of home. But they were reluctant to say goodbye to days of fun, exploring new places, and a break from everyday life, especially when they were with a group of people they loved.

That was particularly true for this collection of women. Finding time for friendship, even in retirement, required strategic planning, negotiating dates and times in order to carve out an hour or two together. Their weekly lunches had nothing on the two weeks of celebrating their bond. They were already planning their next trip together, one they vowed only Luxe Travel would coordinate.

"Hanna, you must promise to visit us whenever you are in California," Hazel insisted over their farewell breakfast.

Their luggage was stored in Madeline's van, ready to drive them straight to the airport once their leisurely meal was complete. Some of the guides Hanna knew preferred to say goodbye to the group the night before they were set to leave, but Hanna felt it ruined the clean exit by saying goodbye and then still seeing them off the next day. Whenever the flight allowed it, Hanna preferred dining with the group one last time before taking them to the airport, that way it prevented prolonged goodbyes.

Hanna never liked goodbyes. They reminded her of all the other people and places she had to leave, and this one hurt more than others.

In the past, she would make vague remarks about how the group could keep in contact with her, leaving the proverbial ball in their court, to limit the level of disappointment she felt if they never contacted her again. But Hanna was closer to this group than any in the past. She had grown fond of Hazel, Mai, Daphne, and even Lillian, and wanted to make promises to see them again.

And then there was Noah. Every day they were together, Noah made it clear that he wanted to continue their relationship, going so far as to create a shared calendar with dates scheduled for times Hanna was back in Los Angeles. He even inquired about future tour locations, suggesting that he might want to plan business trips to those places as well.

The silver lining of the Delgados' cancelled trip meant that Hanna would see Noah sooner rather than later. It still niggled at the back of her mind, not knowing the full reason for the abrupt change. When Noah found out about the cancelled trip, he asked if there was anything he could do to help, but Hanna let him know there was nothing either of them could do. Last minute, she was unable to book the same flight as Noah, and her flight left later that day. Hanna was going with them to the airport to save Madeline from making the trip twice.

"What are your plans before your next tour?" Daphne asked the same question Noah had the night before.

Reaching for her water to hide the blush blooming over her face at the reminder of her night with Noah, Hanna sipped the cool liquid. "Nothing too exciting. Mostly resting and catching up on some personal errands. Then I am going to work on some of those marketing strategies you recommended to drum up more business."

Laundry and a long nap were Hanna's first priorities.

"I hope you set aside some time for fun," Mai said as she reached for another croissant. Mai informed Hanna that she was making the most of their last morning in Paris and was eating her weight in French pastries. "Now that you are done playing chaperone."

The group laughed at Mai's joke.

"Yes, Hanna." Noah's voice was rough with innuendo. "You need to have some fun."

Shooting him a withering glare that was ineffective due to the smile tugging her lips up, Hanna met his smoldering eyes. "I did hear about a new club that opened near Sarah's place, perhaps I will check it out with her."

"What is the club called?" Noah's question reminded Hanna of his constant double checking of her bookings when she was first planning the trip. Before, she thought it was because he was controlling, but now she recognized it for his need to protect the people he cared about. Noah's fingers flew over the screen of his phone when Hanna gave him the name, probably searching the area to make sure it was safe.

While he was distracted, Hanna guided the conversation back to what Hazel and her friends were going to do when they returned home. Mai was preparing for a gala at the museum, one that Lillian was donating several pieces of art from her ex-husband to. Daphne was teaching tennis to a group of kids at an afterschool program for disadvantaged youth and Hazel was inspired to renovate her backyard after seeing the magic of Monet's garden.

Hanna hoped that Hazel and Daphne got around to taking a dance class.

Hearing the group share their favorite memories of the trip filled Hanna with contentment. How the tour ended was just as important as how it began, and guests talking over each other in their excitement to relive moments of the tour was a sure sign of success. It meant that the small blips and deviations in plans were overshadowed by the fun they had together.

"Hanna," Hazel said while pulling two cloth bags from her purse, "before we say goodbye, we wanted to give you a small memento to thank you for all your work. This is one of the best vacations we have ever been on and it's because of you. And Madeline of course, don't think we forgot about you. You kept us safe and without you we would probably be lost and exhausted right now."

"*Non, non. Anna* would not let you get lost. It was a pleasure to drive you around my beautiful city," Madeline said with one of her bright smiles.

Hanna and Madeline reached across the table to take the bags from Hazel. Inclined to wait until she was alone to open her gift, Hanna started to put the bag into her purse before Mai stopped her and told them to open the gifts now. Letting Madeline open her gift first, Hanna watched her friend untie the blue velvet ribbon and reach into the opening to pull out a bottle of her favorite perfume.

Moving around the table, Madeline hugged each member of the group and thanked them for their thoughtful gift.

"*Merci*. How did you know this was my favorite?" Madeline laughed when five pairs of eyes shifted in Hanna's direction. "*Anna*, of course. So thoughtful, thank you."

Madeline kissed Hanna's cheek and gave her a hug. When Hazel and the others asked her what gift they could get for Madeline, besides the tip they already planned on, Hanna immediately thought of the luxury perfume that Madeline always wore. She was pleased that it was well received.

"Go on, Hanna. Open your gift now," Daphne said impatiently.

Tugging on the red ribbon tying the wrapping together, the edge unfurled over Hanna's palm. Nestled inside was a small jewelry box and an envelope. Discreetly looking in the envelope, Hanna tucked the tip into her purse before taking the box into her hands. Lifting the top, sunlight flashed off gold.

Overcome with gratitude, Hanna nearly dropped the box. The thoughtfulness of the gift was more than she hoped for, something unique and customized to her interests and personality, something

Mai noticed her admiring on the tour and purchased without her knowledge.

Artfully draped on red fabric to match the ribbon was the cameo necklace of a birdhouse threaded on a gold chain. Touched by the gesture that meant more to her than any expression of thanks, she felt her heart squeeze. Joy laced with a hint of sadness tightened her throat. There in the palm of her hands was the symbol of the home she longed for, surrounded by the people who knew her well enough to wish it for her too.

"Thank you." Hanna had to fight to whisper the words without crying. Clutching the necklace to her chest, she looked each person in the eyes before speaking directly to Mai. "This is one of the greatest gifts I have ever received and I will treasure it always."

Across from her, Mai opened her arms and Hanna hastily stood to receive the hug. Kneeling to wrap her arms around the petite woman more soundly, Hanna had to tuck her face into the space above Mai's shoulder. Hanna inhaled the scent of the sea and fresh flowers, knowing that the combination of scents would forever remind her of the gifts of listening and understanding Mai gave her that day in the flea market.

"Thank you," she whispered again, just for Mai.

"You're welcome," Mai whispered back. "Whether you wear it or not, I hope that you always remember you are worthy of beautiful things and that the world is a more beautiful and kind place for having you in it."

Hanna moved to hug Daphne next.

"Thank you for a wonderful trip," Daphne said with a crushing hug. "I've already told my friends and contacts in the sports world about you. Expect to get some calls for trips very soon."

Although that was one of her main goals, the rush of professional pride at securing more business paled in comparison to gaining the esteem of a woman so full of life and love.

After a quick hug and thanks to Lillian, Hanna resigned herself to only having a lukewarm relationship with the socialite, she faced the person who had brought them all together.

Hazel was standing with one hand on her hip, the other dabbing at her eyes with a handkerchief. Sassy as ever, Hazel leveled a stern look in Hanna's direction.

"Well, I hope you are happy, ruining my makeup when I could meet a handsome stranger on the plane," she said with mock seriousness.

In all honesty, Hanna would not be surprised if Hazel managed to charm a fellow traveller and end up falling in love over the Atlantic.

Feigning an equally serious tone, Hanna replied, "You only have yourself to blame, picking out such a sentimental gift. If I did not know any better, I would think you were trying to get me to cry."

"Only because I am going to miss you very much," Hazel said as she pulled Hanna into a hug.

Hanna leaned into the comfort of Hazel's embrace, the sensation of being protected and cherished filling her soul. This woman meant so much to her and Hanna would miss her in the time they were apart.

"Don't be a stranger," Hazel continued. "I expect you to keep me updated on how you are and to come visit when you are in town, understood?"

Hanna nodded.

"Good. Bring Noah with you too, I don't see him nearly as often as I want and something tells me he will do whatever you ask."

Hanna blushed at the knowing wink Hazel gave her. So much for being discrete on the tour. Behind them, Noah cleared his throat, a gesture Hanna recognized as something he did when embarrassed. Guessing that he overheard what Hazel said, Hanna shot him a flirtatious wink over her shoulder.

His cheeks darkened in the delightful way that sent Hanna's pulse racing.

Knowing that this was not goodbye for them, Hanna hugged

Noah briefly. If she held onto him too long, she would either burst into tears or never let him leave. And leave they must. A glance at her watch informed Hanna it was time to go, leading the group to the car one last time before they drove to the airport. The closer they got to parting, the more the sorrow at leaving them and hope that they would stay in touch mixed into a cocktail of emotions that had her eyes prickling.

Hanna held her tears at bay as she helped the group through bag check, pressing her lips together tightly in an attempt to squeeze the mix of sadness back into her body. She could do this. She just had to get through security and drop them off at the lounge. Then, she could cry as much as she wanted. Saving her bag for last, a growl of contempt slipped out of Hanna when the screen gave her an error message.

Why did this machine thwart her attempts at a quick exit?

All she wanted was to get through this so she could be alone and sad.

She just needed the stupid machine to find her reservation so that she could check her bag and be on her way.

"Here."

A crisp ticket wiggled in her periphery vision and Hanna's heart leapt with surprise.

Noah was standing next to the kiosk, a smile stretched across his face as he waved the ticket again, mimicking one of their earliest interactions on the trip.

Playing her part, Hanna rolled her eyes at him and said, "I already have a ticket."

"This one's better."

"Why? Because it is printed on first class paper?" Hanna bit back a smile at the playful look in his eyes.

"No, because it *is* first class." He showed her the ticket. Then slid a second ticket out of his pocket. "With me. I moved my flight so we could be together."

Hanna laughed in delight, tears finally breaking free and sliding down her face.

Then, in front of everyone, Hanna kissed him, sinking her hands into his hair as the group cheered behind them.

# 18

## *Expect the Unexpected*

WELL-RESTED and deliriously happy after spending another flight with Noah, Hanna sat in the backseat of their rideshare as the car weaved through Los Angeles traffic. During the flight, Hanna and Noah made plans for the few days she was taking off before starting work again. She joked that Noah's work was going to replace him if he took more time off, but he replied seriously that it was worth it if it meant he got to spend more time with her. That led to a heated makeout session that was interrupted by a flight attendant.

Their ride pulled up to Sarah's house, the native flowers showing off California's recent rainshower by displaying their brightly colored blooms. Hanna smiled as the cheery sight of the bright blue door greeted her. This may not be her home, but Hanna admired how Sarah created a welcoming atmosphere from the matching blue shutters to the smattering of windchimes and hummingbird feeders hung along the trim.

Apparently, it was so welcoming that there was a short, balding man standing on the doormat, running his fingers over a manila envelope nervously. Hanna frowned as they pulled to the curb. The man visibly relaxed as he saw the car, shoulders coming away from his ears as he started walking down the driveway.

"Do you know him?" Noah paused with his hand on the door handle.

Shaking her head, Hanna pushed down her apprehension. "No. He's probably a salesman, or looking for Sarah."

Protective to a fault, Noah stepped out of the car and smoothed the wrinkles in his clothes, standing to his full height to intimidate the approaching stranger. Rolling her eyes behind his back, Hanna climbed out of the car and stepped beside Noah just as the man reached them. Honestly, it was broad daylight and their driver was still sitting in the car, waiting for them to get their bags. What danger did Noah think this man possessed?

Once she knew, Hanna realized she should have been more worried.

The man barely glanced at Noah, focusing his attention on Hanna, causing the hairs on her arms to rise.

"Are you Hannah Poole?" His voice had a slight rasp as he mispronounced her name.

"Yes, I'm Hanna. Why are you here?" She crossed her arms over her chest.

Intrusive thoughts prodded at her and Hanna tried to control her breathing to calm her racing heart. Reminding herself that someone would have called if one of her family members were hurt and that only people trying to sell something came to your address instead of calling. After hours of travel, all Hanna wanted was to get settled in her room, not deal with a solicitor. Noah wrapped an arm around her shoulders, squeezing gently in support.

The envelope hovered in the open air between them. "I was sent on behalf of Trips Ahoy. These are summons for you to appear in court. You have 60 days to answer the complaint within. If you do not, you will get a default judgment against you."

Ice slid through her veins, chilling Hanna despite the balmy Southern California weather. She heard the word "summons" like it was a foreign language and she briefly wondered if maybe the jetlag scrambled something in her brain that rendered her useless at translating it.

The envelope remained suspended in the air, insubstantial until she grabbed hold of it with shaking fingers. How could something with such life-altering contents feel so mundane? The dry paper was coarse, abrasive against her skin when Hanna thought it should feel biting. There should be some visible sign of the damage this envelope was causing her, like bloody fingerprints.

Hanna stared mutely as her body trembled, barely registering that the man was raising his hands in a harmless gesture at something Noah asked him, backing away as if leaving the scene of a crime. How could this have happened? Hanna paid her taxes on time, followed the law, even flossed twice a day. She was a good person, treating people with respect and compassion. Why would anyone have cause to sue her?

Noah bent down to stare into her eyes, holding her face between his hands as he asked her how she was. It sounded like he was speaking to her underwater, the rushing in Hanna's ears drowning out the nuances of language so that she only understood the meaning, if not the actual words, of what Noah was saying. Behind them, the driver rolled down their window and said something. Noah snapped back a reply.

Hanna still could not understand exactly what was being said.

Murmuring something that was probably meant to reassure her, Noah kissed her and then stepped around to get their bags from the trunk. Gripping her own version of Pandora's box, Hanna tore at the flap, ripping off several small pieces before she could slide the folded papers out. Despite wanting to burn them and pretend none of this was happening, Hanna knew that, *"Ignorance is bliss, Your Honor,"* would not go over well in court. A burst of hysterical laughter left Hanna's lips at the thought of saying that to someone as stern-faced as Judge Judy.

It took Hanna four attempts to read through the paragraphs detailing the lawsuit. Phrases like 'ignoring our previous attempts at contact,' and 'cease and desist' jumped out at her. Laden with legalese, Hanna was nonetheless able to make out the finer point of the lawsuit.

She was being sued for allegedly stealing clients from the new owners of Trips Ahoy. They claimed that Hanna used the knowledge gained from her time with the company to use undue influence on clients that rightfully belonged to the large corporation. When her eyes landed on the price they were suing her for, Hanna's head swam. There was no reality in which Hanna could afford what they were asking. The majority of her funds were sunk into the business and her meager savings was a drop in the bucket of what they were asking for.

Damn it! Did she even stand a chance against them? Hanna was unsure how much lawyers cost, but she imagined it was more than she could afford.

Dizzy and out of breath, Hanna felt her knees crumple. Like she was watching herself from above, Hanna slowly descended to the ground. Her heart was beating too fast in her chest and sweat began beading on her back.

"Hanna!" Noah caught her from behind, scooping his elbows under her arms. "Talk to me. What do you need?"

"Just want...to sit down...for a minute." Her limbs tingled and Hanna suddenly felt so tired.

"Okay. Okay," Noah repeated. "Let's sit down."

Avoiding the drought-tolerant landscaping of pebbles and prickly plants, Noah lowered them to the cement driveway. Noah sat Hanna sideways on his lap, bending his knees to better support her body. Cupping her head against his chest, Noah pressed his face into her hair.

Hanna struggled to suck in air. "Being...sued..." she tried to explain, the papers crumpled in her tight grip. The tight constriction of her throat and inability to get out a full sentence just made it worse. This had never happened before and Hanna hated that Noah was seeing her like this.

"We can deal with that later, okay? Let's just focus on your breathing right now. Take a deep breath with me." Noah slowly inhaled, his chest expanding against Hanna's side.

She attempted to pull in enough air to match Noah, but Hanna's lungs were too tight to expand fully. At Noah's direction, they held their breath, then slowly released it. Hanna let herself fall into the hypnotic pattern, unevenly matching Noah's inhales and exhales. An indeterminable amount of time passed as they sat in the driveway and when Hanna's heartbeat began to calm, enough oxygen reached her brain to give clarity to her thoughts. Hanna was surprised to look around and see that the world still looked the same even though her worldview had shifted significantly.

"Thank you." Hanna wiped a sleeve under her eyes. She probably looked like a racoon. "That's never happened to me before."

Noah was still rubbing circles around her back. "Panic attacks are fairly common, especially considering the news you just received. Do you feel steady enough to get up? You will probably still feel drained and shaky for a while, so let's take it easy, okay?"

"Yeah, I am ready to get off the ground." She prayed that her neighbors were all at work or busy in their houses. The last thing she needed was someone staring at them in what was certainly one of the most humiliating moments of her life. "That could not have been comfortable for you."

Her legs were a little unsteady beneath her, but with Noah's warning, Hanna was able to safely get up. Noah watched her closely and when he was certain she was not going to fall back down, grabbed their bags and followed Hanna up the walkway.

"I am more concerned about you right now."

Entering her code into the smartlock on the door (technology made having rotating renters safer for Sarah) Hanna entered the empty house. Having kept in contact with Sarah throughout the trip regarding her housing needs, Hanna knew that she was the only renter currently in the house and was staying in the same room as before. Turning down the narrow hallway, Hanna led Noah into the small bedroom. An unmade queen bed was tucked into one corner with a side table and lamp. A desk and dresser made up the only other furniture in the room, a sparse reach-in closet taking up the remaining wall.

It was hardly more personal than her hotel room in Paris, and Hanna wondered what Noah thought as he looked around. No artwork or personal touches, Hanna's three photos of her family were stored in a box in Sarah's garage along with her basic linens.

This was her life, impermanent, always on the move.

And now, getting sued.

It was all such a mess, and Hanna did not want Noah to see any of it. This was her lowest point. How could Noah want any part of it? They had only known each other for a few months, and been a couple for even less. There was no way she could drag Noah down into this shit. Besides, who would want to tie themselves to a sinking ship?

Noah was better off cutting his losses and finding a woman with less baggage. Fighting this lawsuit would absorb any time and energy Hanna had. What little time she had leftover would be spent salvaging the relationships with her clients and ensuring there was no negative backlash on her business. There would barely be enough time to eat and sleep, let alone give their budding relationship the attention it needed to flourish.

Heart already cracking, Hanna dealt it the final blow. She knew that Noah meant more to her than a fling, but the reality was that their time in Paris was all she could have of him. He deserved so much more than whatever scraps of time she could give him. Now that he was learning to open up his heart and trust people again, he would find someone who could give him everything he needed.

It just would not be Hanna.

"Do you want me to order food? Maybe some of those empanadas you keep talking about." Noah set her bags in the closet before coming back to wrap her in a hug. "We can stay in, relax a little bit, help you get your mind off things."

Why did he have to be so perfect? Hanna let herself sink into his embrace. If this was going to be the last time, she wanted to make the most of it. Holding Noah tightly, she felt his rapid heartbeat beneath her cheek. Her own heart was threatening a revolt, trying to beat out of her chest to latch itself onto Noah, wanting to never let him go. But she could not be selfish. Not with him. Not when Noah already gave up so much to make other people happy. Hanna could do this for him: break her own heart to protect his.

She gently pushed away, trying to fix her expression into something reassuring. Brows lowered over his eyes in confusion, Noah frowned at her.

"No, thank you. I'm not in the mood for food right now. I just want to clean up and maybe take a nap." There was definitely no way Hanna could sleep, not with her brain racing a mile a minute forming to-do lists and questions that she needed to research. The legal paperwork taunted her from where it sat on the desk. "You should go home and try to work off the jetlag. I will not be good company anyway and I do not want you to be bored."

Noah searched her face, eyes dimming when he puzzled out the meaning behind her words. "Don't shut me out, Hanna. Not me. Not after we promised to be real with each other." His tone was laced with hurt, cutting at Hanna's heart. "You want me gone, fine, but don't lie about the reason. At least be honest with me, you never held back before."

Hot tears burned Hanna's sensitive eyes. How were there still any tears left? She felt like she was using up a year's supply in one day. Hanna opened her mouth to respond, but only a sob came out.

When Noah immediately stepped forward to comfort her, Hanna held up a hand. If he touched her again, she would cave and Hanna needed to remain strong. She had to make him understand that this was the best choice for him.

"This mess isn't your problem to deal with. We barely know each other. You have enough on your plate with your own business and family. You don't need my problems on top of it. This is going to bring enough stress to shake a long-term relationship, and we've been together less than a month. And I know you are too kind to call it off yourself, so I'm going to do it for you. You deserve someone who can give you all their attention, not the crumbs that I can spare."

"That's bullshit and you know it." Noah grabbed her hand and pressed it against his chest, right over his heart.

"I don't care how long it's been, this has been yours from the moment you challenged me in that cafe with those gold-flecked eyes. Our relationship might be new, but it is not fragile. I don't want anyone else, I want you. You bring out the best parts of me." His eyes shone with tears. "You need time to take care of things yourself, prove that you can? Fine. I can give you as much time as you need, but do not end this in some misguided attempt to protect me. I want to be right beside you, supporting you, cheering you on, reminding you that you can do anything. But you don't have to do it alone."

Hanna choked on a sob, launching herself into Noah's open arms. One of his hands clasped the back of her head, holding her against his chest as Hanna's body shook with the force of her emotions.

Noah guided them to sit on the bed and Hanna was too drained to protest the fact that their outside clothes were touching the clean bed. At least the sheets were not on yet.

Agony, despair, and fury rose like waves, crashing down in a steady stream of tears. Years of hard work, punishing schedules and missed social events were now at risk because some corporation was greedy and jealous of the success Hanna carved out for herself. Falsely claiming that she was stealing clients they had no ownership of. As if people were like cars, transferring the title from one owner to another when a business was bought. Hazel would balk at the notion.

"Oh, no." Hanna's voice was scratchy from crying. "What is your grandmother going to think? The Delgados must have found out about the lawsuit and that is why they cancelled their trip. If they found out, your grandmother will probably find out soon too. What if she believes what they are saying, that I wrongfully took clients from them?"

Panic threatened to overwhelm her again and Hanna focused on the rise and fall of Noah's chest to steady her breathing. He ran a hand soothingly down her back, stroking her hair with the other. His familiar scent of clean linen filled Hanna's nose as she buried her face in his shirt.

"Mémé will know they are making up lies and will defend you. She knows the truth, that you are a good person and that she was the one who reached out to you about the trip. She loves you."

His lips moved against her hair with silent words before he continued. "Trips Ahoy is scared because you are competition, excelling at your job and connecting with people in an authentic way they could never replicate."

Hanna let out a pained laugh. "Yeah, well I kind of wish I was a little less good at my job if this is the result."

"Do you really?" Noah tipped her chin up so that she could see his questioning look.

She did not have to think about her answer. "No." As much as the threat of the lawsuit felt like her heart was caving in her chest, Hanna did not regret creating her own business instead of working for the large corporation. She was even a little proud of herself for building a reputation and brand that made one of the largest travel companies in the world worried for their business.

"Good." Noah kissed her, wiping away the tears from her cheeks. For once, Hanna did not worry about how she looked, any hint of self-consciousness slipping away under Noah's concern.

Hanna relaxed into Noah's arms, letting her thoughts still in the knowledge that he would keep her safe. When she felt ready to face reality again, Hanna thought about what her next steps needed to be. Pressing up, Hanna caressed Noah's face and gave him a feather-light kiss.

"Thank you for offering to stay with me, but I need some time to work through this on my own." Asking for help was something she did not want to burden him with yet, and Hanna did not even know what help she would need. She had to try to solve this on her own, without adding to Noah's load.

When a panicked look entered his sky-colored eyes, Hanna rushed to reassure him.

"I am not breaking up with you. I am just letting you know that I might not be available for a while. If you want to wait for me–"

"Yes." The word left him in a rush. "I want that."

Like the sun peaking through storm clouds, joy took root in her chest at the prospect of getting to keep Noah. Hanna did not know how much time she could spend with him while navigating the lawsuit, but just knowing that Noah would be there was like the light at the end of a tunnel.

"Okay," she said.

"Okay," Noah repeated. He looked at her like he was memorizing her face and Hanna wondered if Noah worried that it was the last time he would see her. Her heart ached at the thought that she hurt him.

"I will not try to push you away again," Hanna said as she pressed their foreheads together and watched the doubt fade from his eyes.

"I won't let you," he promised. "You are it for me, Hanna, and I will tell you that as often as you need to hear it to believe me."

She hugged him closer. Slowly, Noah's body relaxed in her hold, his head resting against hers. Hanna wanted to own the feeling of his heartbeat against her chest. When she yawned against his shoulder, Hanna felt Noah's smile against the top of her head.

"I'll let you get some rest, sweetheart. Call me when you are ready."

Hanna walked him to the door and waited while his rideshare pulled up, kissing him deeply instead of saying goodbye. Closing the door behind her, Hanna felt any remaining energy drain out of her body. On jellied legs, she made her way to the shower, cleaning off as quickly as possible before collapsing face-first onto the unmade bed.

# 19

# The World Won't End
# if You Ask for Help

RUBBING the heels of her hands against her scratchy eyes, Hanna glared at the book in front of her. Long hours at the library, staring at pages and pages of small font had the words blurring. Law textbooks were a form of modern torture. A convoluted construction of words that Hanna understood individually, but together made no sense.

Tension pounded behind her brow and Hanna pressed her fingers against the pressure points. She was fluent in three languages, almost four. It should not be this complicated to figure out how to rectify the lawsuit filed against her. Next to her laptop, a pad of legal paper (she would appreciate the irony later) sat with notes scrawled in her slanted penmanship. What originally started as a numbered list of items to check off soon became a diagram more closely in-tune with a conspiracy theory board, arrows and lines connecting one thought to another, underlines and circles highlighting others.

If she ever doubted that the legal system was designed to gate-keep regular citizens out of knowledge, her time spent pouring over legislative books and online articles slapped Hanna back to reality. The internet was supposed to help connect people to knowledge, but each search on how to fight a lawsuit against client poaching was like trying to navigate through a maze. Where the walls kept moving. And Hanna was blindfolded. And there was quicksand.

Everything about this process pointed to needing an attorney, but after several phone calls with intake representatives from law firms that specialized in these types of cases, Hanna was left adrift with crippling hopelessness. Yes, her case did qualify for representation and they would be more than happy to take her on as a client, but only if she was able to pay the retainer fee. Which Hanna did not have.

What she had in savings Hanna needed to keep for living expenses in the event this legal battle kept her away from work for months. Hanna already had to turn down a new client prospect because she did not know if she would be available. A few more clients, in addition to the Delgados, called over the past few days to cancel their trips, claiming conflicts of interest, but Hanna knew the real reason was that Trips Ahoy had contacted them about the lawsuit. The loss in business was a hit to both her finances and her pride, and Hanna wanted this settled quickly to prevent more damage to her reputation.

The thought had occurred to Hanna to contact her family and ask for a loan, but her relationship with them was still precarious, and she was afraid that any possibility of their belief in the viability of her career would shatter faster than Venetian glass if she asked for money.

Slumping forward in despair, Hanna groaned into her notes, closing her eyes briefly against the harsh fluorescent lighting of the library. It must be later in the evening than she realized, because Hanna could no longer hear the murmured voices of teenagers discussing a group project over their opened textbooks, or the snoring of an elderly man who fell asleep reading a magazine in an armchair. No, now there was little ambient noise to drown out the constant refrain of *failure* chanting in her skull.

Hot tears built behind her eyes and Hanna let them roll down her cheeks, wetting the pages beneath her skin. She tried to do this, fix the problem on her own, but it was not working. For a self-sufficient, empowered woman who was accustomed to solving every problem on her own and making it appear that there was never a problem to begin with, Hanna was struggling to accept that maybe this was a task where she needed help.

The wet cascade of tears reminded her of the rain at Versailles, huddling with Noah under the limited protection of the window frame in an attempt to keep dry. Cool, late-spring rain dropping onto their hair, collecting along their eyelashes, sliding down their exposed skin before absorbing into their clothing. Hanna remembered the bright glow of Noah's eyes, the resolve in his voice as they argued; her with determination to do everything on her own, him with the desire to help. Calling her stubborn in that fondly exasperated way.

Was she being too stubborn now? Noah's voice replaced her own in her head, replying, *"Yes, but you do not have to be."* She spent every available minute in the library trying to dig herself out of the pit she was in, taking limited breaks to eat and drink, and that was only because of Sarah's notes about leftovers in the fridge and Noah's daily texts reminding Hanna that he was thinking of her.

"Miss?" A hand gently grasped her shoulder and shook. "I'm sorry, but the library is closing. I have to ask you to leave."

Closing time already? Hanna sat up slowly and let the dread over another day with no progress wash over her. Turning to face the librarian, a bespectacled, black man in his early twenties, Hanna clocked the look of pity in his hazel eyes.

"Are you okay? If you need help, or are in a bad situation, I can put you in contact with some resources."

Hanna knew that she looked exhausted, dark circles under her eyes and the dull cast to her usually glowing skin a result of the combination of sleepless nights and lack of sunshine. But knowing you look exhausted and seeing the looks people give you when you clearly are not at your best are two separate issues.

"I am alright. Thank you, though. Just some long days and nights. Sorry to have kept you, I did not realize how late it was. Let me just put these books away before I go."

"No need, I can take care of those for you," he said as he gathered up the books, noting the titles. "I have some friends in law school, and they talk about the intense hours all the time. You could check the books out if you wanted and then you could save time by studying at home instead of here."

Another person eager to help her, even if only because it was his job. Though, the kelly green sweater with the words "Read More Books" covering his torso was a testament to how much he loved his job.

"Thank you, but I think that I got all I could from those books." Hanna stuffed her notepad into her purse, shouldering the strap and following the librarian towards the entrance.

Something about his presence had Hanna opening up to him. "I am not in law school," she explained. "Just someone getting sued, and unless you have a book on where to get enough money to pay a lawyer, I do not think anything else could help at this point."

Hanna's voice cracked on the last word and she stuffed down the painful emotion. The last thing she needed was to delay the librarian's shift ending by breaking down in front of him.

"Hey, don't forget what I said." He shrugged with the books stacked in his arms, "The library is a great place for resources, especially if you don't have anyone else to help you out. We all need help from time to time. "

Hanna thanked him again and walked out the door. In the fading light of dusk, Hanna took the bus back to Sarah's house, the librarian's words stuck in a loop in her head. He made asking for help seem so easy, like it was a given that people would offer their assistance freely, with no expectations in return. Was she letting the past cloud her present, the fight to prove herself against all odds closing her off to the potential that having others' support could bring?

Walking through the front door, Hanna took off her shoes and placed her keys on their hook, pausing briefly at the note taped there.

*Hanna*, it read, *delivery for you on the kitchen table and dinner in the fridge. Don't work too hard. X Sarah*

Taking the note with her, Hanna gasped as she entered the

kitchen. There, centered on the table was a small bouquet of flowers. Tulips, peonies, and roses all burst with color, their perfumed scent filling the room and reminding Hanna of time spent in Monet's Garden. Laughing and painting with Noah, playfully drawing him out of his shell when he was more focused on getting the painting perfect than enjoying the experience.

Bright emotion filled her chest as Hanna reached out to pluck the notecard with her name on it from the blooms.

*I miss the way your eyes light up when you see something beautiful, how you radiate joy and make the ordinary extraordinary. I hope these flowers remind you of the beauty found not in perfection, but in the progress of doing something you love. Selfishly, I hope they also remind you of me.*

*Yours Always, Noah*

The card fell to the floor as Hanna lifted the flowers to her nose, inhaling deeply. She wanted the scent and touch of the flowers to transport her back to happier times, when she was playing in a garden with Noah, paint splatters on their clothing and skin. Her heart was empty without him, like a boat untethered from its anchor, bobbing aimlessly in a churning sea. Reading his words on the card made her ache for him, missing the understanding and acceptance she felt in his arms.

In a rush, Hanna realized that she was hurting for no reason. Noah would never judge her for feeling overwhelmed and lost against the uncertainty of the lawsuit. No, being with him was like having a light shine through the darkness, illuminating the path forward. Needing him, asking for help, would not make her weak, but instead would make her stronger because he would be at her side. And he was not the only one. In her own way, Sarah was showing her support through the containers of leftovers in the fridge, the countless conversations around the kitchen table, and the friendship offered freely. Miles away, Will was texting her daily jokes to lift her spirits, asking if Hanna wanted him to slash someone's tires in retaliation.

Joking aside, Hanna knew that they loved her, not for what she could do for them, but for who she was. Without meaning to, Hanna let these chosen people inside her heart and found a home in their hearts as well. Now she knew that the right people would be there for you, even if you were miles away.

Bringing the flowers with her to display on her bedside table, Hanna pulled out her phone.

"Noah," she croaked when he picked up. Her voice was scratchy after days of crying and spending every waking moment working on a solution to the lawsuit.

His voice was rushed, slightly out of breath as if he raced to pick up the call on the first ring. "Hanna?"

"I need help," she admitted. Instead of feeling like defeat, knowing that she had to rely on someone else, Hanna felt a weight lift off her chest. Relief filled her and made her lighter than she felt in days. Knowing that Noah would not judge her for needing help, Hanna could now see how having others to rely on was a blessing, not a burden. Asking for help did not mean that she failed, it was simply accepting the reality that Hanna could not control everything and was not an expert in all fields.

"I'll be right there," his rich voice reassured her.

AN HOUR LATER, Noah's sharp rap sounded on the door.

"I brought your favorite chocolates." He held out the iconic gift bag tied with brown ribbon. "And some tea."

Hanna rushed into his arms, ignoring the gifts in favor of being held by him. She buried her face in the crook of his shoulder and inhaled his familiar scent. The simple fragrance, free of fuss or frills, was so like Noah that it put a smile on her face. He did not try to be anything other than who he was and as Hanna stood within the warm comfort of his embrace, she felt like she could breathe for the first time in days. Without asking any questions, Noah responded to her request for aid immediately, setting aside whatever she had called him away from to get to her as quickly as traffic allowed. Somehow, Hanna knew that would always be the case with him, that Noah would prioritize her above all else. She could weather any storm if he was beside her and peace sprung in Hanna's chest, spreading to every edge of her body.

Tipping her face up to look Noah in the eyes, Hanna's voice was thick with emotion.

"I love you."

Surprise flickered across his face before it was replaced with a display of joy. The corners of his lips melted into a smile, blue eyes sparkling in the glow of the porchlight.

"That's good, because I am out of my mind in love with you."

Dizzying delight burst within Hanna like fireworks. There was a fullness to her chest that contradicted how light she felt at hearing his words. Still, Hanna could not resist teasing him.

"Out of your mind, huh? It is a good thing I am smart enough for us both then. Luckily, you have a pretty face."

Loud and free, Noah laughed as he picked Hanna up to spin her around.

"Minx," he called her without malice.

Wrapping her legs around his waist, Hanna nuzzled into his neck as Noah carried her to her room. Settling against the headboard, Noah cradled Hanna in his lap, long legs stretched out in front of him—after kicking off his shoes of course. He set her gift down on the nightstand, smiling when he saw the flowers already prominently displayed where she could see them first thing when she woke. Smoothing his hands down Hanna's hair and back, Noah's smile disappeared into a frown when he saw the dark circles under her eyes.

Though his presence and expression of love, both verbal and nonverbal, rejuvenated her, Hanna was running on fumes. Days of endless research drained her, the comfort of Noah's lap relaxing her enough to no longer feel the pressure to keep up appearances and shoulder the weight of her problems alone. With each pass of his hand, Hanna melted further into him.

"Thank you for coming."

"There is nowhere else I would be. I'm just glad you finally called. I was desperate enough to see you that I would have shown up on your doorstep even if you did not call. Do you want some chocolate, tea, wine? We can talk, take a nap, whatever you want."

"A nap? Do I look that bad?" Hanna was only half-kidding.

Noah gently stroked the pads of his thumbs under her eyes.

"Nothing less than beautiful, just a little burnt out."

"I don't think I can rest completely until I have a plan of action."

Noah's chest vibrated as he chuckled warmly. "I thought that might be the case. Why don't you talk me through what you've already been working on, and we can see if I'm more than just a pretty face?"

That was a good way to approach it, very rational and methodical. Hanna proceeded to tell him about her time in the library, the hours and notes resulting in the endless loop that only a lawyer could help her and without money she could not get a lawyer. Just remembering it had Hanna's stomach twisting in knots. As she spoke, Noah listened intently, tugging her tighter against him when her tone shifted to dismay.

Remaining silent for a few moments after she finished, brow furrowed in concentration, Noah's thoughts shifted behind his eyes. Hanna watched as he quickly sorted through the information and disseminated what he needed to move forward, dismissing ideas that would not work. Neither of them were the type of person to present an answer until they knew it was the correct one.

Apparently coming to a decision, Noah's focus snapped back to Hanna's face. "Do you think you could eat something while I make some phone calls? I can't focus unless I know you are feeling better."

Nodding against his chest, Hanna was relieved to know that

Noah had an idea to fix this. Having a task to finally accomplish grounded her, trusting that Noah would not take control over everything, but instead would work as her partner. Sliding out of his arms, Hanna padded to the kitchen, warming two bowls of leftovers as Noah followed behind her, phone already at his ear.

Blowing on the hot chicken soup, Hanna ate while she listened to Noah talk on the phone. Not wasting any time, Noah skipped past pleasantries and jumped right into the conversation.

"Hey," Noah greeted the person on the other line with familiarity, "remember that favor you owe me? Well, I'm cashing it in. You free?"

Noah listened to the response, hearing something that made him laugh deeply.

"Tomorrow?" He raised a brow at Hanna in question. As if she had anything else pressing on her schedule. Hanna nodded.

"Yeah, tomorrow works. Just text me the details."

Hanna puzzled over the brusk, one-sided conversation. Grateful that Noah was wasting no time and curious to find out who he was talking to, she listened closely. At his pointed look toward her bowl of soup, Hanna continued eating. Not even five minutes into the conversation and Noah was already saying goodbye. Setting his phone down on the table, Noah leaned back in his chair.

"That was my friend, Bennett. He's a lawyer and one of the smartest people I know. He'll know how to tackle this lawsuit."

Gratitude warred with embarrassment. "Thank you, Noah. That was really kind of you to call him, but I cannot pay him."

At least, not whatever rate was deemed appropriate for those with the esquire honorific.

"You will not have to," Noah said definitively.

Hanna knew she asked Noah for help, but she still bristled at the idea of him paying for a lawyer.

"Noah, I cannot ask you to pay for that, it's too much."

"Nothing is too much for you." Noah's voice was laced with sincerity. "Bennett owes me a favor and using it to help you is worth it. It won't cost you anything. Helping you does not mean I am going to take over. You still have the final decision. If Bennett cannot help you or you do not think he is the right fit, I will find someone else who can help you. You are not in this alone anymore, remember? We will get through this."

Reaching across the table, Hanna offered her hand to Noah, the weight of his fingers in hers dulling the edge of her discomfort.

"Sorry, I am not used to asking for help and jumped to unfair conclusions. I know that you are just trying to help and I really appreciate it. I want this whole mess behind me so that we can move forward."

Noah brought her fingers to his lips, dusting them with featherlight kisses. "Me too."

"So, what is Bennett like?"

"He's married to his work, brilliant, driven, and fiercely protective of his family. We met in undergrad and he works as legal counsel for his family's company. I should warn you that he can come across as a bit of a dick when he first meets people, brusk and unsocial, but it's just because he is insanely focused and analyzing if he can trust you. Once you get to know him, Bennett is...well, not warm, exactly, but he cares deeply for those close to him."

Hanna teasingly tapped Noah's shin with her foot. "Sounds like someone else I know. Good thing I know how to charm that type."

Noah's eyes flashed with possessive heat. "On second thought, maybe I will keep you far away from him. I know how effective your charm is and I would hate to have to kill my friend for falling in love with you."

Pretending to ponder the idea, Hanna replied with a sassy tilt of her head. "You're right. Orange is not a good color for you."

Her laughter echoed through the room as Noah tickled her until they were both breathless. Feeling more settled than she had in days, Hanna yawned loudly as fatigue swept over her. Scooping her up in his arms, Noah carried her back into her room, silently removing her clothes and tucking her into the bed. Sleepily, Hanna held onto his wrist as he stood, asking him to stay. After cleaning up the kitchen, he returned, stripping down to his boxer briefs and sliding into the bed behind her.

For the first time since they were last together, Hanna slept soundly through the night.

# 20

## When You Do Not Know What to Do, Ask an Expert

BENNETT WAS JUST as broody and disagreeable as Noah described. What Noah failed to mention was that Bennett had the face of an angel to counteract his personality. Honey-colored tresses curled around an angular face, darker brows lowered over stormy hazel eyes. Dressed in a fitted, black suit, the sharp cut of his jaw and unsmiling face screamed uptight and no-nonsense. He reminded her so much of how closed-off Noah was when she first met him that Hanna immediately wanted to befriend Bennett.

As they walked into his office, Bennett rounded his desk to shake Noah's hand, softening the formal greeting by clasping his shoulder and pulling him into a hug.

Noah returned the gesture with a clap on Bennett's back. "Thanks for meeting us."

"Not like you gave me much of a choice," Bennett said dryly. "Calling in a decade old favor, I admit you have me curious what this request is for."

His shark-like eyes pinned Hanna in place and she got the distinct feeling that he was sizing her up, assessing.

"This is Hanna, my girlfriend. She's the reason I called you." Noah stepped back to her side, resting a hand on the small of her back. Hanna warmed at the title, though she wished the first time

239

Noah introduced her as his girlfriend was under better circumstances.

Surprise sharpened Bennett's face, his eyes going between Hanna and Noah.

"Girlfriend, huh? Must be pretty special to get you calling in a favor."

Well, at least he did not add insult to injury by tacking on a placating "no offense" when he clearly meant to offend. Hanna knew she was supposed to be insulted, and there was a part of her that wanted to smack the arrogant confidence off the blonde man's face, but when she studied his posture and tone of his voice, Hanna considered that maybe it was not really about her. She would phrase it differently, but Hanna knew that if it came down to being polite or protecting a friend, she would say a lot worse.

"Bennett," Noah seethed in warning at the implied insult.

Hanna stilled him by placing a hand on his arm. His friend was being an absolute ass, but if Hanna agreed to hire him as her lawyer, she needed Bennett to know that she would stand up for herself.

Hiding her true intentions behind a blinding smile, Hanna held out her hand for Bennett to shake. When his palm clasped hers, Hanna squeezed. Firmly. She really should not feel a giddy thrill at the wince on his face as his fingers were crushed beneath hers, but Hanna was petty enough to enjoy it.

"So *nice* to meet you, Bennett. Perhaps you would like to get to know me first before making a judgement call? Otherwise, you are wasting my time."

Barely restraining the urge to stretch out his fingers after her punishing grip, Bennett met Hanna's gaze, a hint of respect slipping through the look of chagrin.

"Very special then. My apologies. The courts are filled with people using emotional manipulation to take advantage of the other person and I had to check that you were not doing that to my friend."

So Bennett said it to gauge her reaction. Clever. She could use that in a lawyer. It did not hurt that he acted to protect his friend.

Noah needed people like that in his corner. Pleased that Bennett was not too prideful to admit to his faults and apologize, Hanna accepted his apology, pushing their first introduction out of her head and accepting the seat he pulled out for her.

Hanna had never been in a lawyer's office before, but if this one offered a glimpse into the personality of its owner, Hanna was intrigued. She had hosted lawyers on tour before, many of them giving off the general impression of a profession that encouraged the mentality of work hard, play harder. While Bennett's first impression gave off an air of a person who had never heard of the word fun, his office suggested otherwise. His bookshelves were lined with beautiful tomes, spines stamped with gold foil and intricate binding, yet none of them were books on the law like one would expect.

Instead, Hanna scanned the titles of Agatha Christie's complete work, Jane Austen shared space with the Brontë sisters, collections of poetry and scientific theories stacked together. The shelves had no logical order, books that should be categorized together shelved separately. Catching the quizzical look on her face, Bennett spared a glance towards his personal library before returning his attention to Hanna.

"My cousins and I are in a family book club. I keep a separate shelf for each of their selections." Bennett shrugged as if it was nothing, while Hanna thought it spoke volumes toward his affection for his family.

Now that he pointed it out, Hanna noticed that the shelves held additional nods to each of the cousins. A framed photo of them all together had the place of honor in the center shelf, a small canvas painting of a lake house was on another, a medal of valor displayed proudly on yet another.

"How are your cousins? Your uncle?" Noah asked as he folded himself into the curved, low-back chair next to Hanna's.

Designed with natural wood furniture and a sage accent wall, Bennett's office matched the clean lines and tasteful decor of the rest of the converted craftsman cottage. A large window along the right wall provided enough light to brighten the space and offer a view of the garden outside.

"They are good, still pestering me to move back home."

"You are not from here?" Hanna thought she detected a slight accent.

"No, my family is from New York. I came out here for college and it made sense to stay when the company was expanding to the West Coast."

There was an undercurrent to his tone that had Hanna thinking there was more to that story than his succinct summary, but she let it go. She did not know him well enough to pry into his personal life. Though, if he really was a close friend of Noah's, perhaps she would learn the story one day.

Spinning a pen between his fingers, Bennett answered Noah's second question. "Though it might be time for me to visit them. Apparently, my uncle has a new personal assistant for the foundation."

"And?" Noah asked. "That hardly seems concerning. You were saying that he needed help planning the charity gala."

Bennett's voice took on a bitter edge as he clenched his jaw around the words, "She's twenty-four."

The only outward sign of Noah's surprise was his raised brow, the rest of him took on a solemn air, concern for his friend softening his posture. "That's young, sure, but not that young. We were the same age when we got our first jobs out of grad school. What are you so worried about?"

"He does not need to be spending that much time with a girl barely out of school. It's inappropriate."

"We are not in a regency drama, Bennett. She isn't a child. Your uncle can hire whomever he wants. Stop looking for trouble where there is none. She's his assistant. It's not like they are dating."

The pen hit the desk with a resounding clack.

"Don't even joke about that."

Hanna watched them carefully, wondering if she should excuse herself from this obviously delicate conversation or remind them of her presence.

"I am not saying he is dating her, but would it really be so bad if he started getting out there again? It's been seven years since–"

"Enough." The cold steel of Bennett's voice was enough to make Hanna shiver.

There was an invisible line that Noah crossed and Hanna watched as a mask of indifference slid over his friend's face. Pain radiated from Bennett's rigid posture and equal parts of frustration and empathy coated Noah's features. Clearly, this was not the first time they had this conversation, but it was the first time it tripped into uncharted territory. Hanna could see that Noah wanted to help his friend, but it was equally clear that Bennett was not in a place to accept the help. This was an issue he needed to work through on his own.

Offering what comfort she could, Hanna laced her fingers with Noah's, placing their joined hands on his thigh. Bennett tracked the movement, snapping his gaze back to the couple.

"Look, you know that I think of you like a brother, Noah, but you need to drop it. The subject is closed, and if you value our friendship, you will not bring it up again."

Noah sighed sadly. "Understood. I am sorry I pushed too far. I will not bring it up again, but I want you to know I am here for you if you ever want to talk about it."

With a twitch of his mouth, Bennett turned his attention back to Hanna. "Well, I was right, you must be special. In all the years I have known him, I have never heard Noah apologize."

Her laughter broke the remaining tension in the room.

"He just needed a good teacher," Hanna said.

"No." Noah brought their joined hands to his lips. "I just needed you."

Butterflies fluttered in her stomach, each flap of their wings sending shockwaves of happiness through her. Love for him saturated her pores until Hanna was sure it was radiating out of her. There was a matching light in Noah's eyes as they leaned over their chairs so their lips could meet in the space between them. Each touch was a jolt of energy to Hanna's system, giving her a boost of strength.

The clack of a keyboard drew them apart, Bennett's blunt interruption causing Hanna to blush as she remembered where they were. And why they were there.

"We've wasted enough time and my billable hours are quite expensive. Why don't you tell me why you are here?"

Straightening at the reminder of how much this might cost, Hanna tried to temper her expectations.

Some of her apprehension must have appeared on her face because Bennett's glower softened marginally. "I was joking. If I think that I can help, I'll take on this case pro bono. I cannot make the court fees disappear, but we can talk about those after we agree to work together."

The reassurance helped settle her frazzled nerves and Hanna relaxed into the chair. Summarizing the details of the lawsuit as quickly as possible, Hanna pulled out the court summons from her bag and handed it over to Bennett. His assessing gaze reviewed the document, pausing to type notes into his computer or ask Hanna questions.

When she was done talking, Hanna found the resulting quiet disconcerting. Gaze locked on his computer, Bennett scanned the typed words, no hint of what he was thinking revealed in his expression. Worry was a sneaky thing, slipping under Hanna's skin and winding its way through her system, urging her heart into a rapid beat, pressing a hard knot into her stomach, and tightening her skin until it tingled with nerves. If Bennett did not accept the case, that meant he did not think it had a chance at winning, and Hanna did not see how she could continue.

Removing his glasses, Bennett steepled his hands, resting his bottom lip against the tips of his fingers as he took a deep breath. Hanna's lungs stopped functioning, the air trapped as she braced for bad news.

With fire in his eyes, Bennett spoke. "Let's make these bastards pay."

Air whooshed out of Hanna. Beside her, Noah inhaled sharply, as if he had also been waiting to breathe until he heard the news. He remained quiet, though his relief was palpable, and Noah's hand relaxed under hers.

"So it's not a lost cause?" Hanna asked for clarity.

"No." Bennett's curls shook with his head. "Definitely not. Larger corporations scare smaller businesses with lawsuits, the threat of huge fines enough to make most competition give up. This–" He pinned down the court summons with a finger. "–is their way of trying to get you to cave under pressure."

"And you can help?"

His brow creased in befuddlement. "Didn't Noah tell you what type of law I practice?"

Noah huffed out a laugh. "I would have made you help either way."

Rolling his eyes at his friend, Bennett filled Hanna in. "I specialize in mergers and acquisitions. My family owns a lot of companies, investing in startups that otherwise lack access to funding, and help them grow. I do not like bullies, Hanna, and I got into law to fight against groups like Trips Ahoy." His mouth ticked up in a wry grin. "Well, that and to make a lot of money."

"Can you get them to drop the case?" Hanna could not keep the hope out of her voice.

Hanna was glad to have Bennett on her side when a vicious smile twisted his features. She would not want to be on the receiving end of that look.

"Oh, I am not only going to get them to drop the case, but I will do everything in my power to make them pay for the damage they caused you. By the time I am through with them, they will wish they never looked your way."

# 21

# *Don't Underestimate the Value of a Positive Review*

FIGHTING a lawsuit and launching one of your own was more paperwork and tedium than Hanna wanted to deal with for the rest of her life. She thought filing the paperwork to start her own business was intense, but after the heaps of documents Bennett sent her way, Hanna's wrist would be happy to never sign her name again.

After leaving Bennett's office that first day, Hanna was tasked with gathering all correspondence from client's she had at Trips Ahoy, both before and after her time there. According to Bennett, they would use it to prove that Hazel and a few others had reached out to Hanna first, negating the claim that she purposefully poached them from the larger company. From there, the burden of proof was on Trips Ahoy to prove that Hanna intended to steal the groups, which would be difficult since Hanna had documentation of their initial contact.

Hanna spent hours combing through her social media and email, grouping together the messages by person before sending them to Bennett. The second phase of the lawyer's plan was to prove the loss of business due to the lawsuit. Hanna was instructed not to contact any of the clients who cancelled trips herself, Bennett's assistant was handling that, but so far he was unable to reach the Delgados.

Without their testimony, Hanna could not verify that she was losing business specifically because of Trips Ahoy and file for defamation.

In the weeks leading up to the pre-trial meeting, their attempt at a settlement was rejected. Hanna felt like an exposed wire, her nerves frayed and agitated. Refusing to leave her side more than necessary, Noah spent all his available time with her, taking her out of the house for walks in the park, showing her some of his favorite restaurants, and even learning some yoga to put a smile on her face at his lack of coordination. Every gesture reinforced how much he loved her, and despite the uncertain circumstances of her future, Hanna never doubted that they could make it through anything together.

The night before the meeting, Hanna and Noah were sitting together on the couch, watching a nature documentary with Sarah. Hearing the lock on the front door chime, indicating someone was entering, Hanna looked up in confusion. To her knowledge, Sarah had not yet found a short-term renter for the other guest room.

"Honey, I'm home!" Will's boisterous voice sounded from the entryway.

"Will!" Hanna bounced up from her seat to run and hug her friend. "What are you doing here? I thought you were booked for the whole summer?"

"Good to see you, too," Will joked goodnaturedly. "I know that tomorrow is a big day for you, and no matter how it goes, I wanted you to feel supported. So, here I am."

Warmth filled her knowing she had people in her corner to cheer for her successes or pick her up when she was down. But, despite his explanation, Hanna noted the dark circles under Will's eyes and the dejected slump of his shoulders. The bags at his feet were the same ones he used when staying at Sarah's long-term, fuller than what he would need if he was just staying for a few days.

"Thank you," she said, "but you did not have to leave your job to do that. We both know how difficult it is working in a seasonal industry."

He chuckled sadly. "Nothing gets past you, does it? Let's just say there was a misunderstanding with a guest and my schedule became unexpectedly clear. This visit is not about me though, I came here for you, so tell me how I can help. Ice cream and wine?"

Apparently, the men in her life were using the same booklet for how to offer comfort.

"We opted for watching cute animals." Hanna gestured to the living room where the show was paused, Noah a few steps behind her. "Will, this is my boyfriend, Noah."

A teasing smile stretched across Will's tan face. "The infamous Noah at last. So you're the one who finally convinced Hanna to break her rules on dating. Great to meet you."

Cutting a wry glance in Hanna's direction, Noah reached out to shake Will's outstretched hand. "Good to meet you too, though I wish it were under better circumstances. Hanna's told me a lot about you."

Laughing, Will pulled Noah into a quick hug, clapping a large hand on his back. "Hopefully just the good things."

It was Hanna's turn to laugh. "Why would I do that when the stories of all the trouble you've gotten into are more fun?"

So quick that she almost missed it, Hanna saw sadness shadow Will's gaze before it was snuffed by amusement. While he joked with Noah that the stories paled in comparison to the truth, Hanna made a mental note to check in with her friend later. His forced cheer and quick dismissal of trouble at work had her worried.

After greeting Sarah and storing his bags in his room, Will joined them in the living room to finish the documentary. In true fashion, he joked along with the narrator, keeping Hanna distracted from her thoughts as he shared a surprising knowledge regarding the animal kingdom. After a few episodes, the group retired early, knowing that they should at least try to get a full night's rest before the day ahead. Curled up in Noah's arms, Hanna fell into a fitful sleep.

DRESSED in an emerald green pantsuit that felt more like armor than fashion, Hanna met Bennett outside the courthouse. Having already said goodbye to Noah and her friends, Hanna followed Bennett into a private room where they would wait before the pre-trial meeting started. They spent what little time they had reviewing what Hanna should prepare for.

Walking on legs that felt less secure than she would like, Hanna followed Bennett into the courtroom when their case was called. The carpet muffled the sound of their steps. Hanna's heels sunk into the floor as the people seated in the audience benches turned to watch their arrival.

A small spot of comfort broke through her nerves as Hanna saw her friends seated in the second row. Will and Sarah each gave her a small wave, and Hanna's hand trembled slightly as she returned the gesture. In front of them, Noah sat stern-faced, mouth pinched with worry. Over the last few weeks, he'd put on a brave face and Hanna knew he was trying to keep from adding to her stress, but she knew that this was difficult for him too.

When her gaze landed on the people seated on either side of Noah, love broadened her smile. Hazel sat with Daphne, Mai, and Lillian, dressed in powersuits. Each of them agreed to give a character reference, should it be needed. Their presence was not a surprise.

What surprised Hanna more were the people seated on Noah's other side. Long hair braided down her back in a shade that matched Hanna's, Camila Poole sat beside her husband, David, his glasses glinting in the fluorescent light. Seeing her family gathered together to support her had Hanna pausing in the aisle, heart bursting with joy so deep that it brought tears to her eyes. They flew out to see her.

But how? Hanna never told them about the lawsuit. Even with their difficult relationship, Hanna told Noah weeks ago, she still wished her parents were there to support her through the trial.

Her confusion must have shown on her face, because Hanna's father tipped his head in Noah's direction, winking as if to say he approved. Glancing over at Noah, Hanna let the gratitude and happiness shine, mouthing a silent *thank you*. His eyes softened and Hanna stepped forward to go to him.

A hand on her elbow reminded Hanna that there was time for explanations and expressions of appreciation later, she had a court case to win first.

Sliding into her chair beside Bennett, Hanna glanced at the table on the other side of the aisle. The lawyer for Trips Ahoy was a middle-aged man with a receding hairline and large gut. His expensive suit and sharp eyes contradicted his soft features and Hanna knew better than to underestimate him. Large corporations had pocketbooks large enough to attract the best lawyers, but Hanna knew that Bennett was also one of the best and she trusted him.

They rose for the entrance of the judge and the proceedings moved faster than Hanna expected. Each lawyer gave their opening remarks, then presented evidence. The judge, a black woman with grey streaks around her temples, studied the documents with an expression that gave nothing away.

"Does the defendant have any witness testimony?"

"Yes," Bennett responded before calling Hazel to the stand.

Settling into the witness stand with a dignified air, Hazel promised to tell the truth. Responding to all the questions asked by the plaintiff's lawyer with a disapproving scowl on her face, the elderly woman painted a picture of her relationship with Hanna. Their years travelling together and the friendship that developed naturally. She also explained how Trips Ahoy had contacted her after the buyout, but without Hanna working for the company, Hazel wanted nothing to do with the company.

"I followed Hanna on social media for years, so when I saw that she started her own company, I immediately reached out. There was no poaching or whatever nefarious things they are claiming happened. I made the decision to book the tour with Hanna on my own. As you can see from our emails."

If the balding lawyer was frustrated with Hazel's testimony, he did not show it, returning to shuffle his notes. Hanna thought that meant he was done, but at the last moment, he turned back to Hazel with a snap of his fingers, as if a thought just occurred to him.

"Just one more question. While on this tour, did Hanna, the professional tour guide you hired for this trip, enter a relationship with your grandson, Noah?"

Hanna's breath caught in a sharp gasp. There was always the possibility that Trips Ahoy was going to use the relationship to muddy her reputation, but they had been careful, not broadcasting it, and it was a sharp blade to her heart knowing that something as beautiful as the love they shared was being used against her.

Murmurs rose from behind them, shock rippling through the gathered individuals. Even the judge's eyebrow twitched, dark eyes flitting between Hanna and Noah.

"Objection." Bennett rose and addressed the judge. "Relevance."

"Sustained," the judge replied.

With his line of questioning interrupted, the other lawyer returned to his table, thanking Hazel for her time and yielding the floor to Bennett. Unruffled, Bennett stood and asked Hazel minimal questions, pivoting his approach by focusing on Hanna's professionalism and how the initial contact from Hazel proved she was not stealing clients. By the time he was done, Bennett had painted a picture that Trips Ahoy was grasping at straws, incapable of proving their actual complaint. Dismissing Hazel with no further questions, he returned to their table before calling on Mai.

One by one, Mai, Daphne, and Lillian spoke on Hanna's behalf. Since they were not former clients or the one's who booked the tour with Hanna, their testimony was weaker, but Bennett planned for that, using them more as character witnesses instead of evidence that Hanna had not stolen clients.

While Lillian, the last of their expected witnesses, was testifying, Bennett's phone lit with a silent notification and he read it quickly before pocketing the device. He waited until Lillian was finished before addressing the judge.

"I would like to call Patricia Delgado to the stand."

Hanna fought to keep the surprise from her face. Numerous attempts to reach the Delgado family went unanswered and while they were included on the list of witnesses, in case they did appear, Hanna was not expecting them to actually show up.

With a hand on her shoulder, Bennett leaned over to speak directly in her ear, "I was not sure she would be here until a few minutes ago, so I did not have time to prepare you."

Trusting him to know what he was doing, Hanna nodded. Turning in her seat, Hanna laid eyes on Patricia Delgado for the first time. A tall woman made her way towards the rail with powerful strides. Dressed in a flowing, blue sundress, Patricia looked relaxed and professional at the same time, gold jewelry dangling on her arms and ears.

"Sorry I am late, your honor, my family and I were out of the country and came back as soon as we could."

The judge inclined her head to allow Patricia onto the witness stand. Trips Ahoy's lawyer was visibly flummoxed–obviously not expecting the Delgados to attend either–planting a seed of hope within Hanna. If he was not expecting Patricia to show up, then she must have something to say that Trips Ahoy did not want made known. Without proper time to prepare for the unexpected witness, the lawyer deferred the first round of questioning to Bennett.

With a look of a predator having caught his prey in a trap, Bennett thanked his opponent before settling his face into something less terrifying before facing the witness.

"Mrs. Delgado, can you please explain your relationship to Hanna Poole?"

Her gaze met Hanna's momentarily, before returning to Bennett to answer the question. "This is the first time I have seen Ms. Poole in person, but I was referred to her company by a friend and had a trip booked with her that was meant to take place a few weeks ago."

"Was the trip cancelled by Ms. Poole?"

"No, I cancelled the trip."

"Why?"

Hanna leaned forward in her seat, hanging on every word. It was a question that she asked herself often, wondering why the trip was cancelled with little explanation.

"After booking the trip, I received a call from someone at Trips Ahoy, letting me know that Hanna was a former employee who they were taking legal action against due to unprofessional conduct. They led me to believe that she was misleading clients, misrepresenting her business and qualifications. Naturally, I was concerned for my family, not wanting my children around someone untrustworthy."

Bennett put one hand in his pocket, affixing a casual posture that Hanna knew was a front.

"Did you bring those concerns to my client or the person who referred you?"

Patricia's head dipped and her eyes filled with regret. "No, I thought that an established company like Trips Ahoy would be honest. But it was recently brought to my attention that they lied. The friend who originally referred me assured me that Ms. Poole is a professional, through and through. Instead, it is Trips Ahoy that is spreading lies and trying to damage her image so that she loses business."

"Thank you, I have no more questions." Turning to address the judge, Bennett continued, "Your Honor, I move to dismiss the case against my client and instead ask for the following damages."

Pulling a document from his folder, Bennett handed it over to the judge. Listed was the projected loss of income that Hanna suffered from the impact of the lawsuit.

"We will take a short recess and resume in ten minutes." The judge swept up the folder.

Hanna twisted her fingers together as they waited for the judge to return. Bennett leaned over to whisper that this was expected for a pre-trial meeting with a motion to dismiss. The judge would review everything and then return to inform them if the motion is granted or denied. Minutes ticked by as the courtroom sat in silence, the shifting of fabric as people anxiously adjusted in their seats the only sound.

Every one of Hanna's senses were attuned to the door the judge walked through, the weight of the verdict like a physical presence. After what felt like hours, but was only slightly more than ten minutes, the judge entered the room. Everyone rose for her entrance before sitting again. Settling the papers back on the bench, her resonant voice rang through the courtroom.

"Defendant's motion to dismiss, approved with requested damages. Court adjourned."

Feeling like a balloon that had all its helium let out, Hanna sank into her chair. She was dazed, not quite believing what she heard. The room around her faded into a blur, sounds muddled like she was sitting under water. It was over.

They won!

Strong arms wrapped around her from behind, jolting Hanna out of the fog and allowing a tide of elation to rush over her, pushing out any lingering stress and anxiety. There was still work to be done to bounce back from the lawsuit, but at least she still had a business to save.

Folding her arms over Noahs, Hanna leaned back over the railing to lean against him. Bennett raised a brow at their display of affection.

"Save it for later. This is still a courtroom," he groused.

Hanna laughed, feeling lighter than she had in months.

Their group left the building, gathering in the sunlight.

"Thank you for being here," Hanna said as she pulled Hazel into a hug, "and for speaking on my behalf. It means the world to me."

The floral scent of Hazel's perfume tickled Hanna's nose as the tiny woman hugged her back. "*You* mean the world to me, I hope you know that. I am glad this mess is behind you."

"I must admit, I am still reeling from Patricia Delgado's appearance. Anytime Bennett tried calling her, there was no response. If he could not reach her, who did?"

"That would be me." A cool voice came from behind. Lillian walked towards them in a leopard print dress. "The Delgados are old friends of mine, so I gave them a call to straighten this mess out. Honestly, I was embarrassed that they doubted you after the referral I gave."

"That was you?" Hanna's eyebrows shot up in surprise. Out of anyone in the world, she would have ranked Lillian low on the list of people who would vouch for her.

Lillian had the gall to look affronted. "Of course. Hazel would not have recommended you if you were anything less than the best. When Patricia was talking about a family vacation, I passed along your information. After experiencing your services firsthand, I am glad that I was correct in my original assessment."

"Thank you." Hanna's voice rang with sincerity. "Without Patricia's testimony, I am not sure the case would have gone my way."

"It was nothing," Lillian said as she studied her nails. "If the case went poorly, it would reflect badly on me for referring you. I cannot have people questioning my taste."

Biting back a grin at the blush of embarrassment on Lillian's face, Hanna made a noncommittal sound. Having said her piece, Lillian said her farewells, mentioning something about having other plans for the day.

"One of these days," Hazel said with a twinkle in her eye, "I am going to get her to admit that she's actually a big softy."

"*Ana?*" The tentative question sounded nothing like her mother's usual tone.

Over Hazel's head, Hanna watched as her parents approached.

"You must be Hanna's parents." Hazel stepped back to let them greet Hanna. "She is a phenomenal person, you should be very proud." Underneath her sweet tone was a chastisement.

"We are," David said.

"Very much so," Camila added.

"Good," Hazel asserted with a nod. "Then you are invited to the celebration dinner at Sarah's house. Hanna can give you the address."

Like a force of nature, now that Hazel made her statement, she swept away, looping her arms through her friends' before leading them away. Hanna chuckled at the bemused looks on her parents' faces.

"It means a lot that you all came," Hanna said to them. "I know that you are busy with work–"

Her father wrapped her in another hug, cutting her off. "I am sorry that we ever made you feel like you were less important. After our conversation with you, your mother and I talked a lot, and we want you to know how much we love and support you, no matter what your job is. If you are happy, then we are happy."

"And we want you to know that we will be here for you," her mother continued. "When Noah called to invite us, we were disappointed that you had not told us about the lawsuit sooner." Catching the mixed look of frustration and sadness on Hanna's face, Camila rushed to continue. "Not disappointed in you, but in ourselves. Our work is important, but not at the cost of our family. We have not shown our support in the way you needed, and we are ashamed that it made you keep things from us. We want to do better, if you will give us the chance?"

Tears streaming down her face, Hanna embraced her parents. It was not perfect, but it was the start to healing some deep wounds. She did not know what their relationship would look like in the future, but she looked forward to finding out.

"Yeah, I would like that a lot."

Swiping at the tears on her cheeks, Hanna laughed when two handkerchiefs entered her field of vision. Noah and her dad shared a look, ending in David chuckling and putting away his white square. Taking the fabric from Noah, Hanna dabbed at her face.

"So, what's all this about a party?" Hanna pivoted the conversation. Standing in the sun was starting to get uncomfortable, the warm rays heating her face and beading sweat underneath her suit. Only the four of them remained,

Noah took her hand in his, the habitual need to maintain physical contact still sent a thrill through her skin.

"I thought you might like to celebrate after your win. Nothing big, just those of us who were here today. Mémé helped organize the food and drinks, and Sarah offered her home to host it. But if you do not want to go–"

Hanna cut him off with a kiss. He was so thoughtful, always thinking of her.

"It sounds perfect."

There was nothing that sounded better than being surrounded by the people she loved, celebrating life's big and little moments, knowing that they would be there for her.

Always.

# Epilogue
## Nowhere in the World
## Compares to Returning Home

"I'M HOME," Hanna called out as she unlocked the sage green door of their one-story, Spanish revival house.

Wheeling her carryon luggage through the doorway, Hanna dropped her keys in the colorful bowl on the entry table. The clatter as they settled against the fired clay, hand painted in a teal and orange floral pattern with the initials H and N woven together, was drowned by the sound of the oven door closing. Music filtered in from the kitchen, the horns, piano, and upright bass shifting and blending together in the familiar pulse of jazz.

Footsteps sounded as Hanna was taking off her shoes, the dark head of her husband appearing around the corner. Their eyes soaked in each other's presence, checking to ensure that their brief time apart had not caused any harm. Framed in the fading sunlight coming from the kitchen windows, Noah's hair gleamed, the glow paling in comparison to the happiness on his face. It was like this any time work took them away from each other, though the instances were few and far between these days. In most cases, they travelled as a pair, Hanna conducting her tours or working from her computer while Noah met with new sources for products.

This trip was one of the few that Hanna made alone, the tour of Japan for Bennett's uncle and his family coincided with an important meeting Noah had with clients in the United States, and she missed Noah deeply. Any time they were apart she felt like a key piece of her was missing. Even with this beautiful house, purchased in San Diego to be near Noah's family, Hanna only felt at home when she was with Noah.

Evidence of their trips together lined the walls, photos of them wrapped in each other's arms all over the world. Her favorite one was the collage above their fireplace, a garden decorated in burgundy and sage green, people dressed in formal wear laughing around long farmhouse tables. And in the center was Hanna in a knee length white dress, bent over Noah's arm as he kissed her, surrounded by family and friends.

Light shone off the wedding ring on his hand gripping the doorframe and Noah strode forward to sweep Hanna into his arms.

"I missed you." He spoke into her hair.

Hanna kissed his neck. "I missed you too."

"You don't have any trips planned for a while, right?"

Brows pulling together in confusion, Hanna wondered why Noah asked. They still shared the calendar he set up for them over two years ago.

"No, but I did notice that Eric cleared my calendar for the next two weeks without telling me why. You would not happen to know anything about that, would you?'

Eric was the world's best assistant, hiring him one of the best decisions Hanna made after the lawsuit. In an abundance of caution, Hanna planned on saving the money from the lawsuit until she was scheduling enough trips to turn a profit without help from the additional funds. Her plan went out the window when three months later, not the original six she hoped for, Eric called her. A former Trips Ahoy employee like herself, Eric knew Hanna by reputation and laid out a compelling argument for why she needed to hire an assistant immediately and why it should be him.

Hanna hired him on the spot.

Three years and eight employees later, Luxe Travel was continuing to grow as one of the world's premier travel agencies. Hanna was certain that in another two, they would be top of the list. Her role was largely administrative now, handling the bookings and clients. When she missed the allure of taking a group around a new city, Hanna donned her tartan bag and sensible heels, but that was rare, especially if Noah could not join her. Now, when the travel bug bit her, Noah hid her computer and planned a trip for just the two of them.

"Maybe I do." Noah set her back down, kissing the tip of her nose before leading her into the kitchen. "But you won't get any information out of me. That would ruin the surprise."

Hanna was learning to enjoy surprises, but only when Noah planned them.

"Just a little hint?" Hanna pouted playfully, knowing that her husband could never hold out saying no to her for long.

She did not have to wait long. Noah took one look at her exaggerated expression and folded her back into his arms.

"Fine," he grumbled. *"But this is your only hint. One of these days I'll be able to surprise you without hints."*

Hearing Noah speak in French was the only tip Hanna needed. Squeezing him tightly, pleased at the prospect of returning to the city where they fell in love had Hanna bouncing on her feet.

Curling against his back while he worked at the stove, Hanna looked out their window into the backyard. Rows of garden beds and raised planters lined every available space. Slowly, Noah was learning to trust others with running the day-to-day operations of Hazel's company, taking time for what made him happy, planting in the garden and testing new combinations for products. It never failed to bring a smile to Hanna's face when she watched him work outside, relegated to a deck chair because she killed any plant she touched.

"I brought back a gift for you," Hanna said.

"You're the only gift I want." Noah kissed her soundly before Hanna swept out of the room to get his present from her bag.

Keeping it hidden behind her back, Hanna walked back to the kitchen, content to watch Noah pull their dinner out of the oven.

When he wiped his hands clean, Hanna told him to close his eyes and hold out his hands. Rolling his eyes at her, Noah did as she asked.

Hanna placed the delicate object in Noah's outstretched hands. His brow creased at the weight and feel of it, waiting patiently until Hanna had it displayed perfectly and told him he could look.

When he opened his eyes, Noah found a wooden birdhouse, decorated like a traditional home in Japan with tiles on the roof and a round door frame. His face softened with love as he looked from the birdhouse in his hands to their collection in the backyard, mementos from each one of Hanna's trips since they started dating.

Each one, Hanna's way of telling him that no matter where she was, Noah was always her home.

# Acknowledgements

Well, here it is. The part of the book that I thought I would never get around to writing, the acknowledgements. *Lessons from a Tour Guide* was not intended to be my first self-published book. Hanna and Noah's love story was meant to be a palate cleanser after finishing the first in a romantic fantasy series (sign up for my newsletter if you want to be the first to hear about that), but along the way it became clear that their story was ready for the world...so here we are.

While the literal typing of words on a page aspect of writing was largely solitary, I would never have reached the point of actually getting this book out into reader's hands without the help of many, many, many people (if I forget someone, I am so sorry. I do not love you less, my brain is just glitching knowing I am so close to publishing).

First, for the journey of life that brought me to this point, both the highs and lows, thanks to God.

Thanks always to my wonderful husband, my forever home. Your endless love for me gives me the freedom and joy to be unequivocally myself. For all the nights where you brought me snacks and drinks so that I did not have to stop writing, and all the days where you were my biggest cheerleader, thank you. I could write an entire book expressing my love for you and the life we built together, but I guess I already did!

To my sisters, both by blood and choice: Kaitlyn, Robin, Susan, Hannah, and Sam. Thank you for always having my back, for loving all my quirks, and supporting me in this journey. And to anyone else who cheered for me while I was writing, you are my village.

Madison, the first person who ever read a word of Hanna and Noah's story (back when they were nameless FMC and MMC), thank you! Having you as a sounding board for ideas and changes to the book made this version the best it could be. Thank you for all the texts of support and exclamation points when you got to a part you loved.

To my beta readers: Michelle, Kristen, Charlotte, Sasha, Natalia, Susan, Katrina, and Suzie. Some of you have read work I've created before, and some of you had no idea if I could even string a sentence together, but you took a chance. For that, I thank you. You're the best group of beta readers a girl could ask for!

There are no words to express my gratitude to my editor, Cara at edit-my-novel. You challenge me to dig deeper and stick with the tough emotions to make the story better. Submitting a piece of my heart and soul for feedback was a daunting prospect, but your kind words and constructive feedback ensured I felt supported throughout the process. I know that my books are in safe and respectful hands when you are editing them, and your suggestions always make the book better.

Self-publishing is a daunting task and I could not have done it without the help of Becca (TheFairyPlotMother) or Shauna and Becca at TheAuthorAgency. Thank you for giving me the tools to promote my book in the best way possible and walking me through the nuances of book PR. Additional thanks to Sarah at Dragonfly Formats for formatting the book for e-book and print! You made it shine with the page images and chapter headers.

All credit for the amazing cover design and cover illustration go to Kylie Sek. I am not good with color palettes and font styles, but you walked me through the whole process and made sure I had a cover I love. Noah's little smirk? Hanna's cute head tilt? Iconic. Thank you for bringing them to life.

Of course, I cannot leave out the people who made this all possible. YOU! The readers. Thank you for taking a chance on a debut author. Whether you know me in real life and were *gently encouraged* to buy this book, or you saw it at your local independent bookstore, or grabbed it on Kindle Unlimited, I appreciate you. Reading has always been a safe space for me, and my sincere hope is that my books become a safe space for you. Thank you for helping make my dreams come true.

# About the Author

Hi! I'm Kristen, a contemporary romance and romantic fantasy author. A storyteller at heart, I love writing about happily ever afters and the journeys characters take to get there. When I am not writing (or reading), you can find me visiting aesthetically appealing restaurants and coffee shops with friends, dancing, or traveling. I live in Southern California with my husband and two cats.

You can find me on Instagram or my website (kristenjennings.com).

www.ingramcontent.com/pod-product-compliance
Lightning Source LLC
Chambersburg PA
CBHW020125120726
47903CB00007B/2109